SASQUATCH, Love, AND OTHER IMAGINARY THINGS

SASQUATCH, Love, AND OTHER IMAGINARY THINGS

Betsy Aldredge and Carrie DuBois-Shaw

Simon Pulse

New York   London   Toronto   Sydney   New Delhi

Simon Pulse
An imprint of Simon & Schuster Children's Publishing Division
1230 Avenue of the Americas
New York, NY 10020

First Simon Pulse hardcover edition August 2017

Text copyright © 2017 by Betsy Aldredge and Carrie DuBois-Shaw

Jacket illustration © 2017 by Getty Images / Idimair, Bulentgultek

For information about special discounts for bulk purchases, please contact Simon & Schuster Special Sales at 1-866-506-1949 or business@simonandschuster.com.

The Simon & Schuster Speakers Bureau can bring authors to your live event. For more information or to book an event contact the Simon & Schuster Speakers Bureau at 1-866-248-3049 or visit our website at www.simonspeakers.com.

Interior design by Stephanie Hannus

The text for this book was set in Adobe Garamond Pro.

Manufactured in the United States of America

10 9 8 7 6 5 4 3 2

CIP data for this title is available from the Library of Congress.

ISBN 978-1-5072-0280-7 (hardcover)
ISBN 978-1-5072-0281-4 (ebook)

For Ginny, who helps me believe in
imaginary things every day. —BA

For my family and friends who, against all reason, maintained
an unwavering belief in the existence of this book. —CDS

Chapter 1

"Sasquatch: a hairy human-like creature, most often spotted in the northwestern United States and Canada. The animal, which can be up to 10 feet tall, is also called Bigfoot."

—"The Big Guide to Bigfoot," *published by the International Association of Sasquatch Enthusiasts*

On a good day, my parents were just mildly embarrassing. The day the camera crew came to our house was not a good day.

I squinted at the bright lights illuminating our dingy living room, and turned to my older sister, Sophie. "Hunting Bigfoot in private isn't bad enough?" I whispered. "Now Mom and Dad have to humiliate us on national television?"

Sophie shrugged. "You've been complaining for weeks. It's time to suck it up."

Colin, the producer of a new TV show called *Myth Gnomers*, stood behind our scratched-up coffee table shooting pre-interviews with my parents, me, and my two sisters. The awful title of this lousy reality show should've served as an obvious warning we were about to do something ridiculous, but nope, it sure didn't.

Instead of running like hell, all five of us were squished together on our stained, saggy brown couch, smiles frozen in place. At least our butts hid the holes in the upholstery.

"Checking. Checking one, two. Your mics should all be on now." Colin peered over the camera at my parents' matching neon green shirts that read "Ohio Is Bigfoot Country."

My mom's smile tightened. She glared and gestured at me until I put on a Northern Ohio Bigfoot Society hat like my sisters. Each Sasquatch club designed their own logo. My tacky-ass trucker cap had a cartoon footprint and a motto on it in Latin—which probably translated to "We have nothing better to do."

I pulled the brim over my eyes and slumped down, wishing I could join the pennies and crumbs hiding in the dark crevices of the sofa.

At first it made no sense why we were chosen for this show. My dad wasn't the president of his chapter, or even the head researcher. He was the guy in charge of bringing snacks.

Glancing at my sisters, I figured that the producers didn't care about my dad's expertise. They saw his video application and were probably more interested in the fact that he had three fairly cute teenage daughters, which made for better television than the socially awkward dudes with old-fashioned facial hair in my dad's Bigfoot society.

The way Colin hovered over his assistant producer who was checking and rechecking the sound and light levels, you'd think we were going to be on some fancy PBS documentary. Not even close. The show was destined for one of those travel and adventure channels that feature a lot of conspiracy theories about aliens and pyramids. Our three episodes about the search for Sasquatch would launch the series. Lucky us.

I sighed and stole a glimpse at my phone, wondering how long this ordeal would take. I had a buttload of AP biology homework. My family didn't seem concerned with time, which was surprising considering how uncomfortable we were on the couch and how my dad kept rubbing his eyes, exhausted from teaching summer school and Driver's Ed.

Dad perched his reading glasses on the end of his nose, patted the pockets of his safari vest and checked for the notes that he had written on index cards. I had no idea why someone needed a safari vest in suburban Ohio, but that was the least of my issues.

My mom touched up her hot pink lipstick for the umpteenth time and yet, somehow, it still ended up on her teeth. *Classy, Mom.* She had splurged and gotten her hair highlighted for the interview, but they went too blonde, which made her resemble my dad's daughter more than his wife. My parents thought it was hilarious.

Lyssa, my younger sister, gave her best pageant smile and twirled her own bottle-blonde hair. Her short skirt rode up her thighs. I motioned for her to pull the skirt down, but she ignored me and scooted the hem up another half an inch.

Only my older sister, Sophie, totally got how I felt. She had seen the miniskirt exchange and offered me a sympathetic smile. She was lovely, petite with wavy light brown hair and light blue eyes. I looked like a more intense version of her, curvier, with paler skin, deeper blue eyes, and darker, much curlier hair.

Colin's assistant producer, Beth, tucked her mousy brown hair behind her ears and adjusted the camera for the final time. She glanced at her boss for confirmation.

Colin gave her a dismissive nod. "We'll get started as soon as the show's host, Jake Stone, gets here. Beth, do you have his ETA?"

"He was due fifteen minutes ago."

Colin tilted his prematurely graying head to the ceiling and groaned. "I know when he was supposed to be here. Maybe you could try and find out when he'll actually show up?"

Beth quickly riffled through the papers in her folder, no doubt searching for Jake's number.

Colin tapped his clipboard with a pen. "Why is he always late? Actors have no respect for our craft."

"Jake Stone?" Lyssa asked. "Wasn't he one of the kids on that Nickelodeon show *Ghost Grabbers*?"

Colin nodded. "Yeah, right before he was in that failed tween boy band. I forget what they were called."

"Boys Will Be Boyz!" Lyssa made the little squealing noise that I knew to be her cute-guy-alert sound.

"Oh, I know him," Sophie said. "He's the one dating the sweet girl from those teen movie musicals. Melody something."

"Melody Wright. They met on the set of *Teen Marching Band 3*. So romantic," Lyssa sighed.

Colin snorted and paced the length of the room, wearing out our already mangy carpet.

I used the extra time to take off my hat and smooth my hair, which was out of control, as usual. I was the only one of us girls lucky enough to inherit my dad's kinky hair. He at least got to lose some of it, due to male pattern baldness. Mine just kept growing. I heard the camera added ten pounds. I hoped those pounds would go to my boobs and not my hair.

Moments later, Jake Stone made his entrance through the front door. "What's up, party people?" he called out, flashing a toothy grin.

From behind the camera, Beth poked her head up, and raised an eyebrow at him. Lyssa sat up a little straighter and offered a wide smile.

"You're late." Colin made a big show of looking at the clock on our mantel.

"Dude, sorry. Relax." Jake, who was probably my age and height, slid off his black leather jacket, revealing a tight-fitting, deep V-neck T-shirt.

I generally don't like guys decked out in more jewelry than your average pirate, and Jake's hands were encrusted in chunky silver rings. He even had a studded leather bracelet. This guy was trying way too hard to be a bad boy, when in fact he really just looked like a sweet little kid whose mom dressed him up as a punk rocker for Halloween.

Jake strode over to the hallway mirror and patted his overly gelled dark hair, making sure his quasi–faux hawk was still in place. Satisfied, he acknowledged Colin with a tilt of his chin.

"I'm ready, bro. Let's do this," Jake said.

Beth gave the thumbs up.

Jake smirked at the camera, which made me like him a little. I was glad someone else wasn't taking the whole thing too seriously.

Colin put headphones on and stepped behind the camera. "Rolling," he said.

I stuffed my hat behind a cushion, knowing my mom wouldn't say anything in front of the camera.

Colin shrugged and kept filming.

"Deep in the heartland of the Midwest live the Bergers," Jake began, in a game-show-host-type voice. "An average middle-class Jewish family, like any other, but with one very surprising exception. They don't spend their time playing bingo at the synagogue. Oh, no, the Bergers are Bigfoot hunters. On the first three episodes of *Myth Gnomers*, Myron and Brenda Berger and their three lovely teenage daughters will work together to prove, without a shadow of a doubt, the existence of Bigfoot. Our cameras will be there every step of the way, as they face off against a team of some of the country's best and brightest young science students, but first, let's find out more about this family and their unusual hobby."

Jake turned to my father. "So, Myron, tell us a little bit about the Berger Family Bigfoot Hunters."

My dad straightened his spine and folded his hands in his lap. "Actually, Jake, we prefer the term *Wood Ape* over Bigfoot." He cleared his throat. "I'm a middle-school science teacher, and I feel it's important to give these creatures a respectful name. Also, we aren't *hunters*, per se. We're conservationists. Our mission is to conduct research, classify, and preserve the Wood Ape's way of life.

It would be a shame if they became extinct because of our lack of knowledge."

"Presuming they exist," Jake said.

My dad blinked several times as if he didn't understand. I hoped Bigfoot didn't have a sense of humor, because if he did, my dad had no hope of being able to communicate with him.

Dad flipped through his index cards. "Just because we haven't obtained concrete evidence yet, doesn't mean that there isn't an unknown primate species inhabiting the forests of America, and even the world. Science discovers new species every day, for example—"

"And Brenda," Jake cut my dad off, and pivoted toward my mom. "What do you have to say about your family's hobby?"

"Oh, Jake." My mom giggled. "It's more than a hobby. The Wood Ape is part of the family. I'm just so proud of my husband for being singled out for this show."

"Let's talk a little about the other team," Jake said. "What makes you think your family has what it takes to go up against a group of students from one of the most prestigious prep schools in the country?"

"Well," my dad said, cleaning his glasses, "we understand the way the Wood Ape thinks, right, dear?"

"Absolutely! We've spent weeks in the field and at conferences with our colleagues from other areas of the country. We're ready for anything." My mom flashed a winning smile. The lipstick on her teeth? Still totally there.

"Myron," Jake continued, "where does your unusual passion for Sasquatch research come from?"

My dad chuckled. "Ah, that's an interesting story. When I was about eleven years old I was wandering through the woods behind my house . . ." My dad launched into the saga of his one and only dubious sighting of Sasquatch.

Jake's face froze in the kind of polite smile most people use to humor toddlers. I was used to it.

I leaned out of the camera's frame, pulled out my crappy old phone, and tapped out a quick message to my best friend, and fellow outcast, Charlie.

Promise me you'll cancel your cable subscription right about now.

No way! she wrote back. *Then I'd be the weird girl who doesn't watch TV.*

I smiled, thinking of Charlie in all her blue-haired, pink-combat-booted glory. She was well past weird, which was why we were friends. Being the daughter of Bigfoot hunters didn't exactly fast-track me to popularity. Far from it.

I snuck my phone back in my pocket before my mom could glare at me. But I had bigger concerns, like what was going to happen when the rest of the world found out about my parents' obsession. Good thing I didn't want to go to prom anyway.

"Okay, then. Let's hear from the girls." Jake's mouth turned up in a wolfish grin. He swiveled toward my older sister. "Sophie, what are you most looking forward to during your time on the show?"

Sophie sat with both hands folded in her lap. "It will be wonderful to spend some time in nature." Her face lit up the way it always did when she talked about the great outdoors. "The forests in the Pacific Northwest are so beautiful. And honestly, I hope the show inspires viewers to visit parks and forests near them and encourages people to help protect our natural resources."

I wondered if Sophie's Girl Scout uniform still fit and if there was a badge for hunting mythical creatures.

"Lyssa, how about you?" Jake ogled my little sister.

"I'm really glad you asked." Lyssa tilted her head and beamed, an old pageant trick to look sincere.

She was pretty successful on the child beauty queen circuit before an ugly baton-twirling injury permanently weakened her rotator cuff.

"I'm most excited about spending time with my family and stuff," she said. "Family's super important, right? And I think it will be great to be on TV."

She said all that with a slight Southern accent, which would have been fine except for the fact that we're not Southern. We're not even from southern Ohio.

I couldn't take it anymore. My eyes rolled all the way to the back of my head and into the next freaking county.

"Samantha, you seem a bit skeptical about all this Bigfoot hunting. What's your motivation for going on the trip?" Jake asked.

I figured if Sophie was the sweet one and Lyssa the sexy one, I could play the leave-me-the-hell-alone one, which wasn't much of a stretch.

I slouched back into the cushion. "I offered to stay home and take care of the dog, until my family reminded me that we don't have one," I said, forcing a laugh, and ignoring my mom's flashing eyes.

"Cute," Jake said, with a fake chortle. "The producers tell me that you're going into your senior year of high school and hope to be pre-med in college." He seemed determined to get a real answer from me. "I bet the prize money would help with that."

Prize money? No one had mentioned cash before this. I stared at my dad. He smiled and nodded like a bobble-head doll in a fast-moving vehicle. He knew how much I wanted to go to college full-time, and not just part-time like Sophie, who lived at home and worked two crappy jobs to help pay her tuition bills.

So much for playing it cool. My eyes widened and I leaned forward. "What kind of money are we talking about?"

Jake's grin broadened. I was hooked and he knew it. "Enough to put all three of you through college. So, I'll ask again, Samantha, how excited are you to go deep into the forest in search of the elusive Wood Ape?"

A smile broke out on my face bigger than a Wood Ape's footprint. "I'm thrilled for the opportunity, Jake. If Sasquatch is real and hanging in the wilds of Washington State, he'd better make up the guest room, because we're coming to find him."

Chapter 2

"A British guy, named David Thompson, first found
a set of Sasquatch footprints in the early 1800s. Since
then, countless groups of hunters have set off in
search of the hairy guy. Bigfoot, I mean. Not David
Thompson. I have no idea if he was hairy or not."

—*Jake Stone, host of "Myth Gnomers"*

It had taken my dad three weeks and six family meetings to get
organized and four days for my mom to pack our old beat-up minivan. You would've thought we were going to Antarctica, not to the
Pacific Northwest, where I assumed they sold toothbrushes and bug
spray.

"Honey, you remembered to pack the compass, right?" my mom
asked my dad, who was driving for the fifth day in a row. "How
about my battery-operated curling iron?"

My dad patted her hand and gave her an indulgent smile.
"Everything is packed perfectly."

I fidgeted in the back seat, crossing and uncrossing my legs.
Somehow I ended up in the middle between my two sleeping sisters.
Again. The third row of the van was crammed with all our gear.

We hit a bump and a heavy flashlight smacked me in the back
of the head. "Ow! What the hell?" I howled, securing the flashlight
into a backpack. "We remembered the flashlight, so you can cross
that off the list."

Of course we remembered everything. The Berger Family Bigfoot
Hunters—or Wood Ape Conservationists as my dad liked to call
us—were always prepared for anything. We were so prepared that

if a Sasquatch showed up at our camp, we would be one hundred percent ready to welcome him with a five-course meal or a festive block party.

Too bad we couldn't be the Berger Family Holiday Inn Guests or the Berger Family Cruise Ship Passengers. But whenever I voiced my opinion, Mom and Dad would argue that the thrill of adventure was more important than comfort and relaxation. I didn't think they were even capable of enjoying family vacations without damp, dirty clothes and the constant buzz of mosquitoes. Or maybe it was just their way of trying to make us feel better about not being able to afford to stay in a hotel.

Bored, I closed my eyes and tried to get some rest. Several minutes later, my parents started speaking in hushed tones.

"The bank called again," my mom said. "I think I can hold them off another month, but things aren't looking good."

"Did you ask them about refinancing?" my dad whispered back.

"Of course I did," she said behind gritted teeth. "But they say the house is worth even less than we owe."

My dad groaned before my mom shushed him.

"Oh, honey, we'll figure out a way out of this," she said.

"We just have to win that two hundred thousand," my dad said, his regular brightness back in his voice.

Oh. Is that all we had to do to save our house? Find Bigfoot. Well, crap. I knew things were bad, but not that the bank was knocking at our door.

I threw an arm over my eyes and tried to get comfortable and go to sleep for real, but I was too upset.

Two hundred thousand dollars might not seem like a lot to some people, but for us, apparently it meant keeping our house. And for me, it meant going to college without having to work three jobs and being in serious debt when I graduated. It meant a real shot at my dream of being a doctor. If we won.

Giving up on sleep, I blinked my eyes open and tried to focus on the pretty scenery along the highway, which, it turned out, wasn't very difficult because the Pacific Northwest was really beautiful. Dense forests lined both sides of the road, with trees so tall they blocked most of the sky from view. The closer we got to the property where the competition was going to take place, the quieter it got, and the more lush and otherworldly the scenery became. I imagined the tall trees uprooting themselves at night and dancing elaborate ballets with wood nymphs like in one of my nerdy fantasy novels.

I could understand why Bigfoot would rather settle here than in the rural Midwest. Lots of places to hide, plants and fish to eat, and fresh water to drink. Or maybe he just enjoyed grunge music and artisanal coffee.

"Honey, there's the turn ahead." My mom pointed a brightly polished fingernail at a sign on the right that read "Duckworthy Homestead. Private Property."

We turned onto the entrance road, the fog-covered mountains looming in the distance. Only a corner of the gray sky peeked out through the trees. I had hoped for a nice shade of blue, but the sky was gloomy bordering on ominous with heavy rain clouds threatening to burst. No wonder everything was so green. It was the famous Washington rain, good for growing trees, not so much for camping.

I nudged my sisters with my elbows to wake them.

"Ow!" Lyssa elbowed back.

My dad cleared his throat and gave us the stink-eye in the rear-view mirror.

"We're almost there." I gave her my most innocent smile.

"I'm up, I'm up!" Lyssa dove into her purse to get a mirror and lip gloss. "God, who made you boss?"

Sophie woke herself coughing.

I handed her a tissue. "Weren't you supposed to see the doctor before we left?"

She shook her head and coughed some more. "We were so busy getting ready for the trip that I forgot." Her eyes took in the overgrown bushes and moss-covered tree trunks. "Are we finally here?"

"Yup," I said.

"Thank god! I can't wait to get out of this car," Lyssa whined. "I still don't understand why we didn't fly."

My mom fluffed up her hair using the mirror on the visor. "You know your father doesn't like flying."

My dad paled at the mention of flying. He tried to cover his phobia with an extra jolly smile. "Plus, we have a lot of gear we need to bring, and it's just easier to do that with the car. Besides, didn't we have fun along the way?"

"Of course we did, honey," my mom said in her most chipper voice. "Wasn't it fun to see the World's Largest Ball of Twine, girls?"

"Yeah, totally worth going a hundred miles out of our way to see," I said. My mom turned around and gave me the glare of death. Her warning didn't have the same effect it used to when I was younger, but I still got the point.

We followed the winding road and pulled into a makeshift dirt parking lot, a half hour early, as always.

"You don't catch Wood Apes by showing up late," my dad said. He parked the van and we all stumbled out like zombies, legs asleep and necks cramped. I stretched and groaned, dread taking up residence in my stomach as the reality hit. We were about to make complete and total fools of ourselves on national effing television. Normally, I'd protest yet again, but after that overheard conversation about our mortgage, I swallowed my apprehension. My parents didn't need anything else to worry about.

"Let the humiliation begin," I mumbled and scanned the parking lot for the production crew. A few cars were parked, ranging from pickup trucks and Jeeps to expensive-looking SUVs, but I didn't see anyone who belonged to the vehicles. However, a paper sign tacked to a tree at one of the trailheads read: "*Myth Gnomers* Base Camp This Way" complete with an illustration of a gnome holding an arrow pointing the way. I had hoped some interns or production assistants could help us carry all our crap to the base camp. But that was wishful thinking.

I hoisted the heaviest bag onto my shoulders since no one else made a move for it. Then, ignoring Lyssa's complaining, I loaded down my sisters and left a few smaller things for my parents to carry. We set off up the narrow trail and soon saw the film crew.

Colin's assistant producer, Beth the Bland, walked over to us and in a monotone voice said, "You're early. You weren't supposed to be here for another fifteen minutes. Sorry you had to carry your own stuff."

I dropped my pack and the tin dishes and canned goods clanged when they hit the ground. "No problem. Hunting Bigfoot isn't any fun unless you've got half a ton of gear on your back."

Beth didn't crack a smile. In fact, her brow furrowed like I was speaking Martian. I tilted my head, trying to figure her out.

But then I noticed the competition standing across the clearing, and I stopped smiling.

The only thing I knew about the other team was that they were anthropology students, two guys and a girl from Netherfield Academy, a fancy private high school in Massachusetts with a top-notch science and math program. They seemed to fit the profile perfectly, with matching polo shirts like some corporate bowling league. They looked way too pampered to be much of a threat.

Out of the three, the first one I noticed was a really cute Indian guy with slightly wavy dark hair who made me wish I had checked my shirt for ice cream stains. He was impeccably dressed in olive-colored pants and brown leather boots, which made him look like he had just been on an expensive safari. I had no idea Bigfoot hunters came that handsome.

He fiddled with some piece of equipment and laughed with his friends. When he spoke, a touch of a sexy British accent rose through their chatter. Adorable and British? It didn't seem fair to teenage girls with a *Doctor Who* obsession, like me. I didn't realize I was staring at him, until our eyes met.

Busted!

The guy didn't immediately turn away, but instead observed me with a detached, Vulcan-like indifference. I blushed and became very interested in adjusting the strap on my pack. *For god's sake, Sam, pull it together*, I scolded myself. Now that I was here, I was going to win, and I wasn't going to let myself get all boy-crazy over the competition. I'd have plenty of time for boys when I finished med school and my residency in about ten years.

By the time I finally sneaked another peek, he had gone back to talking with his friends.

The other boy was a Korean guy with a laid-back West Coast accent wearing a backwards baseball cap and a generous smile. His team shirt was wrinkled and paired with some khaki shorts. He played with a lacrosse stick while his teammates were unpacking. His grin was charming, if you liked guys who carried around sports equipment, which I sure didn't. The third member of their team was a blonde girl with a face like a horse: pointy chin, big teeth, and waist-length shiny mane. Her tasteful baby blue shorts showed off her long, tanned limbs, which gave the impression that she spent a lot of time playing tennis.

Guy One swatted bugs while the girl wiped dirt off her hands with a baby wipe.

This is going to be a cakewalk. My face relaxed into a smile. If they were already this uncomfortable in the Great Outdoors, the prize money was pretty much in the bag.

My elation fizzled when the handsome, stuffy boy and the girl stopped to stare at something behind me, with matching expressions of disbelief. I didn't have to turn around to figure out what they were eyeing. I already knew. It was my family. Lyssa had put on way too much makeup and bright skimpy clothing, afraid the cameras would wash her out. My mom's baby-blue velour hoodie and lounge pants were accessorized by a fanny pack of monstrous proportions. She looked like a pastel kangaroo. My dad had strapped one of those miner's headlamps on his head, despite the fact that it was the middle of the day. And all three of them were arguing loudly about who should carry the heaviest pack full of food and cooking gear.

Sophie marched in and calmly scooped up the gear. "I'll carry it," she said, wheezing under the weight of the equipment. She trudged off in the direction of the three trailers that made up the base camp and deposited the pack on one of the four picnic tables. Leave it to Sophie to volunteer to carry twenty extra pounds of stuff, just to make everyone else happy.

Well, at least that got my family to shut up and stop embarrassing me for a moment. And Sophie and I had nothing to be ashamed of. We looked more normal, for sure, even though our "work clothes" were far from preppy. We were just lucky they were without ketchup spills. "Bergers and fries are a perfect combination," my mom always said. It was mildly funny the first five times—when we were a hell of a lot younger.

Sophie wore a Greenpeace T-shirt and old cargo pants while I rocked my old, but comfortable Nine Inch Nails concert shirt and cut-off denim shorts. Yeah, the band was retro, but they were from Ohio, and I wanted to bring some home-state pride with me.

Despite my misgivings, I managed a little wave to the blonde girl staring at us. I even took a few steps toward her, to say hello, but she swiveled on one heel and turned her back to me. Then she whispered something to the lacrosse-playing guy. I shook my head and retreated. Screw them.

I was far from surprised by the looks we got from the prep school stiffs. Hell, I welcomed them. I was only there to win the money for college, but beating them would be an excellent bonus prize.

Chapter 3

"Long before the name Bigfoot was first uttered,
Native Americans recounted their experiences with 'wild men.'
The stories varied from tribe to tribe. Some reported
playful, harmless creatures, while others lived in fear
of man-eating beasts."

—"Sasquatch Lore and Legends, Third Edition"

Step one of my new master plan to win was to scope out the enemy.

I sat on a boulder, took out a book, and pretended to read. My parents and Lyssa were going through our equipment list again, but Sophie sat next to me.

"Are those the kids from Connecticut?" she asked in a low voice.

"Massachusetts, I think."

"They're all so good-looking."

"If you like that rich kid thing," I said from behind the book.

Sophie bumped my shoulder with hers. "Be nice. We don't know that they're rich. And even if they are, that doesn't mean they're snobs."

"Oh, dear sweet Soph." I turned down the page of my book and shook my head. "Why are you so kind to everyone? It makes it harder for me to enjoy being mean and sarcastic."

"Yet you seem to manage." She smiled and gazed up at the treetops.

Soon she was lost in her thoughts while I tried to concentrate on my plan, but failed miserably. I couldn't stop thinking about how the other team had stared at my family, and how much I wanted to win and to shove our victory in their smug, good-looking faces.

The preps were struggling with their GPS unit. The sporty dude joked, "Don't look at me. I hate electronics. I swear the microwave tried to kill me the other day. I think the stereo was in on it, too."

I stifled a giggle. He didn't seem so heinous. Too bad he had to hang out with Snob One and Snob Two.

The girl, who was perched on a tree stump with her laptop open on her knee, just shook her head, seemingly unamused.

"How the hell do you get the battery compartment open?" The Brit began to pry the battery cover off with his penknife.

"Don't!" I called out, forgetting that I was supposed to be pretending to read. "There's a latch under the rubber case." The GPS was the same one we had, albeit a much newer, shinier version.

"Oh."

He located the latch and the cover popped open. Instead of showering me with thanks for saving their three-hundred-dollar gadget from ruin, I was rewarded with silence. He squinted his eyes in my direction then turned his attention back to the GPS. So much for gratitude. I didn't know why I was helping them. Maybe I was a really nice person. Or maybe I was a control freak. Or maybe I just couldn't bear to see a good piece of equipment get destroyed because some people were too freaking impatient to read the damn manual.

The sporty guy broke the silence with a laugh and ambled my way. "Thank you—that was nice of you. Especially considering we're the enemy."

"No worries. If you're as good at tracking Sasquatch as you are at electronics, I'm not too concerned," I deadpanned.

He chuckled again. "I'm sorry my friends are so rude. We should introduce ourselves." He waved the others over. They took about three steps and stopped. "I'm Kyle Park, and this is Devan Das, and Caroline Bing."

Devan barely nodded at me, and Caroline looked me up and down, making it obvious she was sizing up the competition. Sophie left her perch on the rock to join the conversation and held out her hand, but Devan and Caroline had already turned back to their gear.

"Hi," I said to only Kyle. "I'm Sam Berger and this is my sister Sophie. Over there, that's our other sister Lyssa, and our parents."

"It's nice to meet you guys," he said, shaking our hands and offering a wide grin. Kyle's expression softened when he made eye contact with Sophie. "Hey, cool shirt. I had thought about being a marine biologist, but then I decided to focus on primatology."

"That's my dream, too." Sophie beamed at him through lowered lashes. "Well, not marine biology, because I get seasick, or primatology because chimpanzees kind of freak me out, but some sort of animal conservation. I haven't figured it out yet."

"Sophie does a lot of volunteering with local shelters and animal rights groups," I said. My sister blushed, but Kyle looked pretty interested.

"That's awesome. So what's your take on Bigfoot? Is he another lovable stray?"

"Maybe . . ." Sophie paused. "What do you think?"

"I'd like to believe he's real. True life can be pretty weird, right?" Kyle said. "Plus, I read that even Jane Goodall thinks they might exist. That's a pretty ringing endorsement."

Caroline snapped her fingers at Kyle like she was demanding the check at a restaurant. "Kyle, we need you here! Stop talking about monkeys and help us get organized!"

Kyle gave a little bitter laugh. "Don't mind my lovely sister. She's the smart one. I'm just here to lift crap and follow orders, apparently."

"Sister?" I asked, not seeing any family resemblance in either the looks or the personality department.

"Stepsister, actually. My dad and her mom are married." He gave me a little salute and walked back over to his teammates. "Caroline, there's always enough time to talk about chimpanzees. Plus, they're not actually monkeys . . ." Kyle added.

"At least one of them isn't a total tool," I said to Sophie.

Unfortunately, an older woman in a wide-brimmed summer hat materialized behind me just then. She roughly pushed past me in a huff. I guessed she had heard my remark and wasn't joining my fan club anytime soon.

Colin followed behind her like she was a big elephant on parade and he was the guy cleaning up after her mess. "Dr. DeGraw, please forgive me, but we're running behind schedule. Everyone really appreciates you coming all the way here to check on the production. We'll get started in just a minute."

"Good. I have a teleconference in an hour with my department and the provost. They'll want me to report back on the team."

Colin simpered. "Like I said, we'll get started shortly."

She dismissed him with a wave and sauntered over to greet Devan warmly. I didn't know who this woman was, but she made me nervous, bordering on petrified. And *I* didn't scare easily.

Colin signaled to Beth and the two cameramen, one a burly, hairy dude, the other a bald, wiry guy. There were also a few crewmembers standing by with huge microphones and lighting gear.

"We're ready, Colin," Beth said.

"Okay, everyone," Colin said, shuffling his feet and surveying the small crowd. "Please gather round."

My parents and Lyssa wandered over and stood next to Sophie and me.

"Before we start rolling, I want to introduce Dr. Roberta DeGraw, Dean of Netherfield Academy," Colin said, his voice squeaking a bit. "Dr. DeGraw holds a PhD in archeology, and is here not only as mentor to the Netherfield students, but also as an advisor for the show. However, she will not be influencing the proceedings."

Roberta waved at Colin to continue.

"We also want to thank Jim Duckworthy for letting us use his 10,000-acre property for the shoot. You'll meet him later, but suffice it to say he's very interested in your findings. I think the contestants have all had a chance to meet each other, yes?"

Boy, did we ever.

Colin gestured at the picnic tables and trailers around him. "This will be our base camp, where we'll film all our group meetings and announce the challenges, and where we'll reveal evidence," he continued, gaining a little more confidence. "During the challenges you'll be followed around by the film crews. However, we're not going to be filming you every second of the day. When the crew leaves your group for the night, they'll take the body mics with them and bring them back fully charged in the morning. But, remember, we've already set up a few cameras in the common areas of each team's home base which will be running at all times to catch any interesting candid moments."

Colin's face lit up, probably from the idea of exploiting our embarrassing moments for ratings. We were going to have to be really careful if we had any hope of preserving our dignity.

Colin paused to look at his clipboard. "I believe everyone already signed the medical and legal documents we sent over. We're all for drama, but don't go overboard. You'll be turning in your cell phones now, but in the case of an emergency, use your walkie-talkies to call Beth, who will arrange for medical care." He pointed with a pen to a basket, which Beth circulated.

I typed out one more fast text to Charlie. *TV people are confiscating our phones. If I don't come back in three weeks, send in the Loch Ness Monster and some scotch.* The phone whooshed as it delivered my message. When Beth came to me, I deposited my last connection to the outside world in the basket.

"Any questions before we get started?" Colin asked.

When no one responded, he glanced at Jake, who was busy checking his makeup in the mirror with the help of the leggy makeup girl. "Jake! You're up first. We'll start with your solo intro. We're chasing daylight. Let's get on with it."

"Dude, chill. I'm almost ready. Mindy here was just working her magic." He gave her a flashy smile. Mindy, who was probably ten years older and at least six inches taller than Jake, flipped her long brunette hair and smiled indulgently at his attempt at swaggering. Lyssa's eyes narrowed a bit. It was her game face. I'd seen it at pageants over the years. She could be very competitive when she felt like it. Not about anything worthwhile like school or sports, but Mindy better watch out.

"Don't even think about it, Lyssa." I grabbed her arm and whispered in her ear. "We're here for one reason only."

"To make Dad happy, so he'll let me take Driver's Ed even though I got a C in science this year?"

"Okay, two reasons. I was referring to the money, but whatever keeps your head in the game."

Jake must have finally been ready to do his thing, because they called quiet on the set. He stood in front of a *Myth Gnomers* banner and spoke directly to the camera.

"The Loch Ness Monster. The Jersey Devil. The Chupacabra. Legendary creatures such as these ignite the imagination of people around the world. On this season of *Myth Gnomers* we'll travel the globe in search of the truth behind those myths and more, starting right here in the Pacific Northwest."

"Great!" Colin said. "Let's take intro number two."

Jake cracked his knuckles then stood in position again. "What happens when two rival Bigfoot teams face off in a race to be the first to find conclusive evidence of the existence of Sasquatch? Can the Berger family from the backwoods of Ohio, armed only with their wits and years of mountaineering experience, beat Netherfield

Academy's brightest young anthropology students equipped with the latest state-of-the-art technology?"

Backwoods? WTF? Sure, we weren't from Paris, but last time I checked we had running water and a Starbucks.

"The winners will walk away with bragging rights and two hundred thousand dollars in cash . . ."

As Jake continued his intro, Makeup-Girl Mindy came around to get us all ready for filming. She patted my face and Sophie's with pressed powder. "You two don't need much. I just want to get rid of the shine."

Her lips curved slightly downward when she got to Lyssa, who had teased her hair into a puffy cheerleader ponytail and slathered on orange bronzer in an attempt to look like a reality television star.

"Can you add more mascara?" Lyssa asked, oblivious to Mindy's deepening frown lines.

"I think you've got plenty, honey," Mindy replied, retreating back to the makeup trailer. Lyssa grabbed a mascara wand from her bag and applied two more coats on her own. I hoped Bigfoot had a thing for raccoons.

Not that we were going to get a chance to see a Sasquatch anytime soon. Television production turned out to be a painfully slow process. We sat and waited for what felt like hours. Jake did about a dozen takes of his two monologues then sauntered to his dressing room. The crewmembers fluttered about adjusting equipment, making jokes, and drinking coffee, while nothing seemed to be happening.

I squirmed in my seat, seriously antsy. What the hell were we waiting for? I just wanted to get this shoot over with so that we could hike to our site and set up camp before it was completely dark.

I looked for Colin, but he had disappeared, so I circled around the production trailer, thinking maybe he was on the other side. As

I rounded the corner, I spied Colin interviewing the Netherfield team. I ducked back behind the trailer before they saw me.

"I feel pretty good about our chances of winning, now that we've met the competition," Caroline drawled to the camera. "They seem . . . um, enthusiastic. But, honestly, I really don't see how *they* think they have a chance against *us*. We're all in the top of our class at one of the best prep schools in the country. It's almost not fair." She paused, glancing at the boys to back her up.

Devan fidgeted like he wasn't sure where to look or what to do with his somewhat gangly arms. Moving them behind his back, he cleared his throat and spoke, too loudly, as if he were reciting a proclamation.

"We've got some fantastic research equipment and are up to date on the latest field study techniques," he said. "We're confident that the Bergmans . . ."

"Bergers," Colin interrupted.

Devan waved off the correction, like it didn't matter. "We're quite confident that the Bergers as *amateur* hobbyists won't have the skills or know-how to compete."

Colin focused the lens on Kyle, and Devan let out a breath, probably of relief. I'd seen enough. I spun around and stormed back to my team. Livid. And worried that the other team was right, that we didn't have a chance.

I clenched and unclenched my fists until I was breathing normally again. It was bad enough we were searching for Bigfoot on television. Now the other team was trashing us on camera. It wasn't just what they said or how quickly they dismissed us that hurt me so much. It was what they didn't say. That they thought my family wasn't as educated and classy as they were.

"Sam! Get over here!" Lyssa hollered at me when I emerged from the other side of the trailer. "We're gonna start soon."

They had herded my family into a formation at the base of the trail that would lead to our camping area. The bigger crew guy was there with a camera, already trained on my family's faces. The cameraman gave me a big grin when I approached the group and pointed to an empty spot next to Sophie. Sophie took one look at my face and her eyebrows rose in confusion and concern. I just shook my head, and tried to stop myself from grinding my teeth. Sophie let it go, probably figuring she'd get the story from me later.

A sound guy handed me a wireless body mic, and showed me how to hook it to my shirt collar, while Beth moved the other team and their own film crew to their trailhead a few yards over.

Colin's megaphone emitted a loud feedback squeal, and he winced. "Okay, everyone. Jake's going to give the intro to the first challenge and we're going to film your reactions. Then, after the monologue, we want you to race up the trails with your gear, so be ready to run."

There was a loud grumble from both teams. Colin added, "You don't have to run the whole way. Just for the first few seconds—we want to create some drama and tension between the teams."

Tension between the teams? *Check!* I was barely holding it together. I really, really wanted to let Devan and Caroline have it, to storm over there and slap the smugness right off their faces.

But then I had a moment of clarity. The best way to hurt them would be to win—puncturing those huge egos of theirs. So I decided to smile, like the rest of my team, and let the preps underestimate us. It was better this way. We would kick their sorry asses and they'd never see it coming.

I peeked over at the other team and to my horror, I caught Devan staring right at me. I glared back defiantly, and after a few seconds he glanced away.

Jake stood between the two teams, facing the camera, feet apart like he was preparing to box.

"We're going to do this a couple of times to make sure it's right," Colin announced from behind the cameras. "Rolling," he added.

"Bigfoot babes and Sasquatch dudes, it's time for your first challenge. Your teams must travel deep into the woods to—"

"Cut!" Colin yelled. "Stick to the script, Jake. You *can* read, right?"

Jake stuck his chest out, which while a fine specimen of what a chest should be, didn't do much to help his case. "I'm just making it sound cool, bro. What you wrote is dry. No one will make it past the first commercial break."

"Let's *not* try to be cool." Colin stepped out from behind the camera holding the pressure points on both sides of his head. "We're taking this seriously because the viewers and the contestants take Bigfoot seriously. I'll allow you the occasional pun, but you are under no circumstances to call anyone 'Babe' or 'Dude.'" Got it?"

"Got it," Jake said with a winning smile and two hands pointed like guns at Colin.

"Take two!" Beth hollered loudly once Colin took his spot behind the camera.

Jake smoothed his hair, and smirked. Lowering his voice to a more serious tone he said, "It's day one of the hunt for Bigfoot, and the two rival teams will travel deep into the desolate woods and call upon their tracking skills to bring back physical proof of the mysterious beast. Big feet, claws, and bodies leave all sorts of clues behind. Our contestants will have one week to scour the area. The trackers who bring back the most convincing footprint, tissue sample, or other piece of physical evidence from the trails will be the winner of this round. Be bold, be creative, and be safe. Now, go Bigfoot or go home!"

I gave Devan and his friends one last look before I took off running up the dirt trail.

Chapter 4

"Bigfoot sightings are common in certain areas, usually
where there is a small population of humans. Either Bigfoot
prefers solitude and certain terrains, or people in
unpopulated areas have more time for Bigfoot hunting."

—*Kyle Park, senior at Netherfield Academy*

"Cut!" Colin shouted a few moments later.

Ugh. We'd only run about twenty yards up the hill when I had
to skid to a halt to avoid careening into the cameraman, who had
stopped dead in his tracks. He had been running backwards ahead
of us in order to capture all the glory of the Berger family in full
gallop.

"Sorry, kid." The cameraman lowered the heavy equipment
from his shoulder and held out a hand to steady me. "Guess we get
to run up the hill again."

"Yay," I said with fake enthusiasm. "Being on TV is even more
glamorous than I dreamed."

The big guy laughed at my joke, and began to lead my family
back down to the starting point. "We probably won't do too many
staged scenes. Mostly I'll follow you around and let you guys do
your thing. You'll forget I'm even here."

"If you say so." I wasn't convinced that this six-foot, two-
hundred-fifty-pound, middle-aged dude with a long red ponytail
and a Yoda shirt would be easy to ignore.

"I'm Hal, by the way." He held out his meaty hand.

I wiped the sweat off of my much smaller hand and took his to shake. "I'm Sam."

"Nice to be working with you guys. We're going to have a lot more fun than those stuffed shirts." Hal gestured down the hill at the other team.

Yup. Hal and I would get along just fine. I was only a little out of breath as we arrived at the bottom of the hill for the next take. Colin and Jake were also there, facing off. There was a lot of pointing, jabbing, and other gestures. "Do it again," Colin glared down at Jake, who was shorter. "And try to be a little more subtle. This isn't one of your ghost shows."

"No shit. Ghosts are real and scary. Bigfoot's just some made-up movie monster," Jake shot back.

"Ghosts aren't real, Jake." Colin sighed. "And for our purposes, Bigfoot is flesh and blood. Just do your job and don't editorialize. You're paid to host, not think."

Jake either didn't notice Colin shaking his head and clenching his jaw, or he just didn't care. "Some of the ghosts I've dealt with could totally kick Bigfoot's hairy ass. Let's lock you in a haunted asylum and see who's scared."

"Back to work. Now." Colin grabbed his heavy-duty binder and held it in the air like a reminder of why we were all there.

Jake coolly picked at the chipping black polish on his nails. "I have to get into character. It's gonna take a while. I need a private trailer and some rap music."

Colin stepped closer to Jake, and growled. "You have two minutes and a park bench. Take it or leave it."

"Not cool, dude. I'm calling my agent! This isn't what I signed up for." Jake's voice rose with agitation.

"Oh, for Christ's sake," Colin said. "We've only shot ten minutes of usable footage. I'll happily start over. And so you know, I can bring in another pretty face from any number of failed supernatural shows. I hear the *Monster Hunt* guys are free . . ."

Jake stormed off, giving Colin the finger over his shoulder. Colin threw his hands up in the air. "Take five, everyone. Come back ready." He walked over to a tree stump, sat down, and massaged his temples.

Finally, Jake decided he was ready to work again. He did a few different takes of the introduction monologue, and each time we'd all lumber up the hill with our gear. The third time, we were allowed to keep going.

The location my parents had pre-chosen for our campsite was about two miles into the grounds, uphill the whole way, of course. My dad had wanted to camp even farther into the wilderness, but the production company insisted that the site be accessible by Jeep so they could get the crew in and out more easily. Unfortunately for us, though, Colin thought it would be more entertaining to watch us hike the whole way, so the Jeep would not be accompanying us.

The mosquitoes, however, would be joining us on our journey, and judging by my already swollen arm, it was an all-they-could-eat buffet and we were the main course.

About a mile into our hike, the trail turned, and we found ourselves on a steep ridge, overlooking a creek running through the valley below. The unmistakable sound of the other team's voices floated up to us.

"You've got to be flipping kidding me," I said under my breath. I dropped my thirty-five-pound backpack, mopped the sweat off my face, and peered at the scene below.

I put a finger over my lips to get everyone else to be quiet so I could listen.

"Kyle! Be careful with that! DeGraw will kill us if we break any of the academy's equipment," Caroline whined.

Kyle lugged one of several big black plastic cases up the steps of a log cabin.

Log cabin was a big understatement.

The house could totally have been featured on an episode of *Hollywood's Famous Forest Dwellers*. The one-story wooden house, complete with a picturesque porch swing, was clearly where the other team would be staying. Caroline was wheeling some huge metal equipment through the front door, followed by the other cameraman. The warm yellow glow pouring out from the windows made it obvious that the cabin had electricity. No doubt there was running water and cable television, too. It was like camping out at the Four Seasons.

"Ooh, they're 'glamping.' I want to glamp," Lyssa said.

"Glamping?" my mom asked.

"Glamorous Camping," she explained. "It's what all the celebrities are into these days."

"Are they going to lure Bigfoot with a continental breakfast?" I laughed and watched Devan unload a huge cooler from the back of the Jeep.

"Oh, Samantha," my dad said, taking out his industrial-sized binoculars, "they'll never catch him from there. But we'll be on the ground, thinking like the Wood Ape, living like the Wood Ape, and sensing his every move."

"And *smelling* like the Wood Ape after a few days," I grumbled. "At the same time they'll have central heating and a microwave. If I were a Wood Ape, I'd much rather hang out with them." I complained, but I hoped my dad was right and that, despite their fancy equipment, they had no idea what they were doing. All I knew was that I had come to win, even if beating them required getting stinky and eating beans out of a can.

"Do you think they'll at least let us use the shower?" Lyssa whined. "Those guys are pretty cute, maybe if I flirt . . ."

"No!" Mom said, more forcefully than usual. "No flirting with the enemy. We can do this on our own. Your dad has a plan. Come on, let's go set up camp. It's not that much further."

Lyssa's eyes were glassy with the threat of tears. I tilted my head toward the camera, to remind her that this was all being filmed, and Lyssa, catching my drift, rubbed her eyes and plastered on a smile.

I heaved my big old backpack onto my already achy shoulders and took one last look at the competition's cabin, wondering what it would be like to be born into that kind of fancy-pants life.

We followed my dad for another mile or so until he located our site, a small clearing surrounded by dense tree cover, not too far from the lake.

I glanced around, spying three remote cameras up in the trees around our site.

My dad clapped his hands with anticipation and waited for Hal to focus the camera lens. "This is the perfect environment for an apex predator, like our Wood Ape. Remote, yet with prime access to a water source and great cover for hiding and nesting during the day. Yes, this should do nicely. A camp fit for a Squatch."

My mom gave him an affectionate squeeze on the arm. Dad and Sophie started setting up one of the tents, laughing and smiling. With slightly less enthusiasm, Lyssa and I worked on another. Even though Sophie and I grew up camping, climbing trees, and building forts outside, Lyssa didn't. Nothing was supposed to get in the way of her pageants. Especially not the sunburns, scrapes, or twisted ankles that come from being a kid playing outdoors. Her struggle with the tent poles made it obvious she didn't know what the hell she was doing.

"Lyssa, pay attention!" Mom snapped at her. "You've got the line all twisted."

Hearing that, Hal turned away from my Dad and swooped in to focus the camera on Lyssa's frustration. I casually stepped in between him and the mess of a tent, earning an annoyed grunt from the cameraman for ruining his shot. Oops.

"It's fine, Mom. We're almost done," I said. I really didn't want to have to sit through yet another argument.

"Lyssa should go help Sophie collect some firewood," my mom said, unpacking the cooking gear.

"Are we having roasted Wood Ape for dinner? Is that kosher?" I teased, trying to diffuse the situation. Seeing my mom's frown, I shrugged. "I know, I know, we would never hurt Bigfoot. We're here to admire him, get to know him; maybe take him slow dancing, and out for ice cream."

Lyssa chortled. She hadn't made any motion toward helping Sophie, and didn't look like she was planning on it.

"Seriously, Sophie's still coughing. Can you help her?" I said, before my mom could scold my younger sister.

"Why don't you?" Lyssa spat back.

"Because Dad and I need to strategize."

"I don't know who put you in charge." Lyssa stuck her tongue out at me but dragged her feet over to Sophie. I finished my tent and beelined it to my dad, who had a map spread out in front of him on a folding camp table. Without looking up from the map, my dad put his arm around my shoulder and said, "What do you think, Sammy? What's our first move?"

Hal leaned in with the camera.

I stared at the map and thought for a moment. "Put out some bait in likely spots; see if anything leaves any tracks?"

"That's my girl! Just what I was thinking." Dad grinned and pointed to the places he wanted to check out.

My sisters were on the other side of the clearing gathering firewood. Mom was putting together a masterpiece of campfire cuisine. Hal grabbed the body mics and started packing up his gear for the night. Everything seemed momentarily under control, so I decided to make a break for it.

It had been a long-ass week of family road-tripping followed by a torturous day of filming and hiking. I was ready to feed one of them to a passing grizzly bear. I desperately needed some alone time.

"I'm going to scope out a spot by the lake for a possible bait location," I announced, taking off my mic and putting it next to Hal's equipment bag. Not waiting for an answer, I grabbed my backpack and headed into the forest.

Compass in hand, I ambled along, enjoying the sound of the leaves crunching beneath my shoes and the twittering chitchat of the birds. I was no bird expert, but I guessed these little guys were wrens, because of their loud songs. The plain gray birds didn't look like much, but they made prettier music than a lot of fancier birds. I knew how the wrens felt. Overlooked. Like I felt in this contest.

Devan and Caroline acted like we were so far beneath them, and their top-notch education. I liked the idea of letting them savor that superiority for a while. When we beat them without high-tech help, they'd never see it coming.

The horizon started to resemble a bowl of quivering orange Jell-O, but I optimistically found a nice flat rock and sat down, leaning my back against a fir tree to observe what kind of animals frequented the area. Settling in for a while, I had just taken out a dog-eared sci-fi paperback when something far less soothing than singing birds interrupted me.

About thirty feet down the hill, someone—or some huge thing—stomped through the underbrush.

What the hell?

I was a skeptic, for sure, but my mind jumped from images of Bigfoot to other imaginary monsters in the thicket who wouldn't mind dining on me. I'd probably be tasty to them whether I believed in their existence or not. Not that I wanted to run into everyday predators like bears or mountain lions either. I was weighing various exit strategies when an obnoxious voice rose above the rustling of the underbrush.

"Come on, baby. Here's a nice spot for us," Jake cooed. There was no mistaking his sultry voice. It sounded like he was trying to impress some girl, and seeing that we were in the middle of nowhere, it certainly wasn't his famous girlfriend.

"Did anyone notice you leave?" he asked.

His body spray wafted in my direction. They were getting closer to my hiding spot.

The side of my brain that was grossed out by Jake and his woodsy rendezvous screamed at me to slip away. But curiosity and indecision got the better of me. I had waited too long and at this point wouldn't have been able to sneak away without being seen.

So I stayed very still, something I was also pretty good at doing thanks to my dad's training. Bigfoot-hunting with him required us to remain absolutely quiet for long stretches of time.

"No one noticed I left," Caroline said.

I took a huge, surprised gulp of air, almost choking on my breath. I coughed into the crook of my arm then peeked from behind the tree to confirm what I heard. Immediately, I caught a glimpse of Caroline's distinctive honey-colored hair.

Whoa. I shook my head in disbelief.

"The boys were busy with one of their contraptions," Caroline said, running her hands through Jake's overly gelled hair.

Yuck. My fingers felt sticky just looking at them.

"They don't know that I took the rechargeable batteries and replaced them with dead ones," Caroline shrugged.

"Nice! *That's* my evil girl."

I guessed that Caroline and Jake had already ditched their mics too.

Jake grabbed Caroline and pulled her against him. They started making out hot and heavy. I shielded my eyes and decided they were distracted enough. It was my chance to sneak away.

"Ooh, baby. What are you trying to do? Get me to tell you all my contest secrets?" Jake snickered.

Like the Netherfield team needed any more advantages. Posh cabin, fancy gizmos, and now insider information.

I couldn't hear her mumbled answer, but I didn't have to.

Caroline was clearly using Jake to get the scoop on what the challenges were going to be. Why else would she be into a twerpy little sleaze who was cheating on his girlfriend?

"Less talking, babe. More kissing." Jake's romantic sentiment was followed by the sound of smacking lips and slurping noises.

The two participants groaned, as did I, but the sound escaping my throat was not one of pleasure. I needed to get out of there or find a magical tree that grew noise-reducing headphones.

In the meantime, I covered my ears and plotted my next move, but it was hard to concentrate when I was so grossed out. Then I remembered why we were there in the first place. The contest. Suddenly, the embarrassment of catching a slimy make-out session wasn't the issue at all. Why should I be embarrassed when Caroline and Jake were cheating, in both senses of the word? My stomach dropped and I bit my bottom lip to stop myself from yelling out. I was pissed and I had every right to be. And there was no way I was going to crouch and hide any longer. I stood and took one last glance from behind the thick, old fir. Jake and Caroline were still sucking face and hadn't noticed me, so I turned to go.

And discovered I wasn't alone.

Chapter 5

"I may be a science teacher, but science hasn't yet explained everything. There is still plenty of mystery in the world. That's what makes science fun."

—*Myron Berger, additional commentary,* "Myth Gnomers: Season One"

Devan stood three feet away from me. His hands were on his hips and a fierce grimace clouded his face as he stared at Jake and Caroline. His frown deepened when his eyes caught mine, like it was my freaking fault his team member was rolling around in the leaves with a barely pubescent TV host. I returned Devan's death glare, right before he stomped in Caroline's direction, loudly. The couple stopped kissing and broke apart, surprised to have company. I stood in my hiding spot, stumped by Devan's attitude toward me.

Caroline sat up and picked pine needles out of her hair. "Oh, great. Dad's here."

"Caroline, what are you doing? We're going back to the cabin. Now," Devan said, scowling at Jake until he stood up.

"What's it to *you*? Is she your girlfriend? I guess you aren't giving her what she needs . . ." Jake said with full New Jersey bravado, tucking in his shirt.

"Bugger off, Jake. Or . . . I swear . . . I'll beat you senseless." Devan's accent was a bit too refined to sound very threatening. He sounded like a cranky member of the British government. Circa the American Revolution, which, by the way, we totally won.

Jake took a step closer to Devan, fists clenched. "Ohhh, I'm *so* scared."

Caroline jumped between the two guys and put her hand on Devan's chest. "Oh, Devan. It's sweet of you to worry, but I'm a big girl. I can handle myself and we were just having a little fun."

Devan's eyes narrowed. "With *this* jerk? Seriously, Caroline? Come on, we're going."

Caroline didn't move, but slowly straightened her hair with her fingers and shot Devan a go-to-hell look. Devan crossed his arms and huffed.

I wasn't sure why Devan cared, but, other than the fact that she was cheating, Caroline had every right to make out with guys, skanky or otherwise. If anyone should have been protective, it should have been Kyle, her own brother.

I narrowed my eyes in Devan's direction. *Pompous, self-righteous, judgmental ass.*

I had seen enough. I backed away a few steps then hightailed it out of there, leaving them to their uncomfortable arguments. I had walked about a quarter of a mile when footsteps pounded the ground behind me.

Please let that be Bigfoot.

In stark contrast to my earlier wish to avoid all things huge and scary in the forest, this time I hoped my visitor was imaginary or mythical. But I knew it was Devan, jogging to catch up to me.

"Sophie, Sophie!" he shouted. "Wait!"

I kept walking. The jerk-off didn't even know my name.

With his long legs, he caught up to me easily and put a hand on my shoulder. "Sophie, I need to talk to you."

I shrugged his hand off. "It's Sam."

He looked at me with a blank expression.

"My *name* is Samantha."

"Oh, sorry." He tried giving me a little smile, but it just looked like he was constipated.

I kept walking.

He followed behind me like one of those elderly speed walkers who frequent my high school track. "I just want to talk to you for a second about what you witnessed."

I stopped abruptly. "Okay. What?"

"I hope you won't mention Caroline's little lapse in judgment. She must have been a bit star-struck, and Jake may have talked her into it."

"Um, she didn't look like she needed much persuading."

"That's absurd. Caroline has far better taste," he said.

Ugh. Cute or not, Devan was such a prick.

"It has nothing to do with taste," I said. "I heard him offer to help you guys cheat."

Devan's mouth dropped open. You could have parked our minivan behind his molars. "You did?"

"Yup." I gave him a huge smirk.

Devan bit his lip and avoided my gaze. "That doesn't make sense. Caroline's smarter than all of us put together. She hardly needs to cheat," he added.

"Maybe she's not smart about everything."

"You don't understand. She's already taking half her classes at MIT. Her IQ is off the charts." Devan was speaking quickly now, his voice rising in pitch with each breath.

"Oh." I'd underestimated Caroline, thinking she was just a pretty and spoiled girl. I wouldn't make that mistake again.

Devan's eyes pleaded with mine. "Please. All I ask is that you don't share this information with Colin or Dr. DeGraw."

"And why would I keep it to myself?"

"I . . . well . . ." This stumped him for a moment. "I promise you a fair competition. I'll keep Caroline and Jake away from each other."

He offered me a boyish grin and some puppy-dog eyes. "I'm begging you for a fresh start," he said.

I raised my eyebrows but didn't say anything.

When he didn't get his desired reaction, in desperation he tried a different tactic. "Listen, I know how much this competition must mean to you and your family. If one team is disqualified they'll probably cancel the whole thing."

I stopped for a moment to think. On one hand, I really hated cheaters, and I didn't want him to think he could walk all over me and get away with it. But on the other hand, he was right. My family needed this contest to happen. We desperately needed that money to save our house.

"Fine. One more chance," I sighed. "But don't make me regret this. If I get even a hint of any cheating, I will go to Colin." I pointed at his chest and gave him the Berger death glare to make sure he knew I was not to be trifled with. "I'm not intimidated by your fancy school or your expensive clothes. Or impressed."

He held his hands up. "I'm not trying to impress you. I was just offering a clean fight, as a gentleman."

"'As a gentleman'? What are you, sixty years old?"

Devan laughed a little and shook his head.

"It's getting dark—I'm going back to my camp," I said. "I'll leave the gentleman alone to his valet and his butler." I gave a little taunting curtsey and began to go.

Devan took a step closer to me. He reached out and touched my arm then pulled his hand back, quickly. "Thank you," he said in a quiet, yet serious voice. "I owe you, Sam." He looked like he wanted to say something else, but instead he turned and walked away.

I stood there, my arm still warm where he had touched it. And when he'd said my name, I had felt a tiny, dragonfly-sized flutter in my stomach, which was pretty confusing. I didn't generally kill dragonflies, but that flutter had to be squashed between two pieces of glass. Pronto. Devan was an arrogant ass and my competition. And Caroline was clearly up to something. I'd have to keep an eye on all of them.

I glowered the rest of the way back to my family's camp. When I got close, the scent of s'mores drifted toward me. I jogged the last few steps, eager to claim my marshmallows before Lyssa ate them all.

My parents were cuddling on one side of the fire while Lyssa and Sophie were laughing about something on the other. I sat next to Sophie, who handed me a stick with a marshmallow impaled on it. I matched her silly grin, grateful for the first time since we arrived. We may not have had money, or perfectly pressed clothes, or Ivy League connections, but I was okay with that. Some kinds of class couldn't be bought anyway.

Chapter 6

"Bigfoot really put the romance back into our marriage.
We love to go to conferences together, or for long
walks in the woods. I tell all my girlfriends they
should take up Squatching as a hobby."

—*Brenda Berger, president and founder of the
Northern Ohio Bigfoot Ladies Auxiliary*

My family got to work right away the next day, scouting for locations that my dad thought a Wood Ape would be most likely to wander through.

"Yes! This is perfect!" My dad enthusiastically pointed at each spot we found. "Let's tie some apples to that tree branch right there . . . no, to your left . . . exactly!"

Colin and the film crew followed closely behind. "Myron, can you explain to the camera, or better yet, pretend to explain to the girls, why you're tying apples to trees?"

"Of course." Dad took an apple and presented it to us as if it were an exotic magical fruit. "Girls, we know that Wood Apes are very fond of apples, because Sasquatches are regularly spotted in orchards in the fall. Our plan is to tie these apples up in the tree, in the hopes that a Bigfoot will be enticed and take them. When it does, we'll have a set of tracks that may lead us to the creature himself."

"Perfect," Colin said and nodded to the crew.

We spent the greater part of the day decorating trees with Red Delicious and Granny Smiths and marking the locations on the map. We only stopped when we ran out of apples.

Back at the camp, Colin, Hal, and Dave-the-sound-guy had packed up their gear and were about to get in their Jeep.

"Oh, girls. Why don't you ride down with the crew to base camp and bring back some more apples?" my mom asked.

Sophie and I crammed in the back seat with Dave and we all bumped along the gravel service road that connected our campsite to the base camp. It was a longer route than the steep footpath we had hiked the day before, but we still arrived at the production trailers in a quarter of the time it would have taken us to walk.

"We have a big bin of apples in that trailer there. Help yourself, girls." Colin pointed us to the main truck.

"This isn't exactly how I wanted to spend this afternoon." I grimaced.

"Why?" Sophie asked. "What else were you going to do?"

"Anything other than lug 25 pounds of produce up that trail."

Sophie opened her mouth to say something, but stopped when we saw Kyle emerge from a trailer and leap down all three steps at once.

"Hey guys!" His smile widened when he saw us. "Whatcha doin'?"

"We're on a very important top secret mission," I said.

"We're getting some apples," Sophie added and Kyle smiled.

"What are you up to?" I asked.

"Just borrowing a cable from the crew so we can hook up our Xbox." He held out the cord.

Not only did they have electricity in their cabin, but a television and free time to play video games? "Is the Xbox part of your Sasquatch hunting strategy?" I asked.

"Nah, just for fun." Kyle looked down at his shoes and shrugged.

"She's just joking." Sophie put a gentle hand on his shoulder.

Kyle glanced at her hand and smiled, but Sophie quickly moved her hand away and put it behind her back like she was embarrassed to have touched him. I'd lecture her later about consorting with the enemy.

She cleared her throat. "Um, how are you guys settling in?"

Kyle rubbed the back of his neck. "The cabin's great. The rest of the team is fine, too, I guess. They were both kinda snippy last night."

"Really? Why?" I asked, knowing full well what was behind their tension.

"I don't know. Maybe it's just stress. It's hard to tell with those two. Caroline's very serious about her work, and Devan's not exactly chatty. He's my best friend, but I don't know what he's thinking half the time."

I got the feeling that Kyle didn't know about Caroline's adventures in the woods last night either. Interesting.

I elbowed Sophie to try to get her attention and failed.

"I'm going to grab some apples," I said to Sophie, who didn't even pretend to follow me. Great. I'd lost her to the other team already.

I trudged over to the pile of apples and started filling up my bags, grumbling to myself until I glanced up at the sky. Crap. The sun was lower than I expected. It was time to get back to camp. I had dragged three big bags of apples across the lawn when Colin joined me, taking one of the bags off my shoulder.

"Hey, thanks!"

"No problem. Are you guys heading back now? I can drive you." His relaxed faced suddenly tensed when he saw Sophie and Kyle together. Was there a rule against chatting with the competition that I didn't know about?

I chewed on my lip. Best not to bring it up, at least until after I got a ride up the mountain and talked to my sister.

• • •

"I don't know what to do, Brenda," my dad sighed, a few days and a whole lot of apples later. He sat by the cold fire pit, poring over the map and shaking his head.

When Jake had announced that we'd have a whole week to track and search for one good piece of physical evidence, we had all thought it would be a breeze. But, apparently, not so much.

We'd been checking all of the bait stations every day, and while sometimes apples disappeared, there were no signs of any monsters. Or any other creatures bigger than a squirrel for that matter. It was strange. And we were screwed. The other team was sure to beat us easily.

My mom rubbed my dad's back. "Oh, honey," she said, "Don't worry. We'll find something soon." They had been so affectionate since they started all this. I would think the Bigfoot hunt was a romantic vacation to them, if I didn't know that our home was at stake. My mom planted a kiss on his forehead. "We've still got a few days."

I wasn't confident. I studied the trees above me. Something wasn't adding up. I just couldn't figure out how the bait kept mysteriously vanishing from some of the trees. Either we weren't any good at tracking in this wet Pacific Northwest forest that was so different from our home terrain or someone was interfering.

Caroline was my prime suspect. I didn't trust her or Devan, and I was determined to make sure they really were playing fair like they promised.

That afternoon, I decided to investigate further. "I'm going to collect some more firewood," I called out behind my shoulder to my parents and then slipped away. Once I was out of range of the cameras, I moved more quickly down the trail toward the ridge that overlooked the Netherfield team's cabin, about halfway to base camp.

As I got nearer, I slowed down and kept a sharp eye out to make sure I wouldn't be caught spying. I crept close to the edge of the overlook, and ducked down behind the underbrush. I pulled out my binoculars and adjusted the focus. *While I'm here, I might as well see if they found anything yet.* If they were having a hard time too, it would take the pressure off us a bit. I knew it was a long shot, but maybe I'd hear something useful.

Then I waited. And waited. Nothing happened. I began to feel ridiculous for playing James Bond in a prickly bush.

But after about twenty minutes, the front door opened and out came Dr. DeGraw, followed by the Preps.

"And under no circumstances should you fraternize with the competition." Dr. DeGraw paused on the porch steps.

"Dr. DeGraw, you have nothing to worry about," Devan said, like the kiss-up he apparently was. "The Bergers are certainly not attractive enough to tempt us. We're completely focused on the contest."

"Oh yes," Caroline replied. "Kyle's been very focused on studying some interesting local creatures—particularly the female specimens."

"Shut up, Caroline." Kyle compressed his lips, but looked down at the ground, possibly hiding a guilty expression.

Dr. DeGraw sucked in a breath causing Caroline to take a step back. "This especially goes for you, Caroline. As a woman, you need to work harder. It's not fair, but if you want to get ahead, that's how it is. Forget being likeable. Just focus on what you need to do."

Caroline nodded and bit her lip.

"You all know how important this is to us," Dr. DeGraw said. "I'm counting on this preposterous TV show to raise money for the academy and our research trip. Don't you want to go into the field on a serious expedition?"

"Yes, ma'am," Caroline and Devan answered. Kyle didn't say anything as the three of them followed her to the bottom of the stairs.

Dr. DeGraw placed her hand ceremoniously on Devan's shoulder. Clearly, she had knighted him the fearless leader of Team Pompous Pricks.

"Well," Dr. DeGraw continued. "We're all on the same page. And I'm very excited for you to share the sample you found with the judges."

"We have nothing to worry about. I've got this all in the bag," Caroline said.

Beth arrived shortly after in the car to pick up Dr. DeGraw. As soon as their mentor was gone, Kyle punched Devan in the arm. "You're such a goddamn snob. Not attractive enough to tempt us . . ." Kyle imitated Devan's British accent. "C'mon, that's bull. The two older girls are really cute."

"Fine," Devan replied sullenly. "But not pretty enough to distract us from the contest."

"And have you seen the rest of the family?" Caroline asked. "I thought this was a serious competition. I'm more than a little insulted that they couldn't get anyone better."

My mouth dropped open. What freaking nerve!

"Jeez, Caroline. That's pretty harsh," Kyle said. "It's not like I really belong here either with you two brainiacs. There's a reason you only ask me to carry boxes and fetch cords."

Caroline raised an eyebrow but didn't respond.

Devan frowned. "Kyle, you do belong. But you have to admit that they're not exactly in the same league as us. But, either way, it doesn't matter. We're here to do some research and win this competition for the school. We're not here to find prom dates."

"That's exactly what I'm talking about, Devan!" Kyle said. "Who cares about leagues? Especially on reality television."

Devan punched Kyle's shoulder. "It's not my fault we have higher standards in London. Or standards at all, really . . ."

"Ow!" Kyle rubbed his arm. "Sure, if by 'standards' you mean a weird accent and slang no one else understands."

The two boys stood glaring at each other, until they both broke into laughter.

Devan wrestled Kyle into a headlock. "Tosser!"

"Loser!" Kyle escaped and the boys continued to laugh and punch each other until they couldn't breathe.

Devan was lucky I wasn't closer because I would have hit him even harder and "loser" would have been a compliment compared to what I would've called him.

And what did Caroline mean by having the challenge in the bag? It could be that their evidence was really good. Or she actually was cheating. Either way, if we didn't find something soon, we were beyond screwed. I'd have to make sure we took full advantage of the short time we had left. Forget the apples. I'd make Bigfoot a freaking apple pie if it would help us get solid evidence.

Chapter 7

"There's a long history of Jews believing in mystical things.
To me, Bigfoot is just an extension of that."

—*Myron Berger, interview in* "The Jewish Journal of Northern Ohio"

It was the last day before the reveal, and we still had absolutely nothing to present to the judges. Colin, Hal, and Dave had shown up at our campsite about half an hour early for our final evidence hunt.

Colin scratched at a bug bite on his arm. "Does anyone have any bug spray?"

"Yeah, sure." I took a big aerosol can out of my pack and threw it at him.

He caught it with one hand and read the label. "This has a lot of chemicals. Don't you have anything less toxic?"

I raised an eyebrow at him. "Really?"

He shrugged. "I have sensitive skin."

"You see those shiny plants over there with three leaves? If you rub the leaves on you, they'll keep the bugs away. Scout's honor." I had only been in the Girl Scouts for the cookies, but he didn't know that.

Colin walked over to a patch of the leaves contemplating my advice, until Sophie grabbed him by the arm. "No! Samantha was teasing," she said. "It's poison oak."

His eyes widened and his voice slightly quivered. "You weren't really going to let me rub poison oak all over myself, were you?"

I gave him my best wicked grin and winked.

Colin took another look at the leaves and shook his head. I worried that I had gone too far, until he erupted in laughter and playfully swatted me on the arm. "You totally got me."

He applied the bug spray, careful not to miss an inch of skin. "C'mon, let's keep walking."

"It's good to have someone around here with a sense of humor," Colin said.

"What, you mean Beth isn't hilarious?" I asked.

Colin's lips straightened into a thin line. "Yeah, she's not the most social, but she can't help it, actually. Beth is on the autism spectrum. I'm used to it, but I forget that other people aren't," he said.

I winced immediately. I couldn't believe I had been such a jerk. "I didn't know. I thought mostly guys got that."

"It's less common for girls to be diagnosed with it, apparently," Colin said.

"I feel like an ass. I'm so sorry."

"Hey, no worries. I know you didn't mean anything by it," he said and gave my shoulder a friendly squeeze. "But I will say this," Colin continued, "Beth's awesome behind the camera. She sees angles that no one else does and knows how to do things with the equipment that guys who've been cameramen for twenty years don't know. I'm lucky to have her."

"All right, gang, let's get going," my dad called out with a strained voice. He was trying to be his usual optimistic self, but I could tell he was worried.

Holding out the map so the camera could see, my dad pointed out our current location and where we needed to go. "I think the soil a little north of us has good potential for footprints. As you know, Wood Apes prefer higher elevation, so we're more likely to see something up there. It's a bit of a hike, but way off the beaten path, so there won't be a lot of interns or anyone else tromping through, mucking things up."

"Perfect! Let's go," my mom said, giving my dad a peck on the cheek.

We all followed my dad like baby ducks north along an overgrown trail. As we hiked deeper into the woods and higher up the trail, the sounds of the modern world faded. The soft distant rumble of cars on the highway disappeared entirely and soon we were surrounded instead by a web of delicate bird songs, insects buzzing, and the soft rustle of wind blowing through the tops of the enormous trees. Only the loud clomping of Hal and Dave's boots trudging along behind us with the camera disturbed the peaceful symphony.

"Hal, are you getting the scenery for B-roll?" Colin asked.

"Yeah, boss." Hal continued filming and stomping on the rocky terrain. If they kept crunching like that, these guys were going to scare away every living creature within five miles, except for maybe an elderly Squatch who forgot to put in his hearing aid.

My mom frowned, and muttered, "For the love of god . . ." under her breath. The strain and stress of the last few days was getting to her too, as much as she tried to hide it. She took a deep breath, pulled herself together, then turned on the Midwest charm full blast. "Guys, can you please keep it down a little?" she said in a sing-song voice. "Let's play who can be the quietest. I'll start." She pretended to zip her lips and throw away the key. That game never worked on us when we were kids, but the crew nodded.

"Sure, sure, I understand." Hal tried to tiptoe through the underbrush. He reminded me of the dancing hippos in *Fantasia*, his huge frame taking dainty baby steps.

Soon we came to a small creek, only a couple of feet deep. It was just wide enough that you had to take a pretty big leap to clear it. Colin and Hal paused to strategize the best way to get the equipment over without getting wet.

"What are you doing?" I glared at Lyssa, covering my mic with my hand and taking advantage of cameras being off.

Lyssa was tugging at her bra straps to make them tighter, probably to achieve some pushup effect. It was bad enough everyone could see her butt cheeks peeking from her shorts. *Short* was a very good word for them.

She smiled and tilted her head, but covered her own mic and whispered, "Duh! If you watched reality television like a normal person instead of your nerdy fantasy stuff, you'd know that you get extra points for sexiness. They never want to boot off the cute girls."

"Um, this isn't Bigfoot Bachelorette, Lyssa, or a popularity contest—and what's wrong with fantasy? At least the chicks carry broadswords . . . Although I usually prefer science fiction."

Lyssa cut me off. "Whatever. It's all nerdtastic to me. I'm just helping the team get attention because it's clear you and Sophie aren't up to it. Geeks and shy girls don't make for good ratings."

I gritted my teeth at her, trying to breathe slowly and calmly. "I want to win for real, not because viewers can glimpse your thong underwear."

"Who cares?"

"I care. I want people to take us seriously. What part of I-don't-want-to-be-humiliated-on-national-TV is so confusing to you?" I asked. "We're not the Berger Family Bimbos. We're going to win my way, so tone it down. Or else."

"You have no imagination. You never know, we could get endorsements or—ohhh, we could be on an infomercial!" Lyssa clapped her hands together in excitement, then remembered her mic and covered it again.

"Way to dream big, Lyssa." I dropped the sarcasm and pleaded with her. "Please listen to me for once. Mom and Dad are too distracted to keep you from embarrassing yourself, and Sophie is too nice to criticize anyone."

Lyssa stared me down. "Luckily that's not *your* problem, huh?" Tossing her hair behind her shoulder, she pivoted on her heel, and sauntered over to Hal, who seemed ready to start filming again.

God! Why was she so determined to make us look trashy? Could she not see how she came off? Like I needed something else to worry about.

My mom let out a low whistle to get everyone's attention. "I think it's time to keep moving."

The group made a strange little parade as we hiked another mile. Sophie chatted with Colin about the different kinds of trees and birds in the forest, while Lyssa stayed in front of Hal, so the camera could pick up her butt wiggle. I led the pack, with my dad, just like when I was little, scanning the surroundings for anything unusual. Dad had taught me how to track other animals, too, and I noticed evidence of all sorts of little critters, but nothing screamed "Bigfoot Was Here."

As the day drew on, I tried to avoid my dad's eyes, not wanting him to see that I was getting anxious, too. I couldn't stand the thought of failing in the first challenge. I knew what it would do to my dad's confidence. And if we lost, the other team's smug self-satisfaction would be freaking unbearable. I was about to ask if we could take a break, so I could rest my sore legs and dig out some ibuprofen from my pack, when my dad stopped and shouted.

"Brenda, Brenda, look at this!" He waved her over frantically, and then crouched down to examine something on the ground.

From behind him, I couldn't see what he was pointing at, but he was poised like a hunting dog that had found its prey. When my mom saw the evidence, she gave my dad a dorky sort of high-five.

"We've got something, girls!" my mom squealed.

I skirted around my dad, careful not to step on anything important. Sure enough, there in the mud in front of him was a huge footprint. I didn't want to jump to conclusions until we could examine the print more closely, but it was definitely worth recording. Sophie and Lyssa hopped up and down, they were so excited. Hal gave us a thumbs-up and circled to get a better angle, and even Colin cracked a smile and nodded.

My dad, still crouched over the footprint, went into team leader mode. Speaking directly to the camera, he said, "As you can see, we have a promising footprint here in sector B of our map. Now, we'll make a plaster casting of it. It'll take some time, and it's a little old-fashioned, but it's still the best way of documenting footprints."

We got to work. I unpacked the camera and Sophie reached for the ruler. We measured eight inches across, which was way too big to be human. The length was hard to tell because it faded into the dirt, but it was well over thirteen inches long. And it clearly had five toes, not claws, which was another really good sign. I couldn't think of any common animals, native to this region, or any region really, that could have made a print like that. While I still maintained a healthy dose of skepticism, it was a huge relief to have finally found something.

My dad surrounded the footprint with a little wall of dirt, mixed the powdered plaster with water in a big measuring cup using a stick, and carefully poured the mixture over the footprint, filling the dirt ring.

I was grateful to be able to sit and relax for the thirty minutes it would take to dry. I think everyone else was too, except for my dad, who danced around, acting like he'd just given birth to a freaking unicorn. He even cried a little, something he usually only did during the movie *Harry and the Hendersons*, which was about a nice family who adopted Bigfoot.

When the plaster casting was completely solid, my dad gingerly removed it from the ground, brushed the residual dirt off, and gazed at it lovingly. "It's so beautiful! I don't think I've ever seen a better footprint. And I've certainly never found anything like this in Ohio. Samantha, take a photo of me with the print!" He grabbed my mom and threw his arm around her shoulder so she could be in the photo, too.

"Say 'Yeti'!" I said, aiming the camera.

They both said "Wood Ape" in defiance, but I got the photo anyway.

My mom wiped her forehead with a bandana. Her face was flushed with excitement, but she looked beat, too. "I guess we should pack and head back to camp."

After fifteen more minutes of shooting scenery shots, Colin and Hal decided that the walk to the camp would probably be uneventful and it would be a lot faster to carry the camera and mics in their cases, rather than film the whole time. I guessed they were eager to get away from the mosquitoes and back to their comfy trailers.

I followed my dad and Colin as they wound their way along the narrow path through the trees. I slowed down, letting the others walk ahead of me, so I could fall into step with Sophie, who was quieter than usual.

"Hey, what's up?" I asked.

"Huh? Oh, it's nothing really. I was just thinking about the other team. I wonder how they did today." She stared off into the forest, squinting like the answer was in front of her carved into a distant tree. A light blush on her cheeks threatened to spread over her whole face.

I nudged her shoulder with mine. "Are you thinking about anyone in particular on the other team?" I knew my sister. When she fell for someone, she fell *hard*. She'd only spent a grand total of five minutes talking with Kyle, but she was definitely a like-at-first-sight kind of gal. Judging by what I'd overheard, he seemed pretty into her as well.

"Yeah, I think I have a little crush on Kyle." Sophie's cheeks got redder by the second. "I'm having a hard time thinking of him as the competition. He doesn't seem that competitive."

I pursed my lips. I needed Sophie to concentrate on winning, but I didn't want to burden her with our financial difficulties. "Then picture Devan and Caroline's smug-ass faces. It's gonna be sweet beating those jerks, right?" I chortled. "Can you imagine them having to go back to their fancy school after losing to us?"

"Yeah. I guess it would be pretty sweet," Sophie said, but without confidence.

"They'd never be able to wear those matching polo shirts again. Netherfield would demand them back."

Sophie usually hated when I made fun of others, but she let out a giggle. I laughed in a far less ladylike manner, which may have involved a couple of snorts.

Chapter 8

"Unfortunately, we don't have genetic
proof of Bigfoot. We can only rule samples out by
comparing them to DNA of known animals."

—*Caroline Bing, Future Geneticists Club*

We arrived at base camp for judging uncharacteristically late. Lyssa and I had gone several rounds over her choice of attire this morning. The only backup my mom offered was, "Well, those shorts are rather short. But Lyssa does have nice legs."

Not helpful.

The other team was gathered around one of the picnic tables and plotting out something. I snuck a peek to see if I could figure out their tactics, but I was too far away. As if he could hear my thoughts, Devan's head popped up and he caught my stare. I quickly turned away, pretending to look for something in my backpack.

Dad put his arm around my shoulder. "Isn't this exciting, kiddo? Look how nervous the other team is." I gave them one more quick glance, careful not to make eye contact with Devan. Unless they exhibited their nervousness by ending their huddle to play Hacky Sack and sip bottled water, they were doing just fine.

"There's no way they have anything as good as our footprint. Right?" Dad added and pumped his fist high above his head, not a good look for a middle-aged science teacher.

After I checked my mom's teeth for lipstick, and everyone's body mic was on and tested, we were ready and waiting. And waiting and waiting. Colin gazed at his watch, and put his head in his hand.

"I'll see what the holdup is," I said to my folks and walked over to Colin, giving him a casual wave.

"Hey," Colin said, his face brightening a little.

Hal and Steve had taken out a pack of cards and were playing poker, and the rest of the crew milled about, gossiping and checking their phones. Even Jake sat idly, reading the *Hollywood Reporter* and looking bored, not bothering to flirt with anyone.

"Are we getting started soon?" I asked.

Colin twisted his mouth in annoyance. "Yeah, we're just waiting for the judges."

A loud vehicle approaching interrupted our conversation. It made a helicopter sound like a six-hundred-pound purring kitten.

It was a big, old truck with oversized off-road wheels, and considering it was a putrid, vomit-colored green and splattered in mud, it didn't look any better than it sounded. The passenger-side door opened and out came Dr. DeGraw. Out of the driver's side jumped a tall, hefty man in his fifties, who sported an impressively long, mangy gray beard. He was either an unemployed Santa Claus or the guest judge. Or both.

"Wait," I said to Colin, grabbing his arm. "I thought you said there were two judges."

He glanced away. "There's one official guest judge for every challenge and they will rotate. This week is Jim Duckworthy, whose land we're on. He's the guy from the show about motorcycle gangs who also make artisanal candles."

I laughed nervously. "Seriously?"

"I wouldn't make up this stuff, even if I could."

Then it hit me. I didn't see any other new faces. "And what about the other judge?"

Colin stared at his clipboard. He lowered his voice, "Dr. DeGraw has generously donated her time to be the off-air, unofficial judge. In case of hard decisions. But she's mostly here in an advisory capacity."

I could feel the bile at the back of my throat reaching the top of my hairline. "What! But, ah . . . what the hell?" I tripped all over my words. "She's clearly not impartial. She's one of them!"

Colin took a deep breath and crossed his arms over his chest, seemingly preparing to stand his ground. "Dr. DeGraw assured me she will be completely professional and won't let her personal feelings interfere."

I opened my mouth to protest, but he looked at me with pleading eyes, begging me to accept the situation. I bit my lip to stop myself from quitting or saying something I shouldn't and shook my head.

"I respect your feelings, Samantha. I get it," he murmured close to my ear. "I don't think you understand, though. I didn't have a say in the matter. This is what the network agreed upon when we pitched the show. Roberta has a lot of connections."

I continued to torture my poor lip and glower at him. I didn't utter a word, but he threw his hands in the air.

"You have to trust that I'll do my best to ensure the show is as fair as possible."

"What choice do I have?" I sighed and watched Roberta make herself comfortable in Colin's folding chair.

Well, that was just fan-freaking-tastic. The mentor of Team Evil was one of the judges. "Someone needs to get me some chamomile tea," Dr. DeGraw ordered, instead of asking like a normal person, or getting off her ass and fixing her own damn cup of tea.

Devan appeared at her side in a matter of seconds. "I would be happy to."

"Oh, don't bother, dear, the girl will fetch me a cup," she said, squinting at Beth and waiting for her to take a hint before Colin hurried over to make her the beverage himself.

"I need Beth behind the camera to help set up the shot," Colin said. "Here you go." He handed Dr. DeGraw a paper cup with some generic tea, a packet of sugar, and a plastic spoon.

Dr. DeGraw stared at the store-brand tea like she was holding a bomb.

Colin hustled back to the set and clapped his hands. "We're ready to go, people. Places!"

Each team's findings were arranged on a table covered by a sheet, to make the reveal more exciting. A chair was placed on set for our guest judge, as well.

We took our spots at our team's table and Devan and company moved behind theirs. Devan stood stiffly with a grumpy expression, staring right at the camera. Kyle shifted his weight from one foot to the other, looking nervous. Only Caroline seemed unfazed by the whole situation. She focused her attention on writing something in a notebook and glancing at Jake. Something was definitely going on between those two and I didn't like it.

Jake stood between the two teams, in red cowboy boots, a tight black shirt, and even tighter jeans. He was pretty hot, especially from behind, and especially when he wasn't talking. Or testing his microphone by reciting Shakespeare—*poorly*.

"But soft, what light goes there? This is the west and Juliet is the south," he said directly into his mic. "Test, test, one, two, three. We're good?" he asked Beth. She nodded and Jake gave her a thumbs-up way above his head. Colin then gave Jake the signal to start.

"Our Bigfoot hunters have had one week to go deep into the woods in search of cement evidence . . ."

"Cut!" Colin put his head in his hand. "You mean *concrete* evidence, not cement."

Jake tilted his head. "You sure, bro?"

"Pretty sure."

"Okay, got it." Jake nodded, and then preened directly at the camera.

"Let's take it again," Colin said.

"Our Bigfoot hunters have had one week to go deep into the woods in search of concrete, physical proof that the mythical creature does in fact exist, right here under our noses. Now, let's see what they came up with. Okay, Devan Das, as team captain, show us what you found."

Jake sounded friendly and professional, especially considering their confrontation in the woods. He may have some questionable morals, but he was charismatic on camera.

Devan's hands shook a little as he took the sheet off the table to reveal his team's evidence.

Trying not to appear like I cared, I took a discreet peek at their table. In a Lucite box was about four inches of coarse reddish-brown hair of some sort.

My stomach dropped. It looked good from where I stood.

"We were lucky enough in our tracking to find a hair sample that could very well belong to a mammal the size of a Sasquatch," Devan announced in a monotone, pointing at the hair. "Based on the color, texture, and length of the fur, we think we have a good case to further investigate the area."

Caroline stepped forward, gave Devan a sideways glance, and gently nudged him to the side. "The cellular structure of the hair is quite unique; clearly non-human. We tried to extract DNA, but the findings were inconclusive. We would need to take more time and use better equipment to do the more extensive testing needed to know for sure if it's Bigfoot or something else."

Just then, a loud popping noise caused us all to jump. "Cut! Everyone hold, please!" Colin shouted. Colin, Beth, and Hal huddled around a piece of lighting equipment with some sort of issue.

My dad's eyebrows furrowed and he strained to get a better view of the other team's evidence. He stepped back and frowned, his shoulders sagging. It was a good thing he didn't play poker—the guy had no talent for bluffing. I had to do something to cheer him up before the cameras started rolling again.

"It could be anything," I whispered. "My guess is it's from a bear," I lied. "A *teddy* bear." I put my hands on my hips. "We've got this one."

"Thanks, honey," he said as he gave me a pat on the shoulder. "I needed that. Don't think I don't notice how you take care of your mom, sisters, and me."

I shrugged and willed myself not to blush. "That's my job. When Lyssa was little and Sophie was in the hospital because of her asthma, you made me promise to help Mom and to take care of my sisters."

His eyes widened. "I'm surprised you even remember that. You were five years old. Listen to me. It's not your job. But that makes all you do more special, even if I'm the only one who sees it, sometimes."

"We're back," Colin said.

Beth cued Jake again.

"The anthropology students have presented an intriguing hair sample for the first challenge. Let's hear from our guest judge." Jake gestured to Mr. Duckworthy who stood. "Mr. Duckworthy, what do you think?"

Stroking his ample beard, he said, "Well, I'm no expert in anything other than motorcycles and sweet ass candles, but I've seen several photos of Washington Sasquatches and none of 'em were redheads. Maybe they come in all different colors, but round here, we only have ones with dark brown fur. At any rate, I'm gonna say that this could just as easily come from a fox or some other critter out there."

Duckworthy sat back down on the metal folding chair and crossed his legs. Jake scratched his chin and waited for the judge to say something else, but Duckworthy remained quiet. "Do you have anything to add?" Jake asked.

"'Nuff said," he replied. I was guessing his motorcycle gang show wasn't heavy on dialogue.

"Okay, then." Jake clasped his hands together. "Myron Berger, it's up to you. Can your team offer something more substantial than an inconclusive piece of hair? Or will you lose your first challenge? Show us what you've got."

My dad gulped, then inhaled a big breath.

Hang in there, Dad. Don't let the bastards rattle you.

He forced a polite smile. "Yes, we *have* found something more noteworthy." Dad carefully pulled the sheet away from the footprint casting and Hal swooped in with the camera for a close-up while Steve, the other cameraman, stepped back to get a wider shot.

"Here, you'll see a massive footprint that, unlike the hair our competitors found, cannot be attributed to a fox or a bear," my dad explained in his best middle-school science teacher voice.

I snuck a peek at the other team to get their reaction. Maybe I was imagining things, but I thought they exchanged nervous glances.

Dad continued, "Based on the shape and size of the print, it's very possible that it belongs to a Wood Ape, also known as a Sasquatch." Having found his confidence, my dad's voice grew stronger. "You'll note by the way the toes are positioned and by the width of the print that this isn't a common bear, but something bigger and more primate-like."

Jake leaned in closer. "Interesting. But I have to ask, can you prove it's not a fake print?"

My dad grinned. "I can, Jake. If you'll direct your attention to the pattern on the toes, like human fingerprints, as well as this scar here on the pad of the foot. Both are difficult to replicate and are generally accepted as proof that a casting is from a living creature."

The hard part over, my dad smiled at my mom, like a kid who was winning a spelling bee.

"Thank you, Myron, and ladies," Jake chimed in before directing the cameras over to the judge. "Mr. Duckworthy, what's your take on the Berger footprint?"

The judge whistled. "That's one mighty fine footprint," Duckworthy said. "I've seen every kind of track, from birds to bears, and this looks like the real deal to me."

"So, are you ready to declare a winner?" Jake asked Mr. Duckworthy.

"Yup. I call this round for the Berger family. There ain't no mistaking a footprint like that. Plus, they're scrappy, and I like rooting for the underdogs." Duckworthy went over to my dad and shook his hand roughly.

I glanced over at Dr. DeGraw, who was gritting her teeth. I guessed she wouldn't be able to influence this round.

"Congratulations, Bergers," Jake said. "Better luck next time to Devan, Kyle, and Caroline."

Of the three, only Kyle wore a small, hopeful grin.

"Keep in mind this is just the first challenge," Jake said. "Now, the challenge winners will receive a special advantage as their prize. Would you like to know what you've won?" he asked my mom and dad.

Please let it be running water or cable.

"You've won a thermal imaging camera! Perfect for late night ghost hunts," Jake said.

"It's *not* a ghost show, Jake. Take that again," Colin said from his chair off screen.

"Okay. Sorry, I got a little carried away," Jake's normally cocky smile was almost boyish. "This camera really helped me out when I was locked in a haunted prison."

"Who let him out?" I whispered to Lyssa.

Jake pointed the scanner at Lyssa. "Look, it gives digital readouts of the temperature and produces infrared images," he said. "Too bad it doesn't have x-ray vision, too." He waggled his eyebrows and waved the thermal imager at my sister's chest. I had no idea how someone as seemingly sweet as Melody Wright put up with Jake.

"It's perfect for night hunting because the scanner detects body heat, so you can see the general size and shape of nearby creatures," Jake added.

My parents, naturally, beamed.

"Oh, this is so exciting!" my dad said. "I've always wanted the Thermo-Meter 360."

Jake shook my dad's hand and nodded. "Use it well. We look forward to seeing what you can do with it."

"Cut!" Colin yelled. "That's it for today, everybody. The crew will meet back here tomorrow morning at five to set up for the introduction of the next challenge. Teams, your call is seven-thirty, and please be on time."

A collective groan came from both teams, as well as some of the crew.

Colin sighed. "The craft services caterer will be here tomorrow with breakfast."

The grumblings subsided and the crew got busy breaking down for the day.

My mom and dad hugged, excited about their victory, and wandered over to chat with Duckworthy. Lyssa crossed her arms and made it clear she'd rather be re-grouting the shower, a job she got stuck doing last spring when my mom caught her sneaking out of the house to meet a boy. However, Lyssa's expression and posture changed when she discovered Jake eyeing her with interest.

Jake took off his body mic and swaggered over to talk to my sister. I stepped closer to Lyssa, intent on running interference. I wasn't sure what that referred to in terms of sports, but for my purposes it meant "keep the slimeball creep away from my sister." From across the set, I could see Devan raking his hands through his hair while talking to Caroline, who was pointing at something in her notebook as if she was trying to explain it.

"Hey, Lyssa. How's it going so far?" Jake asked with a sly grin. He stretched one arm at a time over his head and across his chest, to show off his muscles and tattoos, no doubt.

"It's going really well," she answered, playing with a lock of hair and batting her eyelashes at him.

He leaned closer to her. "Not surprising. You're a natural. You have a beautiful face for TV," Jake said, although it wasn't her face he was actually eyeballing, it was her ample chest again. "I'd be happy to show you some acting techniques, sometime."

At that point, I had to step in. My sister was used to having guys throw themselves at her, but she was playing with fire this time. Jake was an overprivileged teen heartthrob who was used to getting everything he wanted, and I didn't trust him, *especially* with her.

"Yeah, Jake, it's great of you to offer to teach my *much younger* sister," I said. "You do know Lyssa's only fifteen, right?"

Lyssa flashed me a death-ray glare, which I ignored. "I'll be sixteen in October, and Jake turned seventeen last March—I saw the feature about your birthday party on *Celebrity Shindigs*," she said to Jake. "So awesome!"

She crossed her arms and turned back to me. "So Jake and I are only nineteen months apart. That's not even two years, *Sam*."

"Yeah, I can count, *Lyssa*." I returned her glare and then said to Jake, "I just think Lyssa really needs to focus on helping her family win this competition."

"No worries. Just being friendly." Jake's lips turned down slightly like I'd hurt his feelings. "But, if you need a break, let me know. You can come along, too, Sam, although, you don't have the right kind of personality for TV, the way your sister does."

"I think I will," I said at the same time Lyssa said, "No! I don't need a babysitter."

Lyssa scowled at me. "God, Sam, you don't even watch TV."

"Yes, I do."

"Yeah, boring sci-fi stuff from England and other crap. That's not television," she said.

I snorted in response. At this point, I knew I wasn't going to convince Lyssa to step away from the loser. I decided to talk some sense into my mom later. Or maybe Sophie could help me put an end to Lyssa's interest once and for all.

I glanced around for Sophie so we could coordinate our efforts, but she was busy talking and laughing with Kyle. Then I saw Devan crossing the lawn toward them. *Oh, hell no.* No way was I going to let him be rude to my sister.

Again, I found myself running interference for a sister. I jumped directly into Devan's path. He skidded to a halt and stared down at me.

"Thanks," I said with a grin.

"For what?" he asked. His eyebrows rose all the way up to his hairline.

"You were going to say congratulations, right?" Okay, so maybe Jake had a point about my personality.

Devan shook his head. "You win. Congratulations. I hope you enjoy your *one* victory because it's not going to happen again." He smiled, but it was a tight smile that didn't make it past his curled lips. "And really, it shouldn't have happened this time, either."

What an ass. A delusional, arrogant ass.

"You've got to be kidding. We won. Easily."

"Hardly," he said, his smile growing, looking less nervous than on camera. "Even at crime scenes footprints are never the strongest evidence. What you found is purely B-level proof."

Was he joking around? Was he gloating? I couldn't read that smile, so I just waited for him to say more.

After a moment, his grin disappeared and he added, "But why would *you* know about forensic methods and scientific inquiry? Cryptozoology isn't a real science."

It's one thing for *me* to make fun of cryptos, like my dad and his friends. But I sure as hell wasn't going to let Devan trash-talk them. I opened my mouth to make a rebuttal, and a good one was forming in my brain, too, when Caroline came along and threw an arm around his shoulder. She barely gave me a passing glance.

"Dev, I need you to take a look at some DNA data with us. Unless, I'm interrupting something," she said with a sickly-sweet tone. Her voice sounded honey-covered, but her cold grey eyes were like a swarm of bees ready to attack.

Devan hesitated like he was going to say something, but then thought against it. "I'm done here. Let's go."

Caroline's calculating eyes shot me one more look over her shoulder before they turned and walked away, arm-in-arm.

Crap! Of course he would walk off before I came up with a response. My tongue was heavy and numb with words I should have said. I didn't know why Devan was getting under my skin so much, but it had to stop. I needed to concentrate on the game; I couldn't get distracted from my goal, no matter what.

We had won this time, but that didn't mean I could relax.

Plus, I didn't want to play nice anymore. It was no longer just about winning the money for college; I wanted to destroy them.

And I knew the best way to win was to throw them off the Bigfoot trail.

Chapter 9

"Trust me, you don't want to be anywhere
near an agitated Sasquatch. They have huge claws,
and a great deal of strength. So I've been told."

—*Jake Stone, on his blog,* "My Big Fat Bigfoot Adventure"

I made my way back to camp on autopilot. Visions of revenge danced in my head. But none of my ideas seemed practical or vengeful enough. Sure, it would be satisfying to give Devan a Bigfoot-sized kick in the ass, but I needed to get him where it would really hurt—his pride.

A plan began to take shape in my mind, but I realized I was out of my depth. I wasn't devious enough. I had to enlist an expert.

Lyssa was lounging in her skimpy shorts on a beach towel by the water when I found her.

"You do realize it's overcast, right?" I asked. "And you're under a blanket of trees? *And* that tanning not only leads to skin cancer, but gives you premature wrinkles?"

She peered at me over her sunglasses and blew out a sigh. "I know. I was super bored. I miss reality television. And just plain reality, too."

"If you're that bored, you could always read a book." I sat next to my sister, forcing her to make room on the towel for me. "Dad has some stuff on Sasquatch legends, or I could hook you up with this epic fantasy about trolls and goblins competing for land in

Medieval Norway." Lyssa rolled her eyes, and lifted her face to absorb the few pathetic rays.

I glanced at her sideways and dropped the bait. "Or . . . you could help me get back at the other team for being jerkwads."

Lyssa sat up and took off her sunglasses. "What did you have in mind?"

I was glad she didn't ask what sort of jerkwadery they had committed, because despite her crunchy chocolate exterior, Lyssa had a soft center and could be very sensitive. I didn't want to hurt her feelings by telling her what Caroline and Devan had said about us. I was the only one allowed to say snarky things about my family, damn it.

I leaned closer to her. "I want to make them fall for fake clues, and send them on a wild goose chase. It will involve some creativity and some sneaking around. Do you think you can help me?"

"Oh, puh-leeease," Lyssa cackled. "I was skipping gym by ten years old, unwrapping and rewrapping Hanukkah presents by eleven, and sneaking out of the house by thirteen. You've come to the right girl. I may not care about Sasquatch one way or the other, but sneaking around is my jam." Lyssa beamed.

I should have known she would be excited about causing some mischief.

She chewed the bottom of her lip as she thought. "So, what's the plan?" Lyssa asked. "Too bad Dad didn't bring the Bigfoot costume that he wears every Halloween."

Scratching the back of my neck, I pondered the possibilities. "I think I'd like to start with something subtler. They're academic types, so we need to be smart about our strategy."

We both sat in silence for a couple of minutes, trying to devise the right plan to trick them. Finally, we came up with an idea plausible enough that it could work.

"How about claw marks in the trees?" Lyssa suggested. "They'll be looking for something like that, right? We just need a hammer and some nails to design a claw."

"Ooh that's good." I jumped off the blanket and paced. "And maybe some really fake tracks. Devan was so dismissive of our footprint casting, but I don't think he'd be able to tell a real animal track from a sneaker tread. I would love to see him present some super fake, bogus prints and have the judges put him in his place."

"Works for me." Lyssa shrugged. "Tell me what to do and I'll do it."

Wow, that was easy.

I spoke too soon.

Lyssa scrunched up her nose. "Um, I hate to ask this, but won't we get disqualified?"

I stopped pacing and ran my fingers through my hair, forming a messy bun. "Not if we don't get caught. If we do, we can just call it a practical joke. There's nothing in the rule book against that." Besides, we weren't the only ones bending the rules of this game. Whatever it was Caroline was doing had to be just as bad.

Lyssa grinned and stood, too, brushing the pine needles off her legs. "So when do we start?"

"I don't want Mom and Dad, or Sophie to be implicated in this," I said. "They probably wouldn't think it was funny, or, you know, ethical to punk the other team like this. We'll just sneak out the materials, and do it tonight. How does that sound?"

My sister pulled me toward her for a huge hug. "I've never been so proud of you."

"For standing up for our family?" I asked.

"I meant for coming up with such an awesome plan, but yeah, for standing up for our family, too," Lyssa said. "Mom and Dad are total weirdoes, but they're *our* weirdoes and no one messes with them and gets away with it. Right?"

For once I couldn't have agreed with my sister more.

The afternoon went off perfectly. Our parents were making lovey-dovey eyes over their map of the property and barely noticed when we snuck off with a backpack full of supplies and a sorry-ass excuse about getting familiar with the terrain to prepare for the next challenge.

We found some thick branches and took turns hammering the nails in at different angles to approximate claws. Then I cut two footprints out of thick cardboard, one left, one right, and zip tied them to the bottoms of a pair of flip flops.

"Wow, those look wild," Lyssa said. "Think they'll work?"

I stomped around in the shoes. "No one with any kind of tracking skills would believe they were real," I said, "But if the jackasses fall for it, it'll be the most epic prank ever."

"What do we do now?" Lyssa asked.

I grabbed my Swiss Army knife and swung the tool open to the tweezers. "We just wait until everyone's sleeping," I said. "Then your part comes in. The sneaky part."

The next several hours dragged. Eventually the sun began to set, and the bats started fluttering from tree to tree. Marshmallows were roasted and the food hung back up high, away from the bears. Mom and Dad said goodnight and turned in, but Lyssa and I pretended we were really excited about staying up late and telling each other ghost stories. We had purposefully chosen something Sophie wouldn't be into.

Right on cue, Sophie yawned and said, "I think I'll go to bed too. We have to be up so early tomorrow." She crawled into the tent, leaving Lyssa and me to go over the rest of our plan in hushed voices. About an hour later, snores shook my parents' tent. I stuck my head into our tent to make sure Sophie, too, was out cold. We were in the clear.

Lyssa and I had both dressed in dark jeans earlier that evening, so all we had to do was grab our black hoodies and our sabotage gear and sneak away without waking anyone up.

Once the fire was out, the sky was darker than I had thought it would be. The cloud cover was thick and wouldn't let any of the stars twinkle through. I had no idea what phase the moon was in, but even if it had been full, we'd never know.

We couldn't turn on our flashlights until we were far enough away that we wouldn't be seen, so we tiptoed carefully past our parents' tent and deeper into the woods. We had just about made it to the tree line when Lyssa stepped on a twig, breaking it with a loud snap. We both jumped.

"Ouch! Sorry." she whispered.

"It's okay. I think we're good," I said in a more normal voice. "Turn on the flashlight."

"Got it." Lyssa held the flashlight under her chin. It made her look like an especially evil Jack O'Lantern, but at least I could see her.

"That twig you stepped on gave me a great idea," I said. "Why don't we break some big sticks near the claw prints, to make them think the Squatch did it?"

The wicked grin on Lyssa's face almost made me reconsider completing our mission. Lyssa's morals didn't always mirror mine. And Devan had promised to play fair.

But then I remembered the hurtful things they'd said about the people I loved. And Caroline's cheating. My sense of righteousness came back full force. I shook the doubt away, and we crept toward the spot we'd designated for our trap. It was close enough to the cabin that the brainiacs would find it, and far enough away that they couldn't hear or see us setting up the scene.

"Okay, we're here," I dropped my backpack.

I took out the thermal scanner and did a quick survey of the area. We wouldn't want to be surprised by a big mammal . . . or the other team. I didn't know which would be worse. If I had thought to borrow my dad's tranquilizer gun, I could shoot a ferocious beast if absolutely necessary, but I didn't feel right about shooting Devan, as much as I'd have liked to. A tranq dart to the ass might have been exactly what he needed.

I caught sight of something huge on the thermal, and for a moment my heart was in my throat. I grabbed Lyssa's arm and she tensed, too. We held our breath as we watched the orange blob that indicated body heat move on the display. Then, the creature turned to the side and the silhouette became clearer. Phew. Just a deer.

Once our heart rates returned to normal, we jumped up and down together on a big branch we found on the ground nearby. It made a surprisingly loud crack. We froze, and waited to make sure no one was around to hear. I scanned with the thermal again.

"We're good. Let's do a few smaller twigs," I said. Lyssa broke up some more branches, while I put on the footprint flip-flops and stomped around in the dirt. I leapt from one foot to the other, trying to mimic the long strides of a Sasquatch. Then, to approximate where a six or seven foot beast would claw a tree, we scraped the nails of our homemade claw across the trunks of two trees. We took a step back to admire our work.

"Should we do more?" I asked, a little out of breath.

"No. We don't want to be too obvious," Lyssa replied. "We need them to feel proud, like they really found something. It'll be more fun to watch the judges deflate them."

Apparently, my baby sister could be really analytical when it came to crime sprees. If only she put that kind of thought process into real science.

"Good point," I nodded, taking a sip of water from my canteen.

Then, as Lyssa was putting the claw back in the bag, she cut her finger. "Ow! Ow!" She was trying not to yelp, but her blood glittered in the dark.

"Good thing we're not hunting vampires, huh?" I gently took her hand in mine and turned it over and back, examining the cut. One thing we didn't bring was the first aid kit, but the wound didn't look bad enough that it couldn't wait until we got back to camp. And bonus: we were wearing black, so the blood wouldn't stain.

"I'm going to get tetanus and die," she whined.

I took a bandana from my back pocket and wrapped it around her finger, elevating her hand. "No you're not—that's why we had to get those shots before we came here."

Suddenly, she stopped whining and started grinning. "What do you say about adding some Bigfoot DNA to the mix?" Lyssa asked, wiggling her bloody finger.

I had to hold my hand in front of my face to keep from laughing loudly. "That's both disgusting and brilliant. You heard Caroline. Their equipment here is sub-par. Without their fancy labs, they won't be able to tell it's your blood for days." If beauty pageants included a Faking Crime Scenes competition, my sister would have been crowned by now.

"Don't overdo it," I said. "Drop a few spots of blood on the ground, on a leaf, so they can see it and take it with them, then another couple on the tree with the claw marks."

Lyssa followed directions like a champ, then wrapped the bandana around her finger again until the bleeding stopped.

"Ah, quality family time." I smiled. "Other families go bowling or play board games, but we'll always have subterfuge and searching for mythical animals." And despite my grumbling, I wouldn't have wanted it any other way.

Chapter 10

"I'm a little biased, but I'd like to think Sasquatch could take the Yeti in a fight. Unless they were fighting in cold weather, in which case I guess the Yeti would have the advantage."

—*Lyssa Berger, contestant,* "Myth Gnomers"

Despite the enticing aroma of coffee wafting into our tents, neither one of us had any desire to get up the next morning. The nefarious events of the evening before had taken their toll.

"Do you think this is how Peter Parker felt?" I whispered to Lyssa as we groggily tromped down the trail to base camp for our 7:30 a.m. call. "He'd be out all night fighting crime, and then have to wake up in the morning and go to school."

"My Spidey sense says he'd feel better after he had his coffee." Lyssa yawned loudly.

"You actually made a comic book reference. Aw, you do listen to me."

"No, I made a cute boy reference. Hey, isn't the new Spider-Man actor British, too?"

"Yeah, I guess. Why?"

"I saw how you and Devan were talking yesterday. And eyeing each other across the set." Lyssa grinned.

"You've got to be kidding. I can't stand him. At all. He has so little personality, and what he does have is bad." My voice rose in defense, which wasn't helping my case. "Why else would I run around in the dead of night?" I lifted my eyebrows to show her that I meant what I was saying. Really, I did.

Lyssa shook her head slowly. "Last night was fun, but there's a thin line between love and hate. Did you ever stop to wonder why he annoys you so much?"

"I think you've been reading too many of Sophie's romance novels." I ruffled her hair, like I used to when she was younger. On non-pageant days when it was normal little kid hair and not big, poufy beehive hair.

She scooted back out of my reach. "Whatever, Sam. You may know nerd stuff like comic books and robots, but I know guys."

I grimaced. "You're only fifteen. It gets more complicated than hanging out with guys at Dairy Queen, but thanks for the advice."

"And when was the last time you went to Dairy Queen with anybody?"

Damn, she got me. I had no witty comeback. She was right about the whole Dairy Queen situation. It had been a while.

I wouldn't have minded having a date every now and then, but it's not like I had a ton of options considering I was the nerd-girl from a Bigfoot-hunting family. But Lyssa was dead wrong about Devan. Any spark between us was one of anger and righteousness, at least on my end. On his end, well, who knew? Maybe my family fascinated him, the same way a species of rare monkeys would.

I bumped my hip against my sister's, to lighten the mood. "I think we've been in the forest for too long," I said. "Devan's just a mirage of cuteness in the desert wasteland of this family trip from hell."

Luckily, she dropped the subject when we arrived at the base camp and saw the most beautiful sight I've ever seen. The craft services table. It was just a folding table piled with donuts, fruit, some orange juice cartons, and a big coffee carafe, but it might as well have been Thanksgiving at the White House.

Devan, Caroline, and Kyle were just arriving at base camp too, today on foot, sweaty and cranky, like they had gotten lost.

Colin strolled past, mug in hand, which actually said: *Number One Director* on it.

He caught me smirking. "It was a gift from my grandma. She's very proud."

Colin put down his mug and clapped his hands loudly to get our attention. "Okay, everyone! Be ready to go in fifteen minutes!"

I had a few minutes, so I loaded my plate and poured myself a rich-smelling, hot cup of coffee. I dug into a bagel with cream cheese, but halfway through someone startled me by clearing his throat two feet behind me. I jumped and smeared cream cheese on my cheek. Embarrassed, I froze for a moment, then peeked over my shoulder. There stood Devan, holding out a handkerchief.

His mocking eyes sparkled, enjoying watching me make a mess of myself, no doubt. "Do you need some help?"

I grabbed a paper napkin instead. "I'm fine, but thanks for asking."

His eyes crinkled with amusement and his mouth twitched in an involuntary smile. He folded and stuffed his linen square back into his pocket. "Not a problem. I always carry one. You should try it."

"I already have too much stuff to lug around—axes, knives, flashlights—you know, wilderness survival crap. No room for dainty things. But you go right ahead," I said, hoping I sounded badass.

Devan stared down at me, like I was a complicated puzzle.

"What?" I barked. "Why are you looking at me like that?"

"Like what?"

"Like . . . I don't know." Why could I not form proper sentences around this guy? "I mean, why did you come over to talk to me? What do you want from me?"

"I don't want anything. I'm just trying to be friendly."

"Really? Could have fooled me." All the harsh words he had said about me and my family echoed in my ears, making it hard for me to believe him. It was very possible he was just trying to be nice so I wouldn't proactively report Caroline's extracurricular activities. "If you're worried that I'm going to rat you guys out about Caroline and Jake, you can forget it. I made a deal."

"I wasn't. I'm not worried about that. I just . . ." He took a deep breath, clenched his fists, and glared down at me. "Why do you have to be so mean? You're like a frustrating, little . . . hedgehog, aren't you?"

"Excuse me?"

"I just don't get you, Samantha."

Then he turned, shaking his head, and walked away. I watched him go. I was completely baffled by what he had just said. I guess I didn't get him either and I was pretty freaking sure I didn't care.

My mom sidled up next to me with her coffee. "What was that about?"

"Nothing," I grumbled, ignoring her questioning glance.

Jake arrived on the scene in a leather motorcycle jacket. He threw a sultry sort of half smile in our direction. Lyssa's face lit up, but I felt ever so slightly sick to my stomach.

I didn't know why I was immune to his charms, but to me Jake was like a fat-free cookie. Sure, he looked tempting, but I'd rather hold out for something with more substance and less aftertaste.

"Let's rock this," Jake said to Colin, giving him a fist bump and walking past him to his mark, popping up the collar on his jacket. Everyone got into place with their team. Beth, who had been hiding behind Hal, gave the cue and Jake got started.

"We're here at base camp ready for challenge number two—the audio-visual round. In this challenge, our teams will need to record audio, photographic, or video evidence of the elusive Sasquatch. As in the first round, the team with the most convincing evidence will be the winner. Now, it's been observed by Bigfoot hunters around the globe that the creatures are far more active at night. So, both teams will be filmed by our special night vision gear and will be equipped with infrared cameras, to allow them to make the best use of the dark hours.

"And, of course there's a twist. You all did an admirable job in the last round, but now we're going to call in the big guns . . ." He posed for the camera, pausing for dramatic effect. "Without their knowledge, *Myth Gnomers* has chosen one extra member for each team—someone with extensive experience in the field, who will help their team reach their goals."

I glanced over at my dad, who stroked the stubble on his chin. He clearly had no idea what was happening. Judging by the blank expressions on the other team's faces, neither did they.

Jake turned and gestured in the direction of the production trailer. "Now, let's meet our experts!"

"Expert number one, I need you to come out of the trailer in three, two, one, go!" Colin spoke into the walkie-talkie.

We watched the trailer door open and a portly middle-aged man step out. My dad's expression turned from puzzled to excited, like he was about to meet one of the last living Beatles, or that Patterson guy who filmed the most famous Bigfoot footage ever.

I elbowed Lyssa, whose eyebrows lifted in confusion. "Who is that?" I whispered to her.

"No idea. Some old dude?" she answered.

Jake soon ended the mystery. "Joining the Berger Family is Ernie Saposnick, president of the Northern Ohio Bigfoot Society. Ernie's blog has been voted one of the top one hundred cryptozoology blogs by *Cryptid Monthly*."

Ernie smiled and waved to us, then the other team, and finally to the camera before taking his spot next to my dad and enthusiastically shaking all of our hands. He seemed very familiar. I stared, trying to place him. He was short, balding, and potbellied, with an impish grin and a swirly mustache.

"And joining the team from Netherfield Academy, we have Edward "Duke" Mahoney." Jake gestured toward the trailer and out walked a compact man, short but muscular, wearing an FBI baseball cap, khaki pants, a blue button-down shirt, and loafers. He didn't look like the outdoorsy type. I wondered if he was here to arrest Sasquatch and for what. Driving while mythical?

Jake continued, "Duke is a former profiler at the FBI, who has been an expert witness on several major homicide cases. He hosted the true crime series *Babysitters Gone Bad*, and even tracked down eight of the FBI's top ten fugitives. He's here to help the anthropology students profile Bigfoot."

Duke stood still, arms crossed in front of his chest, not showing any expression whatsoever.

"Duke, why don't you go ahead and meet your team," Jake prodded.

That only elicited a nod.

"You can shake hands," Jake said, like he was talking to a shy toddler and not a former FBI agent who could probably kill us all using only a spork.

I enjoyed watching Devan's intimidated expression as Duke marched over to shake his hand. Devan smiled politely and held out his hand. The older gentleman grabbed Devan by the forearm and pulled him close, like he was going to tell him about a secret stash of plutonium somewhere. Duke offered Kyle and Caroline his hand, and then he stood next to Devan and resumed his previous steely gaze. It was more than a little awkward. We got the more affable "expert," for sure, but I was more interested in skills than personality. I would have traded our crypto blogger for a real expert any day.

"And now I invite you to get to know your new team members and formulate a plan, because this challenge is about to get wild," Jake announced. "Each team, with the help of their expert, will have three days to collect their audio-visual evidence. Yeti, Set, Go!"

Colin gave Jake a thumbs up. "You're good to go."

"Sweet." Jake sauntered off the set.

I followed my parents, sisters, and Ernie to a nearby picnic table where my dad unrolled his map. Hal and the sound guy followed as well. "This is where we found the footprint, which won us the first contest," my dad explained. "And this is where we would like to search next based on the direction of the print."

Ernie nodded and studied the map in more detail, turning it around a couple of times. He took a protractor out of his back pocket and started measuring things.

Then it hit me. "Hey, aren't you our mailman?" I asked.

My dad turned red. "Samantha, Ernie's been elected president of our society unanimously the past four elections."

"There's no need to apologize." Ernie waved away my dad's concern. "I do happen to be your mail carrier as well. Although, I hope to retire soon and dedicate myself to Bigfoot preservation full-time." He bowed formally to me.

Lyssa came out from around the other side of the table and poked me in the ribs, hard.

"Where'd they get this guy?" she whispered in my ear.

"The post office," I whispered, poking her back, even harder, and stifling a nervous grin, which completely set her off. "I'm hoping we can return him to sender," I said.

Lyssa turned away to hide her laughter, but you could see her shoulders shaking.

My dad and Ernie walked away to the trailhead that led to our camp. The rest of us had no choice but to follow.

Devan and company walked off in the opposite direction. He caught my eye and I frowned, remembering our last conversation. He hesitated, and for a moment, I thought he was going to walk over to me. But then Duke pulled Devan along, up the trail.

On our way to the campsite to prepare for the hunt, Ernie and my dad debated the best plans for that night's adventure.

"If we wear layers of clothing, we won't get too cold," my dad said.

"Allow me to politely disagree," Ernie interrupted. "With all the walking, we're bound to get hot. I humbly suggest we *pack* an extra change of clothes rather than wear them."

"Then we won't be able to carry as much equipment," my dad countered. And so on and so on. Everything was a huge discussion and nothing ever got decided.

After twenty minutes, I had had enough. I stepped in front of the camera, and turned to face the family, hands on my hips. Their bickering was not going to help us win. "Someone needs to make a decision, so I'll do it. We'll take one backpack of extra clothes and wear jackets and sweatshirts tied around our waists. We'll take turns carrying the heavier equipment, and you two can each rotate being the leader. Is everyone happy?"

My dad flashed a grateful look and Ernie nodded, impressed. "Myron, you've raised very capable young ladies with remarkable leadership skills. Samantha, I do hope you'll run for our junior league executive board in the fall."

"I'll consider it," I said, to appease him. "Let's just move out before it's too dark to see the map."

Ernie practically bounced with excitement. "That was a wise course of action. You'll do us proud, Samantha."

Just my freaking luck. I finally had a groupie and he was a short postman with a Bigfoot fixation.

Lyssa was having a lot of fun watching me squirm. "You know, Samantha, you do need another extracurricular activity for your college applications," she said loudly, to make sure Ernie could hear.

"What a good idea, Lyssa!" I replied, imitating her tone. "You could use some afterschool activities yourself." Then to Ernie, I added, "Lyssa has excellent leadership skills, as well."

Ernie grinned at us. That shut Lyssa the hell up.

From then on, I tried to focus on my compass and the map. Mom, Sophie, and I walked in front, navigating; Lyssa traipsed along sullenly behind us, and my dad and Ernie argued about methods and strategy in the back of the procession.

When we got closer to where we wanted to end up, Ernie enlisted Sophie's help to hang small things from the trees. "What are those?" I asked him.

Again, Ernie smiled at me like I was the teacher's pet. "I'm so glad you are taking such an interest, Samantha. These are pheromone chips." He held out his tiny hand to me. In it were plastic things with a little wire attached for hanging.

"Isn't that supposed to make you feel sexy?" Lyssa asked, eyeing the plastic in his hand as if she were planning to rub it on her skin like perfume.

Ernie wagged his finger at her. "I wouldn't get too excited, young lady. This is made of ape pheromones. We're trying to catch a Sasquatch, not a quarterback."

Our first night out with Ernie was a bust. When no beasties turned up to check out the pheromone chips after a few hours, Ernie decided we should keep moving. He led us in what seemed to me like circles for hours, now and then stopping to check the thermal imager.

Inevitably, he'd get a heat signature "just over there a ways" and after we'd hike to that spot, there'd be no sign of any animals, much less a Bigfoot. My dad deferred most of the time to Ernie and went along on the wild goose chase. By 3:00 a.m. we were all exhausted, except for Ernie.

"Ow!" Lyssa stumbled, and I caught her arm. "Ugh. Sorry, Sam. I'm dead on my feet."

Even my mom, who was usually pretty patient, started whining, "Are we almost done for the night?"

"Can you say that again?" asked Hal, the last person marching alongside our sad little parade. "And can you do the thing where Lyssa trips and Samantha catches her again?"

"No!" Lyssa and I snapped at the same time.

The next day wasn't any better. My dad wanted to show Ernie the location of the footprint that had won us the first challenge, while it was still daylight. Around midday we set off, Dad trotting up the trail with a little bounce in his step.

After a few hours of hiking, Sophie whispered, "I don't remember it being this far. Are we on the right trail?"

"Yeah, I think so," I replied, scanning for identifying landmarks. "I think we're just moving slower than the last time we climbed this path."

Sophie wheezed and took out her asthma inhaler. "Okay. I trust you."

We lapsed back into silence, concentrating on our burning calves and short breath. Eventually we made it to the footprint area. The marking had been eroded away, and even with all of us combing the ground, no other prints were found. There were no signs at all of the elusive beast.

"Myron, are you sure this was where you got that print?" Ernie asked. "Seems like there's no proof of any Squatch, as far as I can tell."

My dad stared at the dirt and, shaking his head, replied, "Yes, this is the spot. I thought for sure there'd be more evidence and that this would be a good spot to set up the recording devices . . ."

Dad's shoulders drooped as we descended back down the trail. I gritted my teeth, fuming that Ernie would be so obnoxious to my dad. But I held my annoyance in check. It wouldn't do anyone any good if I went nuclear on Ernie in front of the cameras. We'd probably all do better after some dinner and a full night's sleep.

Only Ernie was still chatting happily on the long trek back to camp. "Ohhh, I have a great idea," he said to my dad. "Let's do some wood knocking on the way. Maybe something will respond for us to record. Or maybe we'll even catch a shot of it."

"Can we do it sitting down?" Lyssa asked.

Ernie shuffled in circles, hunting for something on the ground. "No, we should be ready to move at a moment's notice."

I had no idea what wood knocking could possibly involve. But I had my doubts about Ernie's research methods.

The FBI guy had probably already cuffed and fingerprinted Bigfoot and we were stuck with a dweeb who thought hanging ape perfume from trees was a scientific endeavor.

Ernie held a couple of thick sticks and started banging them together and smacking them against a big tree. He paused to listen for a response, and moved a few paces further along the trail. At one point, a similar knocking sound echoed itself in the distance. But I didn't think it warranted Ernie's elated expression.

"He's not far! We should head that way." He pointed up to the mountains.

My dad grinned and pulled out some binoculars for a closer look.

Mom cleared her throat pointedly, which was surprising. She had been pretty quiet the whole time. "Um, I think we've done enough for today. The girls were up late last night. I think we could all use some rest." Her stern expression meant she had made up her mind, and everyone else's.

"This is why Squatching should be a solitary action," Ernie grumbled to himself. "You don't see me bringing my family along to hunt. It should be one on one, just you and the beast. None of this 'I'm hungry, I'm tired.' No. You eat when the beast is eating. You sleep when he's sleeping."

He continued, but I tuned him out. I bet the real reason his family never joined him on the hunts was that they probably didn't want to be around him. Sure, I didn't enjoy freezing my ass off in the woods all night, and my parents and Lyssa could be incredibly annoying, but at least they didn't make me want to feed them to wild animals . . . most of the time.

Chapter 11

"Being a cryptozoologist is a lot like being a postman.
You need to know your neighborhood. Once you go
through someone's mail, you can figure out their
habits and desires, and that's how you find someone,
by learning everything about them."

—*Ernie Saposnik, president of the Northern Ohio Bigfoot Society*

We had only walked halfway back to the camp when the sky abruptly turned a vivid purple color that I had never seen before, even in one of those boxes of sixty-four crayons. If there were a crayon that color, it would have been called "Hope-You-Brought-A-Sturdy-Umbrella-Mauve."

I consulted my watch; it was only five-thirty. The crew had just departed for the night in a Jeep. It was way too early for sunset. Icy winds blew dramatic, dark clouds across the sky. The forest became so creepy, I partially expected an alien ship to land and prove me wrong about the whole UFO thing. Sure, I enjoyed all things sci-fi, but I didn't actually believe in the stuff.

Thunder rumbled and echoed throughout the valley. I'd hoped we would make it into the tents before the rain came, but there was still a mile of trekking ahead of us when the storm rolled in, and the torrential rain followed. The ground instantly became slick with mud, slowing our pace even more.

It was a good thing the cameras were no longer rolling, because the entire family looked awful and kind of indecent since our clothes had become see-through in the rain. Like a wet T-shirt contest for mud wrestlers.

We finally made it back to the camp. Sophie and I dove into our tent and stripped off our wet clothes.

"Ugh!" she said, shivering. "I feel like I'll never be warm and dry ever again."

Even in clean clothes, my icy bones creaked. "Yeah, now's about the time I wished I was staying in a tricked-out log cabin with hot soup and running water," I said. "We can't even light a fire until the rain stops."

Sophie sneezed a few times, as if to prove my point.

The pelting rain continued for hours, making for a long, cold sleepless night. The wind howled like a dog with a toothache, and threatened to rip our tents to shreds at any moment. My teeth chattered so loudly, I hoped I wouldn't wake Sophie, who finally fell asleep next to me after hours alternating between coughing, sneezing, and shivering. The calendar may have said it was summer, but if someone had handed me a snowsuit, I would have French-kissed them.

My mind turned to the fake clues Lyssa and I had planted. What a waste. Other than the claw marks, they were probably all washed away in the storm.

Eventually, I drifted off to sleep but Sophie's coughing woke me a few hours later. I found a flashlight and pointed it at her. Sophie's skin was even paler than usual except for the slight sickly yellow tone. Sweat coated her face, and she sported some killer dark circles under her eyes.

"Wow. You'll do anything to avoid being on television, huh?" I teased her.

Sophie struggled to hoist herself up on her elbows. "I'm fine. Just need a sip of water . . ."

I reached out to help her, and immediately felt her scorching, clammy skin. "Shit. Sophie, you're burning up!" My sister had a weak immune system, so when she got sick, she got violently ill. "Lay back down. You're not fine."

For a second, I thought she was going to fight me, but she saw how serious I was and slunk back down in her sleeping bag. My easy victory proved Sophie really felt lousy.

I wiped her forehead with a bandana from my backpack. "This is what's going to happen," I said. "You're going to take some ibuprofen, and I will call Beth on the walkie-talkie and get help. There's no effing way I'm letting you stay outside on the damp ground when you're this sick."

I could be very bossy when I had to be. It was one of the side effects of being a middle child. If I didn't speak up, I didn't get heard.

"Yes, Doctor Berger." Sophie managed a small smile, which barely registered on her face.

"I'm not a doctor yet, but someday, when I'm a kick-ass surgeon, you'll have to listen to me . . ."

"I already listen to you," she mumbled, followed by a coughing fit that shook her whole body and made her gasp for breath.

I cringed and gave her a stern look. "You could use cough medicine, too. And maybe some chicken soup."

"Now you sound like a Jewish mother, and I already have one of those." Sophie tried to laugh, but all that came out was a wheeze and another cough. "Sam, it's the same cold I've been fighting off and on for weeks. I'll be fine."

"I bet the infection's in your chest. You can't ignore it." I crossed my arms and stared at her until she nodded.

She smiled for real, and lay down on the pillow exhausted, like a big vacuum cleaner had sucked all the energy from her body. "You will be a really good doctor," she said.

I hoped she was right. Being a doctor was something I had dreamed about from the time I was a little kid and visited Sophie in the hospital. When I got a little older, I would beg to go to work with my mom at the medical center. She was a receptionist and awesome at dealing with patients and the insurance companies, but I wanted to be the one who actually healed people.

I had volunteered at the local hospital for the past couple of months, helping nurses deliver meals, filing charts, visiting patients, and stuff like that. So that's how I knew Sophie could have the flu or worse. I didn't want to scare her, but pneumonia was even a possibility if her infection went untreated, and that's something you just don't blow off.

I pulled my boots on and stumbled out of the tent. The storm had moved on, but it was still dark outside. I surveyed the campsite with my flashlight. We had the foresight to pitch our tents on high ground, so most of the rain had run down the hill and formed a moat of muddy water around much of the site. The fire pit had turned into a birdbath. Tree branches and debris littered the ground. It was a mess, but it appeared that all the gear and Bergers had survived the storm intact. With the notable exception of Lyssa's little pup tent, which drooped awkwardly on one side, one of its poles clearly snapped in half.

I took a deep breath and braced myself before going over to talk to my parents.

"Mom? Dad? Wake up," I said through the tent fabric.

A rustling came from within and my dad's snores stopped with a snort.

"What's happening? What's wrong?" my mom responded, unzipping the tent flap and peeking her head out.

"Mom, don't freak out, okay?"

That was apparently the wrong thing to say. My mom immediately went into panic mode; turning pale, she asked, "What is it? Is Lyssa okay?!"

"I said *not* to freak out. Lyssa's fine. It's Sophie. She's got a pretty bad cough and a fever. I need the walkie to call Beth. I think Sophie should see a doctor ASAP." I got that all out in one breath, and stepped back, waiting for Mount Mom to erupt.

"Oh my god! My poor baby girl!"

"Mom, it's okay. She's gonna be fine—but I need the radio."

"Right, right." She disappeared and reappeared a moment later with the walkie-talkie.

My father had woken up enough to realize what was going on and he rubbed circles on my mom's back. "Honey, let Sammy call the crew."

"I should make Sophie some soup," my mom said, her face lighting up at the prospect of force-feeding my sister chicken and noodles.

"Good idea," I replied. *That'll keep her busy*, I thought as I walked away with the walkie. I pressed down on the button. "Beth, come in. It's Sam."

"Go for Beth. Hi, Samantha, what's going on?"

"My sister Sophie is very sick. I think she might have the flu. We should get her to a doctor, or even the hospital. She has a compromised immune system because of her asthma."

The other line went silent as Beth paused. "Umm. I'll check with Colin. I don't know if he will move her or not. We'll have to look at the contest rules."

I kicked a tree out of frustration. "I know what I'm talking about. She's having problems breathing. She needs to have a doctor check her out. Immediately." My sister's health was way more important than Colin getting upset about weird-ass rules.

"Okay. Calling Colin now. Over." Beth disconnected and static filled the air. A few minutes passed. Then a few more. I paced and played with the antenna of the walkie-talkie, bending it back and forth, willing the radio to come on again with good news.

When it finally did, Beth said, "We're sending a doctor over in a Jeep."

"Thank you!" I said, my voice cracking in relief. "How long will it be?"

"Twenty or thirty minutes tops," Beth said.

I blew out a huge sigh. "If you could hurry them, I would appreciate it."

"I can't hurry them. It's still early and they said twenty to thirty minutes. Over." She hung up.

I let my parents know what was happening, then grabbed a bottle of water and ducked back inside the tent where Sophie was stretched out like a sick starfish.

"Thanks," she said with a hoarse voice, taking the bottle from my hand. She drank the water and collapsed again. I sat in the corner of the tent and watched her exert way too much effort to breathe.

Thirty-four painful minutes later, the car carrying Colin and a hunky, rugged Seattle mountain-man type doctor arrived.

My parents rushed over to meet him.

My mom wiped her eyes with the back of her hand. "Thanks so much for coming."

"I'm Doctor Sawyer." He smiled at my mom and shook hands with my dad before entering Sophie's tent. Colin stood to the side with my parents and Lyssa.

"So, let's see what's going on here?" The doctor held the back of his palm to Sophie's forehead. He gestured for her to open her mouth, and stuck the thermometer in between her chapped lips. His brows knitted together when the thermometer beeped. "One-oh-three, that's not so good. I'm going to listen to your lungs," he said, offering her a reassuring smile. Then he took out a stethoscope. "Breathe as deeply as you can. Okay, now try to cough."

Sophie's lips formed a grim smile, and her eyes lowered to half-mast. "Not a problem there."

After listening to her cough, Dr. Sawyer said, "Your sister was right to call me. I'm thinking it's the flu. The strain this year has been particularly brutal."

"Do you think she needs to go to the hospital?" I asked.

"I'm hoping not." He gave my sister one final smile. "Don't worry, we'll get you feeling better, Sophie."

"Thanks," I answered for her.

He stood and left to speak with my parents who were standing with Colin several feet away. I followed.

"Well?" Colin asked.

"It's the flu. She's got a moderately high fever and I'd like her to stay in bed—a real bed, not a sleeping bag on the ground—and get some rest for the next few days," the doctor replied.

"So, we're sending her to the hospital, right?" I interjected.

Colin frowned. "I thought maybe we could move her to the Netherfield team's cabin instead. They have an extra suite, so she'll have plenty of privacy and quiet. That way we can film her illness, make it part of the story. It'd be great for ratings. People love that kind of drama."

"What? Are you freaking serious?" I gestured for my parents to back me up, but they seemed unsure what to do.

"Well, that is," Colin fumbled, "unless Dr. Sawyer insists that she go to the hospital."

Dr. Sawyer took a moment to think about it. "No, as long as she's indoors, and kept warm and dry, and has someone to look after her, I don't see why she shouldn't stay in the cabin."

Colin grinned. "I have a feeling that the other team won't have any problem with Sophie being there. They'll take good care of her."

Then it hit me. This wasn't just about showing the recovery of a pretty girl with the flu. This was about Kyle. Colin had seen Sophie and Kyle talking the other day, and was hoping that pushing them together would make for some good soap-opera-style reality TV drama.

"Good," Dr. Sawyer said. "And I can check on her myself over the next few days and we'll figure out if she needs anything stronger than cough and cold medicine. I think really the best thing for her is rest and fluids."

Everyone looked at me, expectantly, but as pissed as I was at Colin's exploitation of my sister's illness, I wasn't going to argue with the doctor. And maybe it would be better to have Sophie nearby so I could personally keep an eye on her. I nodded, "Okay, let's try the cabin. But if she gets worse, she's going to a hospital."

My parents agreed and I left them to radio Beth and get the logistics sorted out.

I crawled back into the tent and whispered to Sophie, "Well, I think you're going to get your chance to know Kyle better."

"What do you mean?" Sophie's voice was rough from all the coughing.

"They're going to send you to his team's tricked-out log cabin until you're better."

"This is awful," she moaned.

I put on my best cheerful face. "You heard the doctor. He said you need to rest for a while. No big deal. I guess you'll just have to do a little glamping."

"I can't impose on them." Sophie patted down her hair and put it behind her ears.

"Bull! You just don't want Kyle to see you looking like this." I pulled out the brush from her backpack and helped straighten her hair.

She exhaled, with some visible effort. "Okay. Whatever you think. I just hope it doesn't affect our team. I know it's important to Mom and Dad."

"Don't worry about the contest. I've got it covered. And I'll come by to make sure you're getting fluids and stuff. Although I bet Kyle won't mind playing nurse either." I winked at her. I hadn't wanted Sophie to get distracted by Kyle, but maybe I was thinking about it the wrong way. It was possible that Kyle would be the one distracted. Maybe he'd fall hard for my sister and not want to see her lose, which could only help us.

The doctor poked his head back into the tent. "Okay, Miss Sophie, we're going to take you to the cabin for a few days. We'll drive you right now in the Jeep." He wagged his finger at her and added, "Promise me you won't push yourself."

"Okay," she replied meekly.

The doctor held out a hand to help her stand.

Sophie's eyes searched mine. I nodded and smiled, then gave her a gentle hug. My dad and Lyssa blew kisses and waved while my mom got into the car with Sophie.

My mom wiped a tear away from her face. "I'm going to get Sophie settled in and then come back," she said.

I draped the dry blanket that Colin had brought over Sophie's shoulders and threw her backpack in the Jeep for her. Once she was all tucked in, Sophie offered a small wave as the vehicle drove away, taking her behind enemy lines.

Chapter 12

"The most important video footage of Sasquatch was taken in 1967 by Roger Patterson in northern California. There is still debate over whether it's real. I think it doesn't hurt to believe."

—*Colin Johnson, producer of* "Myth Gnomers," *in* "Yes, Virginia, There Is a Sasquatch: A Behind-the-Scenes Christmas Special"

I didn't even have time to worry about Sophie that morning—I had to get ready for the camera crew that would be there any moment to follow us on another exciting adventure with Ernie.

I tried to wake Lyssa, who had crawled into my tent after Sophie left because hers was broken from the storm. "Lyssa, get up."

Lyssa covered her face with the crook of her arm to avoid the sunlight. "Ten more minutes," she grumbled into her elbow. "Go make me some coffee."

"No way. You're on your own," I said. "I gotta help Dad."

I pulled my boots on and trudged outside to find him wringing out the clothes that had been drying on the clothesline when the rain started falling last night. "What a night, eh, kiddo?" Dad grinned as he draped a couple of his embarrassing shirts over the line. One read "Gone Squatchin'" and the other said "I'm with Bigfoot." He had many more of those types of shirts back at home.

"That's an understatement," I replied.

"Anybody start building an ark yet?" he asked. "Maybe we can convince two Wood Apes to come on board."

I wished I were a spider, so I'd have even more eyes to roll.

Lyssa finally emerged from the tent, and shortly after that Mom got back from getting Sophie settled in the other team's cabin. Ernie's bellowing snores were still emanating from his tent, so we all tiptoed around, hoping to let him sleep for as long as he wanted. Seems I wasn't the only one who was eager to avoid Ernie.

Everyone was exhausted from a sleepless, stormy night, but I was resigned to get back out on the trail. Sure, we won the first challenge, but time was running out for the second one.

I wondered how the other team was doing with Duke, and toyed with the idea of spying on them again. But I decided against it, feeling like my time would be better used for trying to figure out how the hell we were going to get video of a creature I was still pretty positive didn't exist.

"Okay, Bergers, let's get cracking," Ernie said, once he threw off his sleep mask and rolled out the map. "I've crossed off the site of the footprint. I say we go further up the mountain now."

My dad's lips formed a grim line. "This is a nighttime hunt, which means we should start later in the day. Plus the girls need to rest. We don't want anyone else getting run down and sick."

The two went back and forth endlessly, before my dad finally prevailed. I was proud of him for standing up to Ernie.

By midday, everyone seemed restless and anxious, but my dad was right, we were supposed to be conducting nighttime hunts since that's when the beasts were more vocal and active. And as panicky as Dad and I were about getting something, anything, on tape to present to the judges, we knew we had to be strategic.

Dad ended up going off alone to check the bait stations for the hundredth time that week. Ernie retired to his tent to nap, to everyone's relief. Lyssa took her magazines over to the lake, and Mom and I alternated between cleaning up the muddy camping gear, fretting about Sophie, and worrying that we'd lose the next challenge. Hal and Dave got some footage of us all not talking to each other, then sat down and started playing cards.

And all through the day, I replayed the strange conversation with Devan. "Who calls someone a hedgehog? Could he be any weirder?" I muttered to myself while dragging the pots and pans to the creek to wash them, not that it did much good, considering I accidentally dropped them in a muddy puddle on the way back.

"Crap!" I picked the pots back up and cleaned them again, determined to focus on the tasks at hand for the rest of the day, and nothing else. Unfortunately, we had a whole lot more worrying and waiting ahead of us.

After I spent a few excruciating hours of pacing, trying to read, and pacing some more, the afternoon sun finally started to set and I got busy gathering up our gear and rallying the troops. We marched in silence up the trail, past the location where we found the footprint, and were nearly at the peak of the mountain by full dark. I was second in command, and I wasn't messing around. If we didn't capture some sort of recording of an imaginary beast soon, this hedgehog was going to turn into a full-blown porcupine.

• • •

"Okay, now I feel ridiculous," Lyssa whispered into the pitch-black night a couple of hours later.

"Really? Just now?" I said from the tree next to her. "Not for the past few days or every day since Dad decided he wanted to be a Bigfoot hunter? Don't forget, you're the one who was all excited to be on TV," I said.

Lyssa played with a lock of her hair. "Yeah, that's before I had to climb trees, when I thought we'd actually be staying in a fancy hotel and just pretending to camp out."

I pursed my lips. "Pay attention. No one can see your hair in the dark."

I was using Ernie's night vision goggles to scout for Bigfoot from a low branch of a tree, while Lyssa scanned the area with the thermal cam.

Lyssa squirmed herself into a more comfortable position on her branch. "Oh, so now you're Batman with the x-ray vision."

I was about to tell her that she was actually thinking of Superman, but a loud cracking of twigs and rustling of leaves interrupted me. Startled, I took a step back, forgetting I was in a freaking tree. I had to grab onto a higher branch not to lose my footing.

"What the hell was that?" my sister squeaked.

I focused the goggles, but didn't see anything rustling the leaves. I couldn't see any movement either. "I don't know, but it sounded close. Maybe we'll get something."

"There's something big heading this way," Lyssa whispered staring at the display on the thermal with wide eyes. "Oh. My. God. It's walking on two feet. Wait. I think there's more than one!"

We held our breath and I readied my infrared camera, waiting for the creature or creatures to step into the clearing or make some noise into our recorders. It turned out to be my dad. Followed by my mom and Ernie.

"Girls, any luck up there?" my mom hollered up to us.

"No. Can we come down now?" Lyssa yelled back.

"Just a bit longer, sweetie," my dad replied, just as Hal and Dave caught up. "We need all the angles we can get if we want to get good photos."

"How about we stop shouting? We're basically taking out an ad that we're here," I called down to my teammates. *Seriously, did I have to think of everything?*

"Sorry, sorry," my dad said.

Dad, Mom, Ernie, and Dave each hid behind a tree, and hunkered down with a couple of recording devices. Even Hal tried to hide behind a bush, but he was a pretty big guy, and no amount of ferns and moss could fully conceal his position.

About an hour passed when a quiet snuffling, snorting sound came from a nearby thicket, and all eyes and cameras turned toward it. Whatever it was, the beast was tall and moved in a blur from one tree to the next.

"Lyssa," I called under my breath. "To your right. Now!"

My sister and I started clicking our cameras as quickly as we could. Hal jumped out from his hiding spot with a surprised shout. "I see something, I see it!"

But by that time, the creature was gone.

"Did you get proof?" my dad asked, out of breath from running to the base of my tree.

"I got something, for sure. Did you see anything?" I asked.

"Maybe, I'm not sure," Ernie said. "There was clearly *something* over there, but then this one started shouting and scared it away." He pointed to Hal.

Hal winced. "I was surprised. I didn't think we'd actually see anything."

"Don't get too excited." I swung down from the tree. "We don't know what we caught on camera yet. It could be absolutely nothing."

"We should follow it!" Ernie shouted.

"Too late. It's long gone," my mom said, squinting into the darkness. My sister climbed out of her tree, too, with less grace.

My dad threw his arm around my shoulder. "Oh, don't be so skeptical. We've got something. I'm sure."

"Dad, you've never gotten any good images before. I'm just saying it's highly unlikely. It could have even been someone from the other team in a Bigfoot suit," I said.

My dad scratched his chin. "I don't think any of them is that tall. Or that dishonest. We have a code of ethics among Squatchers."

I winced, thinking of the fake clues Lyssa and I had planted. I didn't regret our prank. They had it coming. But I still didn't want my dad to think I was unethical. "I get it, Dad," I said, looking away.

Having finally captured some possible evidence, we began the trek back to camp. It was still a few hours before sunrise, and the woods were as dark as ever. My parents insisted we all wear the mining headlamp hats for safety. I felt like a reject dwarf from Snow White, but if it got me into my sleeping bag sooner, I was more than willing to take a couple of bites out of that humiliating apple.

Chapter 13

"To hunt Bigfoot, you need to think how he thinks,
eat what he eats, and live where he lives. Only by being on the
ground can you begin to get close to the truth."

—"Squatching for Dummies: A Field Guide to Our Furry Friends"

I woke at dawn the next morning and was ready in record time, needing some hardcore cappuccino action. Jake had insisted on an espresso machine being added to the buffet. At first Colin balked, but then Jake had gotten on the phone with his agent. Despite being Mr. McJerky, Jake had decent taste in coffee.

We'd hiked the two-mile-long trail to base camp enough times at this point that I didn't have to think about maneuvering around the various physical landmarks, rocks, or trees along the way. Absorbed in thought about our strategy, I absentmindedly stepped over a particularly big tree root. However, I forgot to warn Ernie, who was behind me. He flailed and reached out to grab the closest thing to him, which was, unfortunately, me.

He knocked me into a nearby thorny bush and I ended up face down in the dirt with him on top of me. Awesome.

"Ouch!"

After some inelegant clambering to get up, I surveyed the damage. Neither of us was seriously injured, but the bush had given me a nasty scrape on my palm and a few scratches on my cheek. To make matters worse, I was bleeding all over the place.

"I'm so sorry, Samantha. Allow me," he apologized and took a fresh linen handkerchief from his pocket to dab at my face.

I narrowed my eyes and grabbed the cloth from him. "Thanks."

I wiped the dirt from my hands on my jeans and cleaned off my face. There wasn't much I could do about the rip or the bloodstain on my sleeve. I was a hot mess. Again.

"Let's go. We have to keep moving or we'll be late for the judging." I sighed. "Maybe Mindy can lend me a shirt."

Mindy stared at my ripped, bloody shirt and muddy jeans and whisked me off to one of the production trailers to scrounge up something clean for me to wear. The other team arrived noisily by car wearing dry, stain-free clothes.

When I stepped out of the trailer, Devan was leaning against the car door, hands in his pockets.

The moment he caught sight of my oversized hot pink shirt with the *Myth Gnomers* logo on it, his lips curled into a smirk. I bet the frayed purple leggings I squeezed myself into added to his amusement. They certainly did nothing for my slightly pear-shaped figure. Nothing good at least.

"Listen, Sam," Devan said, stepping closer to me. "I know we started off on the wrong foot . . ."

"Um, yeah. You called me an angry hedgehog."

He winced. "Sorry about that. I . . . well . . . anyway, regardless of everything else going on, I wanted to say that I'm sorry about your sister not feeling well." His eyebrows rose slightly, waiting for my response.

Devan's gaze was so intense, I wondered if he was actually sincere. It was hard to tell, considering his disdain for my family. All I knew was that I found it impossible to concentrate with him standing so close. Apparently, intense and confusing was actually my type.

I took a step back. "I'm sure she'll be fine. Sophie's stronger than she looks. Plus, it sounds like she's in good hands." I pointed my chin toward Kyle. My hint of a smile withered when Devan's mouth tensed into a straight line.

Devan glanced away, avoiding my eyes. "I wouldn't presume anything," he said. "Kyle is just a flirt and he knows we're under orders to keep everything strictly professional." He waved his hand in a dismissive gesture.

It was clear he didn't approve of Kyle and Sophie spending time together. I guessed he thought my sister wasn't good enough for his friend.

I gritted my teeth and thought of what it would feel like to unclench Devan's jaw with a good, solid punch. I didn't care if he was cute or not. Kyle liked Sophie and Devan knew it. I glared at him, trying out different responses in my head. None of them seemed clever enough. If only I could remember the British term for giant jerk. I gave up. All this drama was taking away from the more important goal. To win and save our house. No matter what the cost.

Why did Devan have to ruin everything? For a moment, when he expressed concern over how my sister was feeling, he seemed almost human. But with one grimace he managed to make it clear how he felt about me. I meant *us*. How he felt about my family. For the tenth time I asked myself why I cared what he thought. And again, I came up empty-handed.

"I have to go," I blurted. Leaving Devan tongue-tied, I marched across the lot to Kyle, who smiled and waved at me.

"How's Sophie doing?" I asked.

Kyle's forehead wrinkled with concern. He glimpsed down and kicked the dirt with his toe. When his eyes caught mine again, I could see how tired he looked. "She's not great, the flu is kicking her ass. I don't think the cough medicine is helping much. I didn't even want to leave her . . ." he said. "But she claimed she was perfectly happy watching old episodes of *The Golden Girls* all morning. Do you think she was serious?"

"Sophie wouldn't joke about *The Golden Girls*. They're sacred." I smiled slightly, thinking of my sister eliciting that kind of care and concern. Kyle seemed to be a nice guy. Sophie was lucky, except for the major flu part, and the fact that he was on a team with our sworn enemies. But then again, maybe it would help us in the long run.

My happiness waned when Caroline appeared. She puckered her mouth like she had recently sucked on lemons doused in hot sauce. "Kyle!" she yelled across the set. "We need to strategize. Now. God, it's like I have to do everything around here."

If she really was the genius Devan said she was, she did a good job of hiding it behind the spoiled exterior.

Kyle gave me an apologetic smile, and hollered back at her, "Just a sec. Calm the hell down!"

He took his Hacky Sack out of his pocket, and tossed it from hand to hand, burning off some nervous energy. "Sam, I was thinking, maybe a visit from you would really cheer up Sophie. I think she feels bad that she can't help you, and that you have to deal with your folks and Lyssa all by yourself."

I sighed. That was so Sophie. "I would love to visit if Colin will let me. I'll ask."

"Awesome." Kyle tossed the Hacky Sack up and down a few more times, before pocketing it and walking toward his teammates.

Spotting Beth, I waited for her to finish her conversation with one of the crewmembers before approaching her. "Hi, Beth. I wanted to say thank you again for your help with Sophie the other night."

"It was no big deal," she said, looking down at her sneakers. "I'm in charge of making sure people get medical attention if they need it."

"I know, but I appreciate it, especially the extra blanket you sent with Colin," I added. "Everything we had was soaked."

I smiled at her and Beth smiled, too. It was a small grin but it completely changed her face.

"I wonder if it's possible for me to visit Sophie in the cabin?" I asked. "From what Kyle says, she could use some company, and I know I'm going to worry until I can see her," I said.

Beth nodded slowly, like she was thinking through the situation. "I'm sure we can arrange it. I just need to check with the doctor and with Colin, but I don't think they'll say no."

I reached out to touch her shoulder, as a gesture of thanks, but she stiffened so I pulled back at the last second. I gave her a little half wave before sitting down cross-legged under a tree to wait for someone to tell me what to do. I took out one of my dad's Bigfoot field guides, which I promised I would review. I read three sentences before I was distracted. This time it was the sight of Lyssa gawking at Jake. He had his shirt pulled up to show off his six-pack, which, while impressive, was still attached to about 145 pounds of douche. Lyssa reached out a tentative hand to touch his abs, giggling like a drunken girl on spring break.

I groaned and put my head in my hands. *Could she be more embarrassing?*

Apparently, I wasn't the only one who had that thought, because from the corner of my eye I spied Devan, Kyle, and Caroline stop in their tracks to gawk at the spectacle of Jake pretending to be a male stripper. I shielded my eyes, and when I dared to peek through my fingers, he was gyrating and Lyssa was thoroughly enjoying herself.

I slunk against my tree, making myself into a ball. It wasn't the most dignified posture, but I really didn't want to deal with them right now. I figured as long as no one looked down, they wouldn't spot me.

Caroline made a disgusted sound in the back of her throat. "See, Kyle? You're better off avoiding the whole family."

"I appreciate your concern, but I really like Sophie," Kyle said.

"Why bother when there are tons of prettier, smarter girls at school?" Caroline asked. "You can do way better."

"Sophie's different. She's much more laid back and down-to-earth than the girls at Netherfield." Kyle, who seemed like a normally mellow guy, raised his voice. "I've been with private school girls since I was a kid, and they're all the same—boring and only interested in how much money your dad has."

"Good thing your dad has plenty," Caroline said, before examining a pad of paper she took out from her back pocket.

"I have nothing against Sophie, per se," Devan said. "She's cute, but do you really want to be pulled into that uncultured family?"

Uncultured? I contemplated shouting a few things in his face, but didn't want to prove his point. Instead I sat, arms pulled tight around my knees, and tried to fight back hot, angry tears.

"God, you two are such snobs!" Kyle snapped. "Maybe your kind of culture is overrated. Maybe I don't want to summer in Martha's Vineyard and play golf the rest of my life. I hate golf and there are too many flies on the Vineyard."

"Okay, okay. Don't get your knickers in a twist!" Devan tried to joke, but Kyle didn't respond. "I'm just watching out for my best friend. Plus, you heard Dr. DeGraw. Do you really want to face her wrath?"

But it was too late. Kyle had already stormed off.

I couldn't help myself anymore. I was tired of always hiding behind trees. Especially when people said awful things about my beautiful, sweet sister. If they had only been talking about me, maybe I would have laughed it off, but I wouldn't let them insult Sophie. I marched right up to them to give them a piece of my mind. An angry piece.

When I approached, Devan stepped back like I was going to slap him and Caroline wiped the grin off her face.

I felt my chest turning bright red with anger and my hands shaking. "I can't believe you have nothing better to do than to make fun of people who don't have as much money as you. My parents may be ridiculous, but at least they're honest. Unlike you two asshats."

I was about to start yelling again, but a crunch of leaves and twigs startled me. "Good news, Sam!" Beth nearly shouted, oblivious to the fight she interrupted. "You're clear to visit Sophie tomorrow, once she's been on antiviral meds another twenty-four hours."

"Great!" I shouted in the direction of Devan and Caroline's horrified faces.

I left with Beth. I only had so much composure, and I was damn close to running out. My knickers were definitely well beyond twisty.

Chapter 14

"If I had to profile Bigfoot, I'd say he's a middle-aged mammal who no longer needs to hunt for food or find a mate. He's a bit of a loner and feeling a little depressed. That's why he has time to hang out and be spotted. He wants the attention."

—*Edward "Duke" Mahoney, former FBI profiler*

A backfiring car jolted me from my angry meditation. Colin jogged over to the Jeep that had just pulled into the clearing. Dr. DeGraw exited the car in all her frowning glory.

Next to Dr. Heinous stood a slight, twitchy woman with dark hair and birdlike features.

"Do you know who that is?" I asked Beth.

"That's Dr. Matilda Bruckmeier. She's a famous folklorist who has written about Bigfoot. Extensively."

A few hours later we were ready to start filming the presentation of evidence. We flanked one side of the judge, while the other team stood across from us. Based on the way he paced back and forth, I assumed Duke was giving his team a rallying speech before they entered the battlefield. Kyle smiled at us, but turned stone-faced when Duke barked something at him.

Lyssa elbowed me. "Wow. Someone's taking this all a little too seriously on their side, too."

"We'd like to welcome our distinguished guest judge, Dr. Matilda Bruckmeier," Jake pointed at the tiny lady with a flourish once the cameras started rolling. "A noted scholar specializing in American folk tales, now retired from North East Idaho State. She'll be judging you on your research methods and on the audio or visual recordings you collected during the challenge. Dr. Bruckmeier, would you like to say a few words?"

"Certainly." Matilda Bruckmeier pushed her square glasses up her nose. "While I enjoy studying legends and tall tales, I'm a skeptic when it comes to Bigfoot and other cryptids. If these creatures have been haunting our woodlands for centuries, why haven't we been able to closely observe or capture one? And where are the fossil remains? I'd love to be wrong, because it would be great fun to believe in Bigfoot or the Loch Ness Monster, or the Giant Squid."

Dr. DeGraw laughed behind a cupped hand strategically covering her face. "Actually, Dr. Bruckmeier, the Giant Squid is real." She seemed delighted to correct her colleague on camera.

"Oh? Since when?" Dr. Bruckmeier looked out over her glasses.

"Always, dear." Dr. DeGraw bit her lip, presumably to hide her smile.

"Well, either way, my point stands," Dr. Bruckmeier added with a twitch of her head.

"Awesome," Jake said. "Now, why don't we get started? The Bergers won the last challenge, so they'll go first. Okay, Myron and Ernie, and ladies." He offered a wolfish grin. "What do you have for us?"

My dad and Ernie both approached the camera, each wanting to take charge. My dad stood his ground, though, and Ernie eventually got the message and stepped back.

Good for you, Dad.

Steve, playing the part of the audio-visual technician, cued up the video, and a still shot of the first frame appeared on the big screen.

"Before we press play," my dad said, "I want to walk you through the footage. Lyssa and Samantha were up in the trees located here." He pointed to the monitor. The video was from Hal's camera, and you could see our feet in the branches at the top of the screen.

"At about fifteen seconds into the video you will see movement and a dark figure here, in between these other trees, behind the bushes, here." Dad nodded at Steve to roll the footage.

The night vision film was dark and green and the camera was shaky, but *something* big and fast darted behind the trees. However, at full speed, it was hard to decipher. It easily could have been wind in the trees, or a bear, or any number of things.

Jake squinted at the screen. I glanced at Dr. DeGraw and caught her nodding at Devan, like his team had already won.

"Now, let's look at it again, but this time in slow motion." My dad smiled widely.

Steve obliged. Once he slowed the video down, it was clear that the figure behind the trees was upright and about the size of a tall man. But the video still didn't prove the figure was Bigfoot and not a regular gangly guy.

It wasn't the famous Patterson Bigfoot film, for sure. It wasn't even the quality of a bar mitzvah video, if it were taken by somebody's drunk uncle Herbie. "We also have an intriguing still photo Samantha took from her vantage point up in the tree," my dad said.

An image flashed on the monitor. It showed the same dark figure between the trees, but from the higher angle, the moonlight made the furlike texture of the creature's body much more obvious. You still couldn't make out any facial features, other than two dots of light reflecting off of the eyes, but even I was impressed by the clarity of the shot.

"So, what do you say, Judge Bruckmeier?" Jake crossed his arms tightly over his chest, making them look more impressive.

Dr. Bruckmeier tilted her head, walked back and forth past the screen, and then smiled. "I love it! The image isn't conclusive, but it ignites the imagination. We'll have to send it to a film lab to enhance the images. But I think you've captured something very interesting."

My dad lifted his chin.

"Okay, Devan, Kyle, and Caroline, let's see how you and your FBI profiler did on the challenge. Who will present for you?" Jake asked.

Devan opened his mouth, but Duke stepped forward. "I will, of course," Duke said directly into the camera. "I have to applaud my young team members for their enthusiasm and for their technical know-how, but once I arrived, I helped them focus on getting familiar with the perp—I mean the beast—as a living, breathing person. To catch someone, you need to know everything about him, from the cigarettes he smokes to what brand whiskey he prefers. Every detail is important.

"To sum it up, to really get to know someone, I first make rookie agents go through the perp's trash. It's dirty, but it's effective and you don't need a warrant. You can imagine that these future Ivy Leaguers thought they were too good for old-fashioned detective work. They told me Bigfoot probably wouldn't use a trashcan."

Devan's restraint was on full display. He quivered just a little, while Caroline's eyes shot extra-potent poison daggers. Kyle took off his baseball cap and ran his fingers through his hair nervously.

But the former FBI agent didn't pick up on their anger. Apparently, he was just as bad at profiling people as he was mythical creatures. Unfazed by his team's reaction, Duke paced and jingled the change in his pocket.

"So, the best we could do was comb the area for clues and I'm happy to report that we found some interesting evidence," Duke said. "Okay, Steve, show the first slide."

Uh-oh. On the screen was a photo of the fake scene that Lyssa and I set. My stomach dropped. Duke was on to us and he didn't seem like the forgiving type.

Duke pulled out a laser pointer from his shirt pocket and pointed to the right side of the screen. "This is the before photo, taken during the daylight. Over here is Exhibit A: claw marks that were made at approximately ninety inches off the ground. Based on how deep the gashes are, we have reason to believe that they could have been inflicted by a Squatch. We don't feel these could be attributed to a bear because of the size of the claws," he said.

He caught Dr. DeGraw's eye, and she made a gesture for him to continue.

"Let the record also show that several of the twigs below are broken. With this circumstantial evidence in mind, we went back and looked through all the nighttime surveillance footage that we'd captured over the past ten days."

Did they have us on camera? This was So Not Good. "In addition to video cameras, at the start of the contest, my team set up motion-sensitive still cameras in their quadrant of the property, which they set to take photos whenever an animal comes within range. Unfortunately, none of those cameras focused on the immediate area where the scratches were found. However, we did capture this image." Duke gestured to Steve, and a grainy black and white night vision photo of a deer popped up on the monitor.

At first, I thought it was just a close-up shot of a deer, its head tilted in confusion as it sniffed the camera. But then Duke aimed his laser pointer at the bottom right corner of the image, and everyone on set let out an audible gasp. Lyssa and I exchanged horrified looks.

There, in the distance, through gaps in the foliage, was a silhouette of a figure. The fuzzy image showed a pointed head, long arms, and huge claws. I knew that figure was Lyssa or me in a hoodie sweatshirt, about to attack a poor defenseless tree with our fake claw.

Everyone else, though, apparently thought it was Sasquatch. Duke proceeded to give the rundown of the few features that they could see from the photo. My dad and Ernie were glued to the screen, eyes wide, and heads nodding. They were clearly convinced it was the real deal.

Caroline, however, stared me down until I shivered. Yeah, I think she knew it was us. *We were So Screwed.*

Duke raised his arms to quiet the crowd. "We believe the Squatch had been running after prey, perhaps a squirrel or something bigger like a goat. When he didn't catch his prey, he was frustrated and took his feelings out on the tree. It all builds a portrait of a disturbed middle-aged animal with anger management issues. We're seeing Sasquatch more and more because he wants to be seen. It's a desperate cry for help."

Caroline stepped forward and opened her mouth to speak, but Devan pushed her back with one arm.

"Oh, for god's sake!" Devan burst out in a loud voice, like he forgot about being nervous in front of the cameras. "Are you joking? First of all, there's no way Bigfoot would be chasing a *goat* in the forest! Goats don't live in the forest. And there's a deer right there in the photo—why would you even suggest a goat?" Devan threw his hands up then got in Duke's face. "Second, the idea that Bigfoot is some sort of serial killer, slashing at trees because he's desperate for attention, is ridiculous!"

Judge Bruckmeier raised her very thin tweezed eyebrows in surprise. The rest of us gaped, amazed at the way Duke had managed to shatter Devan's usual on-air reserve.

"Actually, there are mountain goats here," Beth said quietly. "They can be dangerous, too."

Duke looked momentarily stricken, but recovered quickly and jabbed a finger into Devan's chest. "I'll have you know that I've been catching dangerous criminals using these methods since before you were born. This is thirty years of experience speaking."

"No, it's utter rubbish." Devan shot back, before turning to Jake and the judge and asking, "Can we start over? Can I present instead?"

"Not up to me, bro," Jake held up his empty hands.

Colin was practically salivating over the drama that he was capturing. "No! No! Keep rolling. This is great!"

"Why don't we take five minutes to discuss?" Dr. DeGraw frowned, but beckoned to Dr. Bruckmeier and Colin to sit with her at one of the picnic tables. Everyone else began whispering in little groups about what had just gone down. Caroline whispered something to Devan, which made him widen his eyes before putting his head in his hands. Duke resumed his pacing and lecturing, but this time his speech to his team was filled with expletives and insults.

They knew. Of course the geniuses found us out. But why weren't they saying anything? Either they couldn't prove it or they figured I had dirt on Caroline, too. Or they were waiting for me to crack and confess. One thing was for sure. I had very few choices and a whole lot to lose. Right then, I chose to wait and bite my lip until it was bloody, trying to figure out my next move.

Soon enough, the judges were back and after some whispered conversation with Jake, they were ready for the pronouncement. "The judge and I have discussed this week's challenge in depth," Jake said. "Dr. Bruckmeier, your decision?"

Bruckmeier put her glasses back on and tucked her wispy hair behind her ears. "I appreciate what both teams brought to the field, however none of the evidence is conclusive. Therefore, I'm going to have to judge you all on research methods and techniques. Duke, your team did an excellent job of trying to get into what you believe is the psyche of Bigfoot, but while I'm intrigued by your images, I remain unconvinced of your profile of the Sasquatch." The last part of the sentence she said like a disappointed third-grade teacher, glaring over the top of her glasses and everything.

"As for the Bergers' evidence, you could use some improvement, there, too, folks," Bruckmeier said. "It was inventive of you to climb trees for visuals, but the video is shaky and inconclusive." She twisted her lips into an unimpressed expression.

Jake nodded too, as if considering each side carefully. "Who would you say is the winner of today's challenge?"

"I'm going to have to go with the Netherfield team," she said with a decisive nod. "Part of being a scientist is keeping up with the latest research methods and I think their use of motion-detecting equipment and surveillance cameras was a good choice for this contest."

I let out the breath I was holding, relieved we were being judged on process, not outcome, and that the other team had no reason to out us now.

Ernie and my dad groaned, but Jake raised his arms and continued speaking. "At this point, we're ready to bid farewell to our special guests, Ernie and Duke. It's been great having you here, but now it's time to send our teams back to the woods by themselves for the next challenge."

After Colin called "Cut" and let us go for the day, I dared to glance at Caroline. One glimpse of her indignant face and I knew this wasn't over, not as far as she was concerned.

Deflated, I punched a bunch of buttons on the espresso machine and listened to the whooshing and churning, imagining it was the mixture of my emotions from the day. I was a premium blend of a mess.

Chapter 15

"Wood Apes are very sensitive. I'm not surprised
they don't like being caught on camera or on film."

—*Brenda Berger, interview with* "Myth of the Month" *magazine*

I was trying to reheat my bland coffee over the campfire the next morning when Beth arrived at our camp.

"I came by to replace the memory cards on the cameras," Beth said. "Samantha, are you ready to go see Sophie?"

"Yes!" I gulped my now way-too-hot coffee in seconds. It burned its way down my throat. "I just need a minute to brush my teeth and stuff."

My mom stopped me on my way. "Let me tell your dad we're going."

Beth frowned. "Mrs. Berger, the doctor thought too many visitors would wear Sophie out."

My mom bit the side of her mouth, something she always did when she was feeling guilty, whether it was about letting us watch too much television or running out of potato chips for our lunches. "I feel bad about not helping. But I also don't want to abandon your father."

"Mom, it's fine. Sophie will absolutely understand. She knows Dad needs you here and she'd never want to do anything that might ruin our chances of winning. I bet you can visit later." I hugged my mom, hoping I made her feel less guilty. When I looked up at her, there were tears in her eyes. "Seriously, Sophie will be okay. It's just a little flu."

My mom wiped away the tears with the back of her hand. "I know, but I'm a mom, I worry. Someday you'll see."

"I hope not. I already worry enough as it is," I joked, rubbing her back gently one more time.

Beth interrupted, "We should get going, Samantha. It may rain."

I craned my neck to scan the sky. "Big surprise there." It had been dark and overcast for days now, and I was starting to wonder if I'd ever see the sun again. "Don't you have the Jeep today?"

"No. We have to walk. Colin needed the car to pick up Dr. DeGraw," Beth said.

Of course she got a cushy ride, while I had to walk in the rain. "Okay, let's go." I grabbed my backpack and filled it with a few more things for Sophie. I figured she would want the romance novel, a couple of her favorite granola bars, and a few extra T-shirts.

"So how'd a nice girl like you end up on a production crew like this?" I waggled my eyebrows to try to make Beth laugh, which didn't work.

"I'd just graduated college with a degree in film, and saw a listing for this job," Beth said. "I didn't want to go to New York or L.A. because I don't do well in big cities. I hate the noise and the crowds, so I figured this would be better."

"Is it?"

She looked straight in front of her and kept walking. "Yeah."

I gestured with my hand for her to say more.

Beth paused for a moment. "I like this job. Colin is smart, although a bit more focused on drama than I thought he would be. And the camera guys are okay, but I don't get a lot of Hal's jokes."

I smiled. "That's actually a good thing. It means you're not a huge geek like me. He references a lot of old science fiction."

She frowned like she was solving long division in her head. "Oh. Okay. I never wanted to ask him to explain."

"Are you going to stick with this for a while?" I asked, trying to gently steer her away from bad feelings about herself.

Beth's face brightened a little. "Until I can save enough money to make my own film. I want to do serious documentaries."

"What, you mean Bigfoot isn't serious? I thought we were going to be on C-SPAN." I put my hand in front of my heart in mock horror.

Beth shook her head seriously. "No. I think most people who watch this show are doing it for entertainment, not for educational purposes."

"I really hope so. I don't want to be responsible for educating anyone about this stuff," I said. "So, what kind of documentaries do you want to make?"

She pushed her hair behind one ear. "I'd like to follow women on the spectrum who have jobs and friends and families. Autism can be different for women, so I want to explore that. A lot of girls with autism deal with depression and eating disorders on top of everything else. I just want to put something out there that's positive for parents who are scared about their kid's diagnosis, and for older kids who feel like different is bad. It doesn't have to be all bad."

Colin was right, Beth was kinda awesome.

"That's amazing."

"It hasn't happened yet." Beth caught my eye before looking away. "I need to learn more about how to run a production."

We were interrupted by huge rolls of thunder, which made some of the tree branches around us shake.

"Man! Is it too much to ask for one lousy day without torrential rain?" I considered the dark clouds threatening to explode any minute, and then remembered I was wearing my canvas sneakers, which had a few small holes in them. I liked wearing things that were broken in and familiar. This particular pair was more comfortable than my hiking boots, but they would be worthless in the rain.

Beth didn't have her backpack with her so I felt around in my bag until I found a plastic poncho and handed it to her. I pulled the hood up on my supposedly water resistant jacket. Just in time, too. The sky opened up and suddenly we were engulfed by heavy rain.

"We're going to have to make a run for it," Beth shouted over the thunder.

"I can make it to the cabin on my own if you want to go straight to base camp," I hollered back.

"You sure?" Beth asked. She seemed relieved that she wouldn't have to go another quarter mile out of her way before getting to her dry, cozy trailer.

I nodded and we parted ways.

One slippery, muddy sprint later, I arrived at the cabin and just stared at the front door. I stomped my shoes on the porch mat, which didn't do anything to make them less muddy. I took a breath. It was time for me to go inside, even though I was completely unexcited to see two-thirds of the other team. Sucking it up, I knocked on the door with my cold, wet fist.

Chapter 16

"I didn't grow up hearing a lot about Bigfoot.
In England we were more interested in the Cornish Owlman,
or the Canvey Island Monster, which is basically a frog
on two legs. Who wants to search for a frog?"

—*Devan Das, team captain,* "Myth Gnomers"

There was no answer, but the distinctive high-pitched sounds of the Xbox came from the other side of the wooden door. I tried the handle and it was unlocked. When I stepped inside, the warm air greeted me like a soft blanket.

Devan and Caroline sat on either end of the couch, Devan playing a video game and Caroline reading, their backs facing the door. They didn't notice me as I stood dripping and giving the place a once-over.

I was surprised the cabin wasn't as fancy as I'd imagined. The living room was filled with sturdy, wood-framed couches and chairs—made for long life, not luxury. The décor was sparse, encompassing a few pictures of ducks and deer and other hunting scenes. There was a brick fireplace with a huge pile of logs stacked up next to it. The cabin was probably Duckworthy's hunting lodge when it wasn't being used for reality television contestants. The adjoining dining room had been converted into a science lab of sorts. Computers and lab equipment took up the large rustic table, and racks of test tubes and microscope slides covered the sideboard.

"Is that classic Space Invaders?" I asked. "Surprised to see you guys playing something so retro."

Caroline gave my mud-covered sneakers the stink-eye. Then without a word, she turned back to her book.

Devan hit the pause button and got up to greet me, banging his knee on the coffee table in the process. "You look like you swam the channel to get here."

I must have looked confused because he clarified, "The English Channel."

"Yeah, I got it. I watch a lot of BBC. *Sherlock*, *Doctor Who*, and other stuff . . ." I said.

His eyebrows joined together like I was a crossword puzzle to be solved.

"Anyway, I came to check on Sophie. Is she awake? Can I see her?"

The eyebrows relaxed. "Yeah, of course," Devan said. He walked over to a closet and grabbed a towel. "You need to take off your clothes first."

I crossed my arms in front of my chest. "Um, I don't think so."

Devan actually stuttered a little. "I just meant that you're wet and we don't want you to track in mud. I didn't mean to say that you had to be naked. Of course. That'd be ludicrous. We'd never do that." He was doing his nervous babbling thing again. He paused and took a deep breath. "We'll find you something dry to wear. You can leave your brolly and shoes on the mat."

"Brolly?" I looked around. "What the hell is a brolly?"

"An umbrella. Some BBC fan you are," he said, but with a teasing smile that completely threw me off.

I gestured to my sopping wet clothes. "I didn't bring an umbrella. Clearly."

I shrugged out of my coat and sweatshirt, left my wet stuff by the front door, and followed him to the bathroom to clean up and change. It felt amazing to wash the mud and grime off of my face with warm water, instead of ice-cold mountain runoff, and then put on the clean, dry clothes that Devan had brought me. They had to be Caroline's because they weren't Sophie's, and I didn't think the Netherfield boys were into expensive floral-patterned yoga pants with matching tunic tops. Plus the pants were too long and the shirt was too snug—definitely sized for Caroline's tall, slim Elvish build and not my short, curvy Hobbit bod.

Returning to the living room, I held my arms out wide and turned around in a circle. "Now, can I see my sister, or do you want to check me for fleas, too?"

He looked me up and down and issued a weak laugh. "You're good to go. I'll bring you and Sophie some chai."

"Um, thanks." I wasn't sure what chai was, but I hoped it was warm. It turned out Devan had nice manners, when he wanted to be polite, which wasn't very often as far as I could tell.

Something was off, though. Why was he being so pleasant? Maybe Caroline hadn't told him that I was behind those bogus scratches. Or maybe they truly didn't know it was me in that photo of the deer. Most likely they didn't think I was smart enough to fool them with fake evidence.

Devan pointed me down the hall and I opened the door a crack. Sophie was propped up against a few pillows. Kyle was sitting on the foot of the bed and the two of them had their heads bent over a Scrabble board. It was a sweet scene and I hesitated to ruin the moment. Sophie giggled at something Kyle whispered in her ear, but the giggle quickly turned into coughing.

I went over to her and handed her a glass of water from the table next to her. "Hey, Soph. How're you doing?" I asked.

She stopped coughing long enough to nod, and take the glass in two pale hands. "More or less okay," she said with a weak smile. "I'm so happy you're here!"

I gave her a hug in response. I examined her color, which, while still pale, was a little better. "What did the doctor say this morning?"

I turned to Kyle for an answer, since I knew my sister would downplay it.

Kyle frowned. "The antiviral medicine isn't working as well as he hoped. She may be getting a bit worse, but he thinks she just needs to wait it out."

Sophie put her head back on the pillow. "I've felt better, that's for sure. But Kyle's been great. He's even let me beat him almost every time."

He chuckled. "I only let you beat me the first time before I knew how good you were," he said. "Now I'm out for blood. And I'm still losing."

"Okay. You're on," she said. "Best three out of five."

"Your funeral," Kyle joked, while he carefully moved the board and tiles off the bed. "But maybe not right now. You guys probably want to catch up, I bet."

"Yeah, how's everything going with the contest?" Sophie asked, her nose wrinkled in concern. "How are Mom and Dad behaving?"

I laughed. "The usual. It's like refereeing a kids' soccer game. Noisy. Chaotic."

Kyle said, "Your parents seem pretty cool though. Seems like you have a lot of fun together."

"Ha. Fun is maybe *not* the word I'd use," I said dryly.

"I would. My mom died when I was really little, and my dad works a lot, mostly traveling to Korea to help launch new tech companies in Seoul. We never did family road trips or anything, even after he remarried." He stared down at the Scrabble board.

"Oh, sorry. I . . ." I wasn't sure what to say. I felt bad. He was right. As embarrassing as they were sometimes, at least my parents were around for us. I ended up blurting out, "That's rough."

He shrugged. "It's fine. My dad's a good guy, just busy. Caroline had it much worse. She hasn't even spoken to her real dad in years. But now she has us. I wanted to adopt a puppy, but I got a pain-in-the-ass sister instead." Kyle laughed, but his usually sunny grin seemed partially cloudy.

He moved toward the door. "I'll be in the other room if you need anything." He squeezed Sophie's hand, then left, closing the door quietly.

I gave Sophie a smile. I hadn't wanted her to get distracted by Kyle, but seeing her so happy, even when sick, changed my mind. "Wow! Pretty cute nurse, huh? He's risking getting the flu and he'd rather hang out with you than play video games—that's devotion."

Sophie sighed. "I know. It's been so nice to spend time with him, even though I feel awful. He says he'll come visit us in Ohio on his winter break from school. Isn't that sweet?"

"I'll say," I replied, trying not to let jealousy creep into my voice. "No one hangs out in Ohio in the winter for the scenery."

"I know, right?" She started to giggle again, but her lungs weren't strong enough for it. I helped my sister with her inhaler. On top of the flu, she had severe asthma, which was usually under control, but one little cold or sinus infection could really compromise her breathing.

"Better?" I asked, putting my hand on her forehead to see if she had a fever, but she felt more clammy than anything else.

Sophie grabbed my hand and held it tight. "I'm just glad you're here."

I sat down on the bed next to her. "Me, too. I've missed you. Plus, look around. It's like a fancy mansion compared to our tents. Poor Lyssa." I shook my head. "We don't even have regular TV, never mind cable and video games."

"I know! I bet she would kill for a frozen pizza."

"You have pizza? I only got offered chai, whatever that is. I didn't want to ask." I stood.

"It's tea with spices in it. His grandmother showed him how to make it. Isn't that sweet?" Sophie asked.

I imagined Devan cooking with a grandmotherly figure, which was a pretty cute image, as much as I hated to admit it.

"I guess, but I need some actual food, too. I'll get us something real to eat from the kitchen."

"You'll have to sneak it by Caroline, or else you'll get a lecture about the dangers of wheat and gluten."

"Really?"

"Yeah, she's a pretty serious health food nut."

I frowned. "She's a serious something, all right."

Now Sophie frowned. "Come on, Sam. She's not so bad. She's been really nice to me since I got here. I know she comes off as elitist, but I think she's just, sort of, shy."

"Hmmph. As shy as the plague."

"Okay, maybe not shy, but, I don't know," Sophie searched the ceiling for the right words. "Not good with people, maybe? I think she has a hard time letting people get to know her. Kyle says she has trust issues."

I chewed on my bottom lip. "Huh." That made sense, considering what Kyle just said about her dad.

Sophie continued, "The whole time I've been here, she's been mostly in the lab, hunched over a microscope, like she'd rather deal with germs and microbes than people. But then yesterday, she came in here with some delicious garlicky soup and gave me a whole rundown about how the ingredients are anti-inflammatory and antimicrobial and stuff. She made it just for me. To help me get better. That's pretty nice, right?"

"Or she wants you to get well so she can kick you out of here," I deadpanned. *And keep you away from her brother.* I stopped myself from saying more.

"Well, either way, it was a nice thing for her to do. And I think the soup actually helped. So, maybe try to be civil to her, Sam, okay?"

"Fine. I'll try." I smiled at Sophie, to show her I meant it. "But now I'm getting us lunch. And not some hippie-ass health soup. I'm going for the good old-fashioned overly processed deliciousness."

The kitchen wasn't exactly gourmet, but it was decent. I found a small microwave pizza in the freezer. While it cooked, I wandered to the doorway of the living room to see what the preps were up to. They had switched off the video game and were watching the news.

Devan had his fist over his mouth like he was trying not to scream. Caroline and Kyle exchanged concerned looks, and Caroline put an arm around Devan's shoulder.

"Is everything okay?" I asked.

"Not really," he said in a husky voice, shrugging Caroline's arm off. Without even glancing at me, he stormed down the hall and slammed the door to his bedroom behind him.

"Something I said?"

Caroline jumped up out of her seat. "I'll go see if he's okay," she said.

Kyle held out his arm. "Let me. After the Jake thing, I think you two still need some space." He took off down the hall to Devan's room. *Ouch.* I guessed that Kyle had been filled in on Caroline's pine-fresh make-out session.

Caroline slumped back onto the couch and glared at me. "This is your fault."

"Excuse me? How do you figure that?" I asked, peering down the hallway, as Devan's door opened and Kyle stepped inside. The door slammed shut again.

"You told Devan I was cheating, which is bull. And now he won't talk to me."

I gritted my teeth. "I know what I saw. And heard."

"No, you don't," Caroline said. "I was only fooling around with Jake because he's hot and I was all kinds of bored. And now Devan's acting like I stole the crown jewels and I blame you."

"Hey, don't blame this on me! I'm not the one who was screwing around with the host of the show, on the first day of the competition."

"I can fool around with whoever I want. But I wasn't cheating. And do you really think I would need to go to Jake for help? I'd hack into the production computers if I cared enough, which I don't."

"Really?" I said skeptically. "You don't care about winning two hundred grand?"

Caroline turned back to the television, like the conversation bored her. "Not at all. The money's going to the school, not to us."

I didn't respond. It was so freaking unfair. They didn't even need the money.

"So is that what Devan was so upset about, just now? The whole Jake thing?"

"No. It's about something else. I guess you don't know who his parents are," she said, only half paying attention.

"How would I? It's not like we have visiting day here at Sasquatch summer camp." I may have had streaks of compassion like my sister, but I sure as hell didn't have her patience.

Caroline huffed a little and picked at one of her nails. "Dr. Das is a huge deal in the archaeology and art conservation worlds. He deals with ancient artifacts and saves them from natural disasters, war, and stuff. He's been on *60 Minutes*."

"So? What's that have to do with anything?"

"His dad is in Syria right now. There were more bombings last night. It was on the news just now." Caroline flicked the TV off.

"Oh my god! Is his dad okay?"

Caroline finally looked up at me. "We don't know. Devan got special permission to use the phone. He left four messages on his mom's cell, but she apparently doesn't get much signal over there."

"His mom is there, too?" I didn't blame him for being freaked out. I got nervous when my dad drove during snowstorms, but that was nothing compared to having both your parents off in a war zone.

"She's an art history professor at SOAS University in London, so she sometimes goes with him to help." Caroline stood up. "They shouldn't have been anywhere near where the bombing happened. They were working further to the south. But Dev usually gets at least a text from his parents every day. So this is strange."

"Wow." I was glad my dad stuck to the occasional exploding Bunsen burner.

"Wait, what happened to your sweatshirt?" Caroline had stopped in her tracks and was staring at my black hoodie which was hanging up on the back of a chair near the kitchen.

"Huh?"

"Your sweatshirt. How did you rip it?"

I peered over at the sweatshirt across the room, confused at her sudden change of subject. "I don't know. I guess it happened when I fell. Why?"

She continued to stare at my sleeve for a moment. "What? I don't care. Just curious," she answered sharply. "I could fix it for you, if you want. While you're here. I have a sewing kit."

"Uh, okay." What was happening? Caroline held out her hand, and I took the slightly damp sweatshirt off the chair and handed it over to her. She folded it in her arms, so the rip was on the top, and headed into the dining room laboratory.

"Well, thanks," I replied, but she had already disappeared into the lab. *That was weird.*

The microwave dinged and I grabbed the two plates and headed into my sister's room, wondering if maybe I had misjudged Caroline. She seemed so concerned about Devan's parents. And then she offered to fix my sweatshirt. Maybe Sophie was right, and Caroline just took some getting used to. Or maybe she had some MIT genius trick planned and was several steps ahead of me.

Sophie and I nibbled our lunch, trying not to drip cheese all over us. "This is so good!" My sister said in between bites. "I've had nothing but soup for days."

"Hey, Sophie?"

"Mmm," she said with a mouth full of food.

"Have you noticed anything strange about Caroline or Devan?"

She reached for a napkin to wipe her chin. "Not really. Devan sings bad '80s music in the shower when he thinks we can't hear. That's kind of funny."

Not exactly what I had in mind. I couldn't really pry further without giving her a reason for my suspicions. I wasn't about to tell her what Lyssa and I had done, or that I was worried Caroline had figured out it was us. Plus, I still didn't want Sophie to know about Caroline and Jake's little rendezvous, because then I'd have to explain why I didn't report Caroline's cheating to Colin. Sophie's angelic conscience wouldn't abide cheating on either side, and she'd want us to come clean. However, we needed that prize money to save our house and pay for college. Risking having the contest cancelled just for the sake of a little honesty wasn't an option. So, I'd just have to scope things out myself when I got the opportunity.

When we were done with lunch, we hung out in her room. Halfway through our second made-for-television movie, Sophie fell asleep curled up in a ball. I pulled the covers over her, snuck out of the room, and closed the door behind me.

I wandered into the now-empty living room and stared out the window. The storm had only gotten worse as the day had turned into afternoon. The wind pummeled the windows and the rain beat down on the roof like an endless drum roll. The mud puddles had become lakes. Even the sturdy trees looked like they could uproot at any moment.

"You're not going to be able to leave tonight," Caroline stated, leaning in the doorframe from the other side of the room. I hadn't noticed her come in. "Beth called. They've moved your family into a nearby hotel, but figured you'd rather stay with Sophie. They're worried about mudslides."

"Oh." Of all the effing luck. I couldn't imagine anything worse than spending the night with these guys, other than staying in all that mud. "I hope Sasquatch knows how to swim."

Caroline raised a perfectly plucked eyebrow at me, and handed me back my hoodie. The sleeve was patched and mended so well it was almost like brand new. And she had washed it too.

"Thank you."

"Whatever. You need to take better care of yourself," she sighed before settling onto the couch with an issue of *Scientific American*. I turned back to the window, as Caroline started flipping through the magazine.

"I guess they'll have to postpone the next challenge, right?" I asked in a monotone voice.

"I suppose. I hope this shoot doesn't go over schedule too much, I'm supposed to meet my friends in Aspen. They have a house there."

"How nice," I said, arranging my face into a neutral mask.

"I'm trying to persuade Kyle to go, too. He loves it there and my friends adore him. I've been trying to set him up with my friend Elle. She speaks three languages and is majoring in biochem next year. And she's gorgeous."

Boom. That was it. She wanted me to know that Sophie had competition. Caroline noticed how close Kyle and my sister were getting, and she was clearly trying to sabotage their possible romance. She wanted me to go back to my sister and tell her she didn't have a chance. Screw that. Sophie may have only finished her freshman year at a state college, but she was kind and smart, and probably a lot more fun to hang out with than Caroline and her friends.

I didn't dignify Caroline with a response.

This freaking storm needed to clear soon, so we could win our money and go home. I was more determined than ever to get my sister feeling better, and the two of us out of here, even if it took all the goddamned tea in the British Isles.

For now, all I could do was wait. All afternoon, I paced around the house, like a miserable caged animal. Eventually, I settled into an armchair and out came my trusty paperback. But I had a hard time concentrating. Every time I heard a creak or a bump, I would glance up to see if it was Devan. I was curious to know if he had heard from his parents, and, I admitted to myself, to see if he was okay. Sophie wasn't the only one who cared for wounded animals, even those that bit their handlers.

I heard a door open in the hall, and my head involuntarily snapped up to see who it was. It was Kyle. He plopped himself down on the sofa next to my chair.

"Hey Sam, how's it going? Sophie asleep?"

"Yeah, poor bunny. You okay? You look tired." I hoped he wasn't getting Sophie's flu.

"I'm fine." Kyle straightened up in his seat. "Just been a long day. Devan finally heard back from his parents. They're fine. Totally safe."

I exhaled and realized that I had been on edge all afternoon. "Oh good. I'm so relieved."

"Me too." Kyle nodded. "I thought Dev was gonna lose it there for a while. He won't admit it, but I think he was pretty scared."

"Jeez. Who wouldn't be?"

Kyle yawned and stood back up. "I guess I am tired. I'm gonna go to bed early."

I sat in the living room for a while longer, wondering if Devan would reappear, but soon my eyelids started to droop. The rhythm of the rain on the roof was mesmerizing and I was exhausted.

In my sister's room, someone—probably Devan, our perfect host—had left a pillow and blanket on the chair for me. Seriously, the guy could have opened a bed and breakfast. He thought of everything down to the extra toothbrush in the bathroom. I sat on the floor next to my sister's bed and pulled the blanket over me. The floor was hard, but at least the cabin was dry and warm.

Sophie stirred. "Sam, is that you?"

"It better be, unless you're sneaking boys in here," I teased her.

Sophie lifted a corner of the blanket. "Don't sleep on the floor, come share the bed with me, like we used to at Grandma's house."

I sighed, but climbed in, warmer and happier than I had been in days.

Chapter 17

"Every single state except for Hawaii has had
sightings of Sasquatch. If we look at it logically, how can
all those people be imagining it?"

—*Beth Randall, assistant producer, "Myth Gnomers"*

As cozy as Sophie's bed was compared to the hard ground I had
been sleeping on for days, I was restless. I was positive Caroline was
up to no good, and determined to find out what it was. There was
no way that gorgeous, snooty Caroline would ever make out with
a creep like Jake unless she wanted something badly. I just needed
proof.

Finally, when the house was silent, I got up and pulled my newly
mended black sweatshirt on, partly because I was cold and partly
because it felt appropriate to wear black when conducting an illegal
search.

I tiptoed down the hall into the living room, ears perked for any
noises. The lab seemed like the most logical place to keep evidence
of illicit activities. I wasn't exactly sure what I was looking for, but I'd
kick myself if I let this prime snooping opportunity pass. As I rifled
through the stacks of papers and notebooks filled with numbers
and formulas, I began to better understand how serious these guys
were about their research. Everything was meticulously recorded.
I had no idea what all the statistics indicated, or why there was an
entire notebook full of phonetic notations, but it was fascinating
and nerve-racking. We'd have to get equally hardcore to beat them.

I would have kept looking if it weren't for the loud, sudden howl, which jolted me out of my reading, making me stub my toe on the desk and hop away silently swearing.

"What the hell was that?" I raced to the window but couldn't see anything in the absolute darkness outside.

The desperate howling erupted again, and by the sound of it, the beast was close by.

Caroline rushed into the living room and moved to the window next to mine.

"What do you think it is?" I asked. "A coyote?"

She shook her head. "No, coyotes don't howl like that," she replied. "I've been analyzing audio recordings of animals as research for this project, and I've never heard *any* animal sound similar to this one."

It took me a second to realize that something was very different about Caroline, besides the fact that she wasn't insulting me. She was wearing a fleece nightgown and sporting a retainer and ugly square glasses.

My eyes widened in surprise. Caroline was a secret geek, trapped in a hot girl's body. That explained a lot, really. Maybe she was just insecure.

She caught me staring at her. "What the hell are you looking at? Yes, I wear glasses. Big freaking deal. We need to get a recording now." She snapped her fingers in my face. "Pay attention."

She dashed into the dining room and started searching through equipment boxes.

"Are you really thinking of going out there?" I asked.

Caroline returned with a clunky piece of equipment that looked like something out of an older episode of *Doctor Who*. "Sure. We'll just go out on the porch and set up the high-powered parabolic mic to record for the rest of the night."

The strange howling continued. "We? Are you kidding? I'm not going out there," I blurted.

"What? You're scared?"

I couldn't tell if she was daring me or if she was surprised at my reaction. Either way, I was mostly just trying not to laugh at the way she said "scared" while wearing her retainer.

I always considered myself fairly brave, but if there was a nice thick wall and a locked door between me and a hungry, hungry carnivore, I knew which side of the door I preferred.

"No, just practical," I said.

Caroline held the recorder tight in her hand. "You don't have to come," she said. "But if you weren't such a chicken, I'd ask you to keep lookout while I set this up. I'll get one of the boys."

The superior sneer on her face was enough to make me want to let whatever was out there eat her and her parabolic mic. I knew I shouldn't help the rival team, but I also thought Caroline was taking a big, unnecessary risk. And if tonight was the night Sasquatch decided to prove he was real, I wanted to be the first to see him.

"Fine," I sighed. "For the record, this is a goddamn awful idea, but I'm not in the mood to see you mauled by a mountain lion."

Caroline gave me a triumphant metallic smile, probably the first real smile I had seen from her since the contest started, but it promptly disappeared when the growls outside grew louder.

I gazed at Kyle and Devan's doors, wondering if they were too scared to come out of their rooms. Caroline followed my eyes.

"They're probably sleeping through the whole thing," she sighed.

"It's getting closer," I said, trying to stop my voice from shaking. "Do you have a tranq gun or any kind of weapon?"

Caroline put the recording device on the table and backed up, all traces of confidence gone. "You really think we need a gun?" she asked.

Duh. "That's generally what 'I'll cover you' means. How else would we fight off an attack?"

"Well, maybe we *should* have the boys do this," Caroline said. She removed the retainer and shoved it in her pocket.

"Now who's chicken?" I raised an eyebrow. "And seriously, of all the people in this cabin, who do you think has more experience with firearms? The boys may have taken fencing at Netherfield, but I doubt they brought their dainty swords with them."

Caroline and I shared a quick giggle. I could just imagine Devan and Kyle trying to fence with Bigfoot.

"Point taken," Caroline said. "We don't have any sort of gun, but I can give you a baseball bat."

"You have thousands of dollars worth of fancy electronic equipment and not even a freaking BB gun? Okay," I said, grabbing the bat. "Let's do this quickly. Don't close the door in case we need to rush back in."

I opened the front door and flicked on the porch light. Bat in hand, I took a few steps off the porch and scanned the surroundings. The rain had let up but the growling was closer than ever.

Peering through the darkness, I squinted at the area surrounding the house to get my bearings. The underbrush at the edge of the clearing rustled, accompanied by the loudest howl yet. I glanced back at Caroline in the doorway and she too was staring at the spot in the bushes. She crept out on the porch to set up the mic. Hands shaking, she fumbled for a couple of moments, then mouthed "almost done" and got back to work on her task. I held my breath and planted my feet, ready to stand my ground.

There was something giant and yellow out there. *What the hell*? I took a step closer not sure of what I was seeing. A human silhouette pushed through the trees, only twenty feet from where I was standing then turned in my direction. And waved.

"Hey, Samantha!" it said in a singsong voice.

It knew my name. I walked towards the figure and saw that the huge, yellow beast was actually Hal, the camera guy, in a really bright poncho, and with him was a big German shepherd.

"We thought you were a bear!" I said to him, clutching my chest and breathing normally once again.

"Is it the yellow poncho? Is it too Winnie-the-Pooh?" Hal asked as I climbed down the stairs to see him.

I reached over and punched Hal on his beefy shoulder. "Not that kind of bear. We heard strange growling."

"Oh, that was Chewbacca." He pointed at his dog, whose ears perked up when it heard its name. "Chewie hates going out in the rain and mud. Don't ya, girl? She's very vocal about it."

"Chewie's a girl?"

"Yup. I named her that because *Star Wars* rocks, of course, and also because of the noises she made as a puppy when you gave her a bone." He noticed the baseball bat. "It's a little muddy for baseball."

I blushed, "Oh, that was for the bear."

"Bears play baseball? Evolution moves fast around here," he laughed.

"No, it was more of a preventative measure. Never mind. What are you guys doing out so late at night?" I asked.

"She's an active dog but won't go out in the rain, so I had to take her out the minute it let up a bit."

I laughed a little hysterically, relieved at the outcome of this odd night.

Caroline let out a deep breath behind me. Clearly she was more nervous than she had let on.

The dog sat at attention, but her wide, sad eyes begged for some affection. I reached down to pet her. "I can't believe we thought you were a bear," I said, and she wagged her tail, as steady and fast as an up-tempo metronome.

"Chewie's a total sweetheart, but definitely noisy. Aren't you, sweetie?" Hal said to the dog in one of those cutesy voices reserved for pets and babies. She jumped up, covering him in mud with her filthy paws.

"Oh, I should warn you," Hal added. "Colin wants behind-the-scenes footage of you guys in the cabin waiting around, and of Sophie recovering and stuff. We'll stop by in the morning and take some posed shots, if the storm lets us. I just wanted to give you the heads up. We'll try to be as quick as possible. Unless you have steamy romantic stuff going on?"

I scratched the dog's ears. "I don't think you'll get anything more exciting than footage of the boys wrestling over the video game controllers."

Hal held up his hand in a Spock-like Vulcan salute. "Sorry to have scared you guys." He looked at the dog. "Keep it down, Chewie."

Chewie let out one last bark. I swung the baseball bat onto my shoulder and walked back toward the cabin.

"So I set all this up for some ridiculous dog?" Caroline asked when I got closer. She leaned on the doorway, her arms crossed. "Granted, that dog does have a very strange bark. I wonder . . ." Caroline froze midsentence.

Sophie had come up behind her and stood with her mouth and eyes open wide in fear. She pointed behind me and not in a gentle "oh, hey, look here's a pair of shoes you would like" way. It was more of a "oh my god, there's a scary monster behind you" sort of gesture.

I slowly turned around and two bright eyes in the darkness at the edge of the clearing were looking directly at me. This time I knew it wasn't Hal and Chewbacca, who could be seen in the distance going in the opposite direction. Based on its height and bulk, I assumed it was a wolf.

I backed away slowly, one foot at a time until the first porch step hit my ankle. I crept up the stairs, holding onto the railing with one hand, while keeping my eyes focused on the wolf. I was just two steps away from the safety of the house. Two steps until someone could hand me a huge cup of tea, and I would happily take it. I took one step, then felt a well-manicured hand pull me inside the cabin, then slam and lock the door.

"Ouch!" I said, rubbing my arm. "Is that a French manicure or a claw?" I glared at my rescuer.

"You're welcome," Caroline said, inspecting her nails. "You're lucky I didn't chip one."

I strained my neck to peer out the window, and imagined the wolf was laughing at us. *Silly humans.*

"Thanks for your help tonight," Caroline said, as she packed her microphone away. She looked me in the eyes, as if she were reconsidering her original assessment of me.

"Any time," I replied with a hollow laugh. "It was actually kind of fun, in a twisted way. Not that I would recommend wrestling with any other wild animals." She shook her head and sauntered off to her room while I grabbed the walkie-talkie on the table and made sure Hal and Chewie were okay.

Two seconds later, Sophie came into the room, gave me a hug, and sank into a kitchen chair.

"You were supposed to stay in bed, Sophie," I said.

"You're kidding, right? You almost got eaten by a wolf, and you're worried about *me* getting out of bed?"

"When you put it that way . . ." I laughed. "Can I get you anything?"

"I fell asleep before I could take my medication, so maybe some orange juice and my pills from the bathroom?"

"Sure thing. Just stay there. Don't try to fight off any wild animals," I said.

Sophie attempted a thin-lipped smile, but it didn't quite make its way to the rest of her sleepy face. Even her nose looked tired.

I ran into Kyle on my way to the bathroom and started to laugh. His hair was going twelve different ways, none of them the right one. And I was giddy with adrenaline.

He yawned. "Did I miss anything?"

"Not unless you count finding Bigfoot, who ended up being a bear who actually was a German shepherd. Oh, and then, escaping from a hungry wolf. You know, average day."

"For who? Goldilocks and Little Red Riding Hood?"

Kyle followed me back to the kitchen and sat next to Sophie while she took her pills. She leaned on him to stand, and he supported her by putting his arm around her waist.

"Okay, back to bed with you," I said, waving her off toward her bedroom.

"Is she always this bossy?" Devan's amused voice drawled behind me. I jumped. I hadn't heard him come in.

"She's awesome," Sophie said. "But she's a control freak. Don't ever try to change the radio if she's driving."

"That's it. You're done," I said to my sister and gave her a gentle shove in the direction of her room.

"See what I mean?" Sophie did the giggle and cough thing and Kyle half-dragged her back into the bedroom. She didn't seem to mind.

"Goodnight, Sophie," Devan said. I glanced over my shoulder at him.

"Goodnight, Captain Bossy Pants," he added, saluting me with two fingers. I wanted to salute him with just one, but somehow managed to refrain.

I took a few steps down the hall but decided to let Sophie and Kyle have some time to themselves. I headed back into the kitchen where Devan stood quietly leaning against the counter. "Did you need something?"

"No, I wanted to . . ." I examined my cuticles, hoping they held some answers about what to say, but all I found was dirt from the evening's exploits. "I mean, Caroline told me about your parents being in Syria, and I just wanted to say that I'm glad they're okay."

He lifted a surprised eyebrow. He probably expected a snarky quip or a sarcastic comment from me. "Thanks." He played with the spinning spice rack on the counter and avoided my gaze.

"Yeah, you seemed pretty upset earlier today."

"I overreacted," Devan said. There was a long pause before he continued. "I should know better than to worry so much. This isn't the first time they've been near that type of danger. They've been all over Iran and Pakistan, and other places, too."

"It doesn't sound like an overreaction to me."

"Perhaps, but they travel constantly. I should be used to it by now." He rubbed his forehead and plunked down on a stool at the kitchen counter. I hadn't expected our conversation to continue. I had been planning on going back to bed, but he seemed so sad. I wanted to help.

I sat down across from him.

He sighed. "Usually when I'm at school they text or call every day, just to check in, so when I don't hear from them, I worry. But a lot of times they're somewhere without Internet or phones."

"Wow. I don't think I could handle my parents being away so much. Don't you miss them?"

"Yeah. Of course, but it's fine. I know they're busy doing important work. I don't want them to worry about me, especially when they're in dangerous situations and need to focus. As long as my grades are good at Netherfield and I don't get into too much trouble, they can concentrate on work." He choked out a nervous laugh. "I don't know why *I* worry about them so much."

"I can't imagine ever getting to the point where I wouldn't worry," I said.

"I'm surprised," he replied, knocking over the red pepper flakes from the rack. "You seem pretty unfazed by everything."

I snorted, which was kind of rude, but his assessment of me was beyond absurd. Devan's forehead creased slightly, and for a moment I thought I'd really hurt his feelings.

I quickly explained. "I've made worrying into an art. A fine art. I practically have an MFA in worrying. I worry constantly about everyone and everything. Ask Sophie. She'll tell you."

His face relaxed and he almost smiled at my rambling monologue while he cleaned up the spices.

"So when I'm stressed out, I usually find something ridiculous on television and gorge myself with junk food." I flashed him a conspiratorial smile. "Bad for the diet and the brain cells, but good for the soul. How 'bout it?"

"What?" he asked, looking at the wall clock. "Tonight? It's already pretty late, and I don't want to keep you up. You're probably exhausted from fighting a wolf with a baseball bat."

"You saw that?"

He nodded. "I can see the yard from my window."

"Why didn't you run out to help?" I smacked his arm harder than I meant to.

"You seemed to have it well under control." Devan grinned, but rubbed his arm, attempting to cover his embarrassment. "I'd admire your bravery if you weren't so utterly frustrating."

Huh, what the hell did he mean by that?

Unsure how to answer his backhanded compliment, I changed the subject.

"So, movie?" I said, grabbing some pita chips from the counter, ripping open the bag, and taking a handful out.

Devan opened his mouth, and I thought he was going to protest my stealing his chips.

"Hey! I totally saved your lives, I deserve a few chips," I said with my hand in front of my mouth, which was full of the aforementioned snack food.

He stretched a long arm past me to the cabinet behind. He was so close I could smell the woodsy scent of his cologne or deodorant or aftershave. It was intoxicating. He pulled a big bowl from the cabinet and poured some of the chips into it.

"Oh, a bowl. Aren't we fancy?" I said.

He sat back down.

"Nope, just well-mannered." He crunched extra loudly and handed me a paper napkin. "See, super posh."

"Well, I approve of your snack food choices," I said. "You have frozen pizza, chips, and salsa. All good. But where's the chocolate?"

"The pizza is Kyle's doing, I'm really more into spicy snacks, and Caroline only eats organic food. We weren't expecting any other guests, so there's nothing sweet," Devan said.

"Except me," I chuckled. "Kidding. I'm pretty far from sweet. Obviously."

Devan folded his hands and leaned on them. "That's not really true, is it? You may act like a hard-ass, but I see how you are with your family. You'd fight a wild animal for them. Barehanded."

"I'd at least need a baseball bat," I snickered. It wasn't even that funny of a joke, but the stress of the last few days and the wolf encounter released all this anxious energy and I couldn't help it. I cracked up and in a few moments he was laughing too. My giddiness was contagious. We laughed until we both had tears streaming down our faces.

It was the first time I had seen Devan actually enjoy himself for more than a few seconds, and much to my dismay, he was kind of gorgeous when he was grinning like a fool. I stared at him and we caught our breath. He ran his fingers through his dark hair and smiled. I glanced away, but not soon enough. My stomach did the mother of all back flips and the butterflies flew back in swarms. It was a butterfly infestation. I sighed and reminded myself that butterflies were insects, even if they were attractive.

I grabbed the chips and beelined it for the living room. "How 'bout that movie?"

"Sure." He followed me to the couch. He stood back, though, unsure where to sit. I scooted over on the couch so that he knew it was okay for him to sit next to me. If he wanted.

I grabbed the remote and turned on the TV. "So, what'll it be? Something spooky?" I flicked through the digital menu. "Ooh or how about *Shark vs. T. Rex*?"

"Sure, whatever you want." He sat on the couch with a shallow smile. His posture was very stiff and he was as close to the opposite arm as he could get. I was reminded of my first junior high dance, in which the boys stood on one side of the room, staring at the girls on the other side of the room with a vast chasm of awkwardness between them. Unfortunately, I never got past that phase and it seemed like Devan hadn't either by the way he drummed his fingers on his knees.

"You definitely need some shark and gator battle scenes to help you relax," I said.

"I thought you said T. Rex?"

"The gator just has a cameo. But it's amazing. Just watch. All will be revealed." This time his grin was genuine, and he made himself more comfortable on the couch, hugging a pillow to his chest.

My heart beat a little faster. It was probably because I was so glad that I could cheer him up a bit. Because that's what I did, I helped people who were sad or sick. It had nothing to do with the way his hair flopped in front of his face, or the fact that his shoulder looked so inviting next to me. Nope. I was just being a buddy by hanging out with him on the couch. Sharing a snack. You know, like friends do. As I reached for some chips, my hand brushed his, making me blush.

I gulped down some water so I wouldn't get even more flushed.

"Are you okay?" he asked.

"Yup. Just thirsty." I put the glass down and tried to concentrate on the movie, but the storyline wasn't getting through my Devan-filled brain. Eventually, though, as the shark and the T. Rex duked it out in the swamps of Louisiana, the adrenaline from my wolf encounter wore off and my eyes grew heavy. I tried not to sleep through the rest of the movie, but failed.

Music partially woke me up, but I snuggled against a warm pillow. My eyes fluttered open to find that it wasn't a pillow. I had fallen asleep on Devan's shoulder and he hadn't moved me.

"Oh. Uh. Hi." I stammered, still a little confused. There was some reason why I wasn't supposed to be sleeping on his shoulder like that, but it felt so nice, I couldn't for the life of me remember what that reason was. "Sorry."

"It's okay," he said. "I didn't want to wake you. You seemed so tired. I don't mind. Least I could do. You know, in return for taking my mind off everything tonight." He gazed down at me with a tentative smile.

Then the fog parted and I remembered that we were on opposite teams, and we weren't exactly on cuddling terms. I sat straight up and inched away from him a little. "Yeah. I'm very distracting. It's one of my charms."

He leaned closer to me. "I noticed."

Hypnotized in my flustered state, I found myself leaning toward him too.

Devan's lips parted slightly and he placed his forehead close to mine like he was preparing to kiss me. Oh my god. Did I want him to? My heart did a double-time tap dance in my chest, making me think I did, indeed, want him to kiss me.

Until I remembered the cameras. Shit! We had no privacy in the cabin and I completely forgot. I glanced around and spotted a small blinking light in one corner of the room, which would perfectly capture us on the couch. Oh, yeah, and there was one in the kitchen, too, which was no doubt recording the backs of our heads.

Kissing the captain of the competition on camera, even if he was completely dreamy, was a bad idea. A horrible idea. The worst idea ever. I leapt up and gave him a super awkward pat on the back, tripping on the coffee table as I tried to make my escape.

He stood up too and gave me a small smile, and nodded formally, shaking off his own fogginess. "Goodnight, Sam."

I backed away a few steps, not sure what to think. "'Night."

Devan paused for a moment, looking at me as if he had never seen me before. I stared at his beautiful lips, waiting for him to say something. He just tilted his head with a puzzled grin and turned to go into his room.

I went to mine, also pretty damn puzzled. I lay awake for a long time, confused, replaying the late-night conversation with Devan over and over. Why did he let me sleep on him? Why did he almost kiss me? He must have been trying to play with my mind before the next challenge. I couldn't help but assume the whole thing was just a game—a battle of wits like Sherlock Holmes and Moriarty. That made the most sense, right?

Unless he liked me. It was bizarre, but I could have sworn there were forest-fire sized sparks on that couch. I sighed. What would it have been like if we had met in some other circumstance—if we weren't sworn enemies?

Sworn enemies? I scolded myself. This wasn't *Romeo and Juliet*. It was reality TV, and there was a big prize at stake. A prize my family was counting on. Even if we weren't enemies now, if my team won this ridiculous contest, I was pretty sure the only sparks he would be feeling for me would be angry sparks.

Chapter 18

"As American Squatch hunters, we don't like to admit it, but
the term *Sasquatch* was first coined by a Canadian,
J.W. Burns, in the 1920s. Other than bacon, and maple syrup,
the name Sasquatch is the best thing to come
from our northern neighbors."

—"50th Anniversary Handbook," *Northern Ohio Bigfoot Society*

I never thought indoor plumbing, hot-water heaters, and micro-waves were luxury items, but it turned out that living in a muddy forest, even for only a week and a half, changed everything. The morning after the great German Shepherd Incident, I towel-dried my hair, thinking about the previous night with Devan and what had happened or almost happened.

He wasn't up yet, which just led to more anxiety about seeing him in the cold light of day.

I pulled on my freshly washed T-shirt and stepped into my now mud-free jeans. I was glad to be back in clothes that fit. When I was dressed, I wandered into the living room and waited on the couch, fiddling with the remote control, nervously waiting for the rest of the cabin to wake up.

Sophie walked in, looking a little pale, but definitely healthier. "I feel so much better today. I barely even coughed last night."

"I know. I was in the room with you. But you did hog the covers, so you must be almost back to normal."

The sound of mud splashing and someone kicking their boots on the front porch suggested that we had a visitor. A brisk knock confirmed it. I jumped up to open the door.

"Hi, Sophie." Dr. Sawyer wiped his feet on the doormat and nodded at me. "Samantha."

Colin, Hal, and the rest of the crew were behind him. Hal's shadow, Dave, was holding a huge boom mic, which got caught in the doorway. I waved at Hal who took the camera off his shoulder and frowned.

"Cut! Samantha, you need to pretend we're not here," Colin said.

"Oops. Sorry."

"Also, before I forget," Colin added, "we are holding off on shooting the next challenge one more day, just to let the ground dry up a bit. The base camp is basically a lake right now."

"Got it." I turned my attention back to the doctor and Colin indicated for filming to continue.

"Okay, Sophie," Dr. Sawyer said as he went over to the kitchen sink and washed his hands with the lemony antibacterial dish soap. "You seem like you're feeling a bit better. Yes?"

Freezing in front of the cameras, Sophie nodded but didn't say anything.

Dr. Sawyer warmed up the stethoscope in his hands, and placed it on Sophie's back. "Breathe in and out as normally as you can."

He whipped out a tongue depressor from his kit and unwrapped it. "Ahhh." He opened his mouth and Sophie did the same. "To be safe, I'd like you to take one more day off, but after that I think you're good to go. But don't push it."

"Can my mom come visit?" Sophie asked.

"I don't see why not," Dr. Sawyer said. "I'll have Beth arrange a time to bring her here later on today."

He held out his hand for Sophie to shake, and then for me.

"Bigfoot doesn't stand a chance next to you girls." Dr. Sawyer waved goodbye, but the camera crew didn't follow him.

I sank onto the couch next to my sister, trying to ignore Hal and friends standing in the middle of the living room, taking panoramic shots of everything. It was hard to act normal.

"So, what next?" Sophie asked.

"I guess we wait for instructions." I gazed out the window. The sun was shining, as much as it ever did in this area of the country, meaning the sky was a light gray as opposed to a scary dark gray. "I don't think they'll hold off production for much longer. It's got to cost a ton of money to shut everything down."

Sophie sighed. "You're probably right." She lowered her voice, even though the guy with the boom mic had made his way down the hall. "I hate the idea of having to compete against Kyle again."

"What I hate is the idea of giving up indoor plumbing." I nudged her shoulder with mine, feeling guilty I didn't tell her about my almost kiss, but there wasn't really anything to tell at this point.

Sophie rubbed her shoulder even though I hardly made contact with her. "I bet Mom and Lyssa are about ready to kill each other without us to mediate," she said.

"No doubt. That's the exact reason why we never had to join model U.N. We lived it at home. It's sad when I'm considered a diplomat." I snorted.

"Actually, *I'm* the diplomat," Sophie said. "You're the enforcer."

She nudged me back until we were both laughing.

When Sophie finally caught her breath, she said, "On the bright side, it will be good to get out of these pajamas. They're cramping my style."

"What style?" I asked.

Sophie playfully smacked my arm, then put her head on my shoulder and we stayed like that for a good ten minutes, thinking and relaxing and tuning out the noises coming from the other rooms. Even when we were children, we got along, for the most part. Other kids would complain about their siblings, but I worshipped Sophie.

She was always patient with me even when I ate all the good cereal or broke one of her toys. We were still quietly resting when the boys came out of their caves, followed by Hal and friends.

My skin got all clammy when Devan entered the room. He stretched out his arms and put them behind his head, showing off surprisingly sexy muscles. "Morning," he said, with a brief nod. His eyes found mine and then quickly darted away.

I glanced away, utterly embarrassed. *Imagine what a mess I'd be if I actually had kissed him.*

"I'm going to wake Caroline," he told Hal. "You may not want to go in there, if you value your life."

"I'll take my chances," Hal said.

Devan knocked lightly.

"Go away!" Caroline said through the door.

Devan opened it anyway.

I giggled to myself. Caroline was not going to like being filmed with bed head and circles under her eyes, not to mention the glasses and retainer.

"Sophie's stuck inside for another day," I said to Kyle who squeezed onto the couch next to my sister.

"The doctor said I'm almost back to normal," Sophie replied.

"Well, he must not know about your *Golden Girls* fixation. That's far from normal," I said.

Kyle beamed. "That's great!" He played with the fringe on the pillow and gave her a sideways glance. "I mean, I'm glad you're getting better but I wish you didn't have to go so soon . . ."

Not wanting to be a third wheel, I pushed myself off the couch. In the kitchen, I helped myself to some potato chips directly out of the bag and sat on the bar stool at the counter.

From where I sat I could watch Sophie and Kyle leaning in toward each other and laughing. Kyle did some funny robot dance and Sophie cracked up. They even had private jokes already. I was happy for Sophie. She deserved someone who appreciated how awesome she was and didn't mind looking ridiculous in front of her. No one looked cool doing a robot dance. And if Kyle still found my sister attractive in her worn-out kitty pajamas from middle school, he must've liked her a lot.

Hal and company sneaked out of Caroline's room looking like they had barely survived a rough battle. Colin's eyes sparkled when he saw Sophie and Kyle together on the couch and he immediately directed the cameras in that direction. Of course.

I was in the middle of devouring the potato chip crumbs at the bottom of the bag when my favorite obnoxious-yet-fascinating person reappeared. I tried to act cool, nonchalant, as if last night was no big deal.

Devan put a saucepan on the stove and filled it with water and milk. "I'm sorry, I never got to make you the chai I promised," he said.

"What's that?" I asked as he grated something over the pot and put in a pod of something else.

"Gingerroot and cardamom," he said, before plopping in a cinnamon stick and finally carefully measuring out some loose tea. He tapped his fingers on the counter while the mixture simmered. He didn't make eye contact the whole time.

"That's a very elaborate process," I said, trying to break the silence.

He strained the chai over two mugs, one for himself and another which he shoved across the table at me. "I make it for all my guests," was all he replied.

Did that mean I was special, or just one of many? I guessed that he must have been regretting our weird-ass encounter. Not that anything happened. And actually he was the one who was acting awkward and pouty. He was the one that let me sleep on his shoulder. It wasn't my fault things got uncomfortable. I was just trying to be nice and cheer him up. And now he was giving me the silent treatment. Jerkface.

But it was hard to stay mad once I took a sip, and the delicious liquid warmed my throat and even made my lips tingle a bit. Yum.

"Okay, I think we've got enough here," Colin said.

"Later gators." Hal saluted us and they all took off.

Laughter floated in from the living room. Devan and I turned to see what was going on. Kyle had picked an eyelash off Sophie's face, and held it out for her to make a wish. Cuteness overload.

Devan's jaw tensed and any trace of a smile vanished from his face.

"It really bothers you that Kyle's interested in Sophie, doesn't it?" I probed.

His eyes flashed back to me. He didn't say a word. I got the feeling that my boldness surprised him and he was trying to decide how to answer. He glanced up at the little camera in the corner.

"I don't know what you're talking about," he finally responded, through gritted teeth. "Kyle's a nice guy and probably wants to make sure your sister feels comfortable here. I don't think there's anything going on between them. He's not really serious about her."

The way he said "her" made me put down the chai and clench my fists at my side. "Why not? What's wrong with *her*?" I whispered harshly, so my sister and the kitchen camera microphones couldn't hear.

He recoiled. "Nothing. But Dr. DeGraw made it clear . . . I don't want Kyle to get in trouble . . . Sophie's just not . . ."

"Not what? A rich boarding school bitch? A future Ivy League snob like you?" I stood abruptly, scraping the tiles with my chair. *Screw the cameras.* I was livid.

Devan winced at the sound but didn't reply. He just stared at me for a breath, with a pained expression, and then glanced again at the cameras.

At that moment, Kyle turned around to see what was going on. He grimaced when he noticed our expressions. "Sam, pay no attention to Devan. He's just a stress ball."

"Clearly," I said, grabbing my backpack from the kitchen floor and storming through the living room. On my way to the door, I paused. "Sophie, I'm going back to camp. Mom should be here later. Call Beth if you need anything," I said, covering my anger with a measured tone and a weak smile.

Sophie had burning questions in her eyes, but I avoided her gaze and slammed the door behind me. I stole a quick glance at the house, and stomped down the wooden porch steps and onto the muddy trail. I kept up my pace until I was out of sight of the cabin. Then I stopped and bent over to take a deep breath and a moment to clear my head.

I kicked my sneaker against a tree imagining Devan's smug face. *Pompous ass.* Although, if I was being honest, I felt more foolish than angry. I should never have let my guard down around Devan. Of course he had said something hurtful. Why did I expect otherwise?

The rest of the trek to my family's camp was uneventful. I unclenched my shoulders and tried to enjoy the woodsy smell of pinecones, the chirping of various woodland creatures, and the canopy of the trees. However, the serenity was short-lived. I arrived at the site to find my mom and Lyssa bickering loudly.

Lyssa clomped toward me. "I don't see why it's such a huge deal!"

My mom opened her mouth to respond, but when she spotted me, she hurried over and gave me a big hug.

"Sam, honey," she said to the back of my hair. "How's Sophie doing this morning? How did it go last night?"

"Fine—Sophie's fine—last night was fine . . ." I chose not to mention the wolf. Or the near kiss with Devan. Mom gestured for me to continue. "Sophie's doing a lot better and should be back with us tomorrow, but the doctor said you can visit her later on today if you want."

"That's fantastic news," my dad said.

"I knew some rest would do her good," my mom said. "We're relaxed, too. The hotel was a nice treat."

"Yeah, we're lucky we stayed there." Lyssa wrinkled her nose. She was right, the campsite and everything in it was covered in mud.

Noticing how my mom and Lyssa avoided each other's eyes, I sighed. "I hate to ask, but what were you arguing about this time?"

Lyssa gave me a why-did-you-have-to-bring-it-up glare.

My mom pushed Lyssa's hair behind her ear, which didn't go over so well. Lyssa made a frustrated growling sound that could have given Chewie a run for her money.

"Samantha, tell your sister that she shouldn't wear a bright pink thong with white shorts," my mom said, crossing her arms in front of her.

My dad quietly backed away to examine his map, shaking his head. He knew enough to stay the hell out of these battles.

I shrugged. "Why do you think she'd listen to me? I spend most of my time trying to keep underwear out of my butt crack."

Lyssa giggled. "I like thongs, they're more comfortable."

My mom pursed her lips. "I don't want people to look at Lyssa and get the wrong idea. She's a smart girl. She doesn't have to dress that sexy."

"Whoa!" I said, wiping some dirt off my hands. "Why can't a girl be smart *and* sexy, Mom? When she's older, I mean."

"In my day, if you wanted to date nice boys, you dressed like a nice girl." My mom's voice strained with tension.

Lyssa rolled her eyes.

"Good job, Mom. You just set the women's rights movement back fifty years," I said. I loved my mom, but she could be super old-fashioned. "Although, Lyssa, what's the rush?" I added. "When I was your age I was still sleeping with my stuffed animals."

"Yeah, that was less than two years ago." Lyssa crossed her arms over her ample chest, looking like a copy of our mom. "And you're a total dork."

I nodded in agreement. "And proud of it."

"When did you get so wise?" My mom hugged me again.

"Don't know. Maybe when Lyssa was shopping for thongs," I said.

My mom laughed, but my sister scowled at me.

"I don't know whether to thank you for standing up for me or be mad at you for discussing my underwear like I'm not even here," Lyssa said.

"Your choice."

She shook her head and stalked away.

Chapter 19

"Did you ever stop to think that maybe
Bigfoot doesn't believe in you either?"

—*Hal O'Brian, cameraman,* "Myth Gnomers"

"Sophie!" my dad bellowed as we arrived at *Myth Gnomers* base camp the following day. Sophie smiled and waved from her seat on a bench, almost spilling her tea in her enthusiasm.

My parents bounded over and took turns hugging their eldest daughter.

"How are you feeling today, darling?" my mom asked, pressing her hand to Sophie's forehead.

By then Lyssa and I had reached the bench and joined the hug fest. Poor Sophie still had bags under her eyes and pale skin, but her face glowed from her cheery smile.

"I'm okay, Mom. Just tired. The doctor said I had such a severe flu that it may take a couple of weeks to be one hundred percent back to myself. So I need to walk slowly, but otherwise, as long as I don't push myself too much, I'm good to go. Dr. Sawyer said I was lucky to get such good care." She smiled in the direction of Kyle. "They really were great to me."

My raised eyebrows must have spoken for themselves. "They were great, or Kyle was great?" I asked.

Sophie shook her head. "Devan was, too. He washed my clothes, and made me his delicious tea. And Caroline . . ." her voice trailed off. "Well, she kind of grew on me. She let me read her magazines and borrow her clothes."

My Sophie, always trying to see the good in people. Quite an annoying trait, really.

"You know what else grows on you? Toe fungus and belly button lint," I teased, once the rest of my family had left to get ready for the shoot. I was grateful that the Netherfield kids took care of my sister, but I was still really upset about Devan's latest insults. I clenched my fists, as I did every time I thought about them. But I kept smiling for Sophie's sake.

Shaking out my hands, I threw an arm over her shoulder and gave a little squeeze. "So are you ready to rough it in the tents again? Or are you too fancy for us now?"

She leaned her head on my shoulder. "I'll never be too fancy for you." Her gaze suddenly shifted and she whispered, "Incoming," and I saw that we were surrounded on all fronts.

Colin walked toward us from the left side while Devan approached on the right. There was no escaping either of them.

Colin got to us first, but stopped several feet away. "Sophie, I'm glad you're up and about," he said. "Ready for the next challenge?"

"Don't worry. The doctor says I'm not contagious, right, Samantha?" she replied.

"Yup. You could probably make out with her and be totally fine," I said. "Unless you think Kyle would mind?"

Devan cleared his throat, and Sophie and I turned to see him staring at the ground. He'd overheard that last sentence.

"I'm sorry to interrupt," Devan said with a prim expression.

What a prude. Seriously, a little teasing about sucking face and he looks like I just took my clothes off at temple and started belly dancing. He really needed to lighten up. "Can we help you with something?"

"I have Sophie's cough medicine. The doctor dropped it off after she left." Devan carefully avoided looking at us and took a small bottle and a handwritten note out of his pocket.

I glanced over at the note. "That's pretty spiffy handwriting for a doctor."

Devan made a face. "*I* wrote down the directions for Sophie, so I wouldn't forget anything."

"Wow, does Netherfield require you to take Fancy Penmanship 101?" I asked.

"It's something my mother insisted I practice," he replied. Then, standing a little taller like he was getting ready to make a point, he added, "But, I think nice handwriting can say a lot about an individual. I can only imagine that your handwriting resembles a kindergartener's."

Colin laughed at Devan's barb and I turned to Sophie to back me up. Her mouth fell open, out of astonishment, I assumed.

"Look who just stooped to our level," I said to Sophie.

Shaking his head, Devan walked away in the direction of the trailers until Sophie called out to him to stop. "Devan, I wanted to thank you for everything you did for me over the past few days. I really appreciate your help."

"Yes, well." He frowned a little. "My mother also taught me how important it is to take care of one's guests. I would've done that for almost anyone."

"*Almost* anyone?" I asked. I couldn't help but assume he meant me. Despite the fact that we had been sparring and arguing for days now, my cheeks burned from his spite. I opened my mouth to launch a biting comment at him, but when his eyes met mine, the hardness in his jaw softened.

"No, I wouldn't help out an ass like Jake." Devan held my gaze for a moment, before he turned and walked away.

"It wouldn't kill you to be nicer," Sophie said, turning to me.

"It might, actually." I twirled one of my curls around my finger. She was right. As usual. Or she would be, if she knew the whole story.

"I'll try," I told her, letting out all the air in my lungs.

Colin rubbed the bridge of his nose. "Bad blood between the pretty boys?" he asked.

"You have no idea. Shouldn't we get started soon?" I asked, changing the subject. "We're ready to win this thing," I said with a pointed look at my sister.

An intern ran past us with a huge stack of papers and a frantic expression. Colin made a motion for him to speed it up and then took off. The crew was also in overdrive, reorganizing gear. Even Beth hurried around the set with a clipboard. I'd never seen the crew so wound up and frenzied.

"What's going on around here?" I asked Sophie.

She shook her head.

"Something's up," I said with a frown.

"I guess we'll find out soon enough."

Jake had just stepped out of the makeup trailer studying what looked like a script. Unfortunately, he was followed by Lyssa who was carrying his coffee cup and gazing at him with rapt attention. I let out a small groan as I watched them cross the lawn. Sophie saw me chewing my nails and pulled my hand out of my mouth. "Don't worry," she said. "Lyssa's a big girl."

I examined my cuticles and sighed. "I know. I don't think she realizes who she's dealing with. He may enjoy flirting with her, but I doubt he cares about letting her down easy."

My sister rubbed my back a little like she used to do when I had a bad day at school.

"It's not up to you to save everyone. I'm the big sister, remember? And we have parents, too. Let them worry about Lyssa."

"I just get so anxious. I even have nightmares that I'm a shepherd and you guys are all sheep, and my job is to keep rounding everyone up, and then another one runs away and I have to start herding again." All the stress of the last few weeks hit me like a huge linebacker—on steroids. Panic welled up in my throat and hot tears flooded the corners of my eyes.

"Stop!" Sophie probably hadn't raised her voice at me since the Great Barbie Haircut Disaster of 2005. I thought Barbie wanted a pixie-cut. Clearly I was wrong.

Her eyes flashed at me. "We can all take care of ourselves. I think I can speak for Mom, Dad, and Lyssa. We all know how much you love us and how you worry about us, but you need to let us take care of you sometimes, too. It's not worth making yourself sick with worry."

I tried to let her words permeate my brain and to calm myself down. It didn't work. Sophie had no idea how worried I was, because she didn't know the full story about Mom and Dad and the bank.

"But I can't help myself. I'm Jewish, therefore I worry."

Sophie shook her head. "All those years of Hebrew school. Didn't you learn anything? Of all the rich aspects of our Jewish heritage, you couldn't have picked being able to make kickass chicken soup, you had to go with being a worrywart?"

"Okay. Fine. More cooking, less worrying." I gave Sophie a hug. Part of me felt better, but the other part of me wished desperately that I had never heard the name "*Myth Gnomers*" or the words "Bigfoot" and "reality TV" in the same sentence.

Jake put down his coffee, apparently ready to start filming. He stretched his neck from side to side and jumped up and down, like a boxer. "Okay, Colin, I'm good to go."

Colin nodded once and held up his megaphone. "Let's get everyone on set, please." The cast and crew took their places.

Colin pointed at the cameras. "Rolling," he said.

Jake looked straight at the camera and with a well-placed grin, began, "As Bigfoot hunters, you all know that part of a cryptozoologist's skill lies in being able to distinguish the real from the fake. Ladies and gentlemen, for this next challenge, you will be split up into pairs. Each pair will have three days to find five pieces of fake evidence that we've planted in your quadrant. And it won't be easy, because we've had a team of special effects and set dressing experts from Hollywood come in to set the scene . . ."

Ha! If anyone knows about fake evidence, it's us Berger girls.

"But, don't get too comfortable, Squatch hunters, because we're going to completely mix things up this round. Contestants, please shake hands or hug your teammates . . ." Jake paused and made a gesture with his hand like he was serious.

I followed his directions, hugging Sophie first then Lyssa, before embracing my mom, who looked worried—big surprise—and my dad, who was still pretty enthusiastic, but a bit confused.

I glanced at the other team. Kyle and Devan exchanged full bro hugs while Kyle and Caroline gave each other a quick peck on the cheek. When Caroline approached Devan, she hesitated like she wasn't sure whether to hug or kiss him. She leaned over for a kiss, but he offered her his hand to shake instead. *Ouch!* Maybe it was a British thing, or maybe he was still mad at her because of her fling with Jake.

"Just so you know," Jake said. "That was goodbye for the next three days, because for the next challenge some of you will be paired off with members of the other team."

Excuse me? WTF?!

"Each pair will be given points for their findings. So, that means you'll have to put aside your differences and work together. Yeti or not, let's find out the pairings." Jake clasped his hands together like an evil villain, plotting to take over the world.

Beth snuck by the camera to offer Jake a fishbowl with little pieces of paper in it. I caught her eye, and she mouthed that she was sorry. Not a good sign.

"This is gonna be fun!" Jake smiled, picking two pieces of paper from the bowl. "Our first couple, sorry, I mean pair," he said, but didn't really look like he slipped on that word at all, "will be Kyle and Sophie, who got really close when Sophie was recovering from the flu at the cabin. Let's see if they can work together as well in the forest."

Sophie and Kyle offered each other genuine smiles. I was happy for them and glad someone would enjoy the next few days.

"Next up, we have Lyssa and Caroline."

I couldn't imagine them both getting out of the woods unharmed. Neither was an experienced camper, but both were experienced divas. Caroline's face seemed stuck in a frown, but Lyssa had plastered on her best pageant smile. My sister was a pro. The audience was going to love her.

"And lastly," Jake softened his voice, like he was on a matchmaking show. "We have . . . Devan and Samantha."

Of freaking course! Trapped for three days with Her Majesty's Royal Pain in the Ass.

Devan nodded at me, but he didn't look any happier than I felt.

Jake continued, "Myron and Brenda, you can sit out this round, and watch from the production monitors. You can even stay in the guest house since no one else will be there."

My parents held hands and nodded. "Like a second honeymoon," my dad said, kissing my mom's hand.

Ew, gross. In general, I knew that I was lucky my parents were still together and in love, but I just wished they could act like normal people.

"Contestants, please stand with your new teammates." Jake gave me a particularly wicked grin.

Kyle and Sophie practically floated their way to each other. Kyle even threw his arm around my sister's shoulder. Sophie, of course, blushed.

Devan, on the other hand, made his way over to me like I was going to give him a root canal with a rusty spoon. Caroline scowled and stomped toward Lyssa, who was going to permanently injure her cheek muscles if she kept smiling that hard.

Colin and Jake exchanged a nod.

"Here're your assigned quadrants." Jake handed each pair a map. "And remember, you and your partner will be judged not only on the amount of clues you are able to find, but also on how well you work together. You have thirty minutes to plan and pack!"

And then to add insult to injury, before Colin called "Cut," my mom shouted, "Love you girls! Kick butt!" loud enough that Lyssa, Sophie, and I could hear, not to mention the other team, and oh, yeah, all of America and most of Canada.

The moment the camera was no longer on Jake, he dropped the bravado. His phone rang and he picked it up. "Hey, Melody. I miss you, too, baby," he said and slunk off to the espresso machine.

Everyone else began talking and arguing. Devan peered down at me with a withering glare.

Before he could say anything, I blurted out, "I hate losing. So don't make me lose."

"Oh, you think I'm the weaker link?" he scoffed.

I didn't bother answering. Instead I muttered, "I'm gonna go get some snacks for the road." Without bothering to see if he was following me, I took off toward the craft services table.

On my way, I eyed the glass fishbowl that had determined the pairings. No one seemed to be watching, so I ran my hand through the papers in the bowl, feeling them slip through my fingers. Out of curiosity, I picked one up and unfolded it. The paper was blank. *What the hell?*

I picked up another and another and they were blank, too. It wasn't fate that brought us together at all. It was Colin. He had seen the footage of Devan and me on the couch that night, and our fight the next morning. He knew that Kyle and Sophie were smitten, and that Caroline and Lyssa hated each other. This was all about manufacturing drama. Looking around at the rest of the cast, I didn't think Colin would have long to wait.

Chapter 20

"For as long as scientists have been searching for Bigfoot, there have been hoaxes. Anthropologists must differentiate these frauds from the real evidence of actual primates."

—*Dr. Roberta DeGraw, dean, Netherfield Academy*

I stared at the snack table, wondering how many donuts we could pack, and whether I'd have room for anything with real protein and vitamins and stuff we needed. Devan followed me, wearing a small frown.

He leaned on the table right in a pool of coffee. He hastily tried to wipe off his sleeve with a napkin, then opened his mouth to speak. "Sam, I know this is far from ideal." He didn't get any further.

Dr. DeGraw strode up behind me.

"Devan, if I could have a minute," she said. It didn't sound like a question.

She didn't bother to address me, ignoring the fact I was standing a few feet away from her. She probably expected me to leave, but I stood my ground.

Dr. DeGraw cleared her throat, and grabbed Devan by the arm. Her eyes bore into his without blinking. "I'm very disappointed with the way your team is conducting themselves. As captain, I expect you to rein them in," she said.

I smirked. Being invisible had its advantages. Devan seemed to forget my presence, too. It was nice to see him cut down to normal-guy size.

"Yes, ma'am, I—I—" he stuttered, trying to get out an answer. But Dr. DeGraw wasn't finished.

"I need you to act like a leader," she said. "You know how important this is for the school. Kyle is behaving like a lovesick puppy, and Caroline is letting herself get distracted from her work by a prepubescent James Dean."

Devan's eyes flashed at her. "I have no idea what you mean."

"You three are supposed to be representing the hallowed history of our illustrious school, and you are failing."

Dr. DeGraw pointed a bony finger in the direction of Devan's chest. "You must focus on the tasks ahead of you, and not on trying to undress any halfway attractive people you meet. This is supposed to be an intellectual pursuit, not spring break."

Devan's head drooped with the weight of her tirade. "I'm sorry to have caused you any disappointment or to have embarrassed the academy," he said, drawing out the words as if they took a lot of effort.

The professor gritted her teeth. "Never mind Netherfield, what about your father? He's one of the leading archaeologists in his field, and you can't even hold your own against rural rednecks from Idaho."

That was it. I opened my mouth to tell her off, but Devan's eyes flicked over to mine, pleading with me to keep my opinion to myself.

"They're from Ohio," he said, finding the courage to meet Dr. DeGraw's gaze.

"I don't care if they're from Antarctica. You need to do better. Otherwise you may want to find a new school in the fall. I would hate to have to tell your father you've failed out of the program, especially when you're so close to getting into a top university. With my help, of course." Dr. DeGraw scowled at her watch, as if she had wasted enough time with Devan.

"There's no need to tell my father anything." Devan stiffened. "I'll handle it."

Wow. What a bitch on wheels. I suddenly felt sorry for Devan. She could call my family all sorts of rude names, but at least I wouldn't ever have to deal with her again once the show was over.

Devan turned and walked away as fast as his dignity would allow. I followed, but glanced back at Dr. DeGraw, who seemed surprised to see me there.

"What a charming woman," I muttered. His dark expression didn't change as his long legs propelled him up the trail toward the cabin. I struggled to keep up.

"You don't know her," Devan sighed, walking even faster. "She's difficult, but brilliant. She was one of the first women to direct an excavation in her twenties, right out of grad school. She's won lots of important fellowships in her field and had guys in their fifties and sixties working under her on digs. She had to be tough to get people to follow her. And yet she still couldn't get tenure. I don't blame her for being a little bitter."

"I guess so," I said.

"And she's right, you know. There are expectations I have to meet. And this television show is the last thing I need my parents to worry about while they're abroad." His voice rose as if he was trying to convince himself, too.

I jogged after him. "So what happens if you fail?"

"I don't think it's too much to ask Kyle and Caroline to keep their heads in the game."

"Maybe. But she really has no right to treat you like that. *I* think you should stuff your brolly up her . . ." I paused. "I'm sorry, I don't remember the British slang for *ass*."

"Oh, is there not enough swearing on the BBC these days? It's *arse*." His lips twitched a little, or maybe it was a smile. It was hard to tell.

"Oh yeah, I knew that."

We had arrived at the cabin and Devan held the door open for me in grim silence. He gestured for me to follow him past a very cuddly Sophie and Kyle whispering on the couch, barely looking at the map in front of them.

We headed into Devan's bedroom. Gulp.

"I don't usually invite girls into my room," Devan said, rubbing the back of his neck. "I mean, I've had girls in my room, you know, for study sessions, and Caroline, of course . . . I don't want you to think . . ." He paused, took a breath and started again, more calmly. "It's important the other teams don't overhear our plans. Plus there are no cameras in here. I'm so tired of always being filmed."

I found myself enjoying it when he got flustered. It was a rather adorable look for him.

"It's okay. I think my virtue is pretty safe with you. That is, what's left of it," I joked, but stopped when I saw his expression, part intrigued and part horrified at me making an off-color joke. "I'm kidding," I said. I think he was worried I was going to jump his way-too-attractive bones. Which I hadn't even considered. Much.

"Samantha," he said my name softly, which sounded wonderful in his proper accent. "Thank you for trying to cheer me up, or whatever it is you're trying to do, but I am quite capable of handling things myself, despite what Dr. DeGraw thinks."

"I know. I just have a terrible habit of trying to take care of everyone." I shrugged. "Don't take it personally."

His eyes twinkled a little bit. "I'll try not to take anything you say personally."

"Good deal. So, where are we with the map Jake gave you?" I put my hands on my hips.

Enough chatting. We needed to get organized, and quickly, to win this thing. I assumed Kyle and Sophie wouldn't get around to making many decisions anytime soon; they were both too mild-mannered and polite. But Caroline and Lyssa could be a shrewd team, and big competition for us, if they didn't kill each other first.

He squirmed and made room for me next to him on the bed.

A little nervous, I didn't sit right away, but instead stood looking at a photo on his shelf. It was of Devan with what I assumed were his parents and his sister on the stairs of a beautiful old building with carved stone pillars of some sort. His dad was also tall and slender, like Devan, and his chin jutted forward proudly. His mom, who was petite with thick dark hair, squinted in the sun, and his sister had one of those please-take-the-photo-already forced smiles. Devan looked the most casual, wearing a cotton vest and white shirt, his hands in his pockets, sunglasses on his face. They were a good-looking family. No surprise there.

It was sweet that he hung a photo of his family. I would have done the same thing if I were away from my family for any length of time.

He cleared his throat. "We were in India for my cousin's wedding last year."

"It's beautiful." I pointed to the photo. "What's this building?"

Devan stepped behind me, closer than I would have expected. His breath tickled my neck, which made me shiver.

"That's the Sun Temple at Konârak. It's a pretty important heritage site near the Bay of Bengal. It was built in the thirteenth century."

"I'd love to visit." I felt my face redden, hoping he didn't think I was inviting myself to hang out with him and his family.

He walked over to the other side of the room and picked up a small statue off a shelf, and held it in his hand before placing it back. I breathed a sigh of relief, and stole a glance at the rest of the room, which was a disaster area. "I wouldn't take you for a secret slob, Devan."

An assortment of papers, books, and random socks was strewn on the floor, along with a pair of boxers with the TARDIS from *Doctor Who* on them. If it were a T-shirt I would have asked him about it, but I really didn't want to discuss his underwear while we were alone in his bedroom.

"I *am* a bloke. I reserve the right to be a bit messy," he said, kicking some of the dirty laundry under the bed, including the boxers.

"So, the map." He rolled the map out on the bed and stuck a book on either end of it, to keep it from curling up. "We'll be here," he pointed, "in quadrant six at the north side of the lake, along the edge of the mountains. It should be about a sixty-minute hike from your camp. We can run by and get anything you need on the way."

"That's probably not a bad idea," I said, curling my hair around a finger, while coming up with a mental list of supplies. "I have some field notes that could be helpful, along with my sleeping bag, and clothes, and we can figure out what equipment we need."

He ran his hand through his hair, messing it up in a really attractive way, like he just got up from a nap or something else that involved a bed. And of course I blushed as the butterflies turned into huge bats playing rugby in my stomach. "Do you really think we'll need to stay over in the woods?" he asked.

"I really don't think we have time to trek back and forth from the quadrant every day. We should just set up camp there."

"Aren't there bears and whatnot?"

"You're hunting Sasquatch, but you're afraid of bears?" I teased. "Don't worry. It's not a big deal."

Devan's lovely brown eyes grew wider. "Not a big deal? I think we're a bit more likely to run into a ravenous bear or wolf than a mythical creature."

I shook my head at him. "I'll protect you. I just need a baseball bat." I surveyed his mess again. "But you definitely can't leave candy wrappers around. Anything that smells like food will be a problem."

"So I should leave my fish-and-chips-scented cologne at home?"

"Unless you want to attract some wild animals," I said.

"Maybe I do," he said pointedly, with a cheeseball grin and a wink.

I snorted and busied myself by pretending to examine the map. "Pretty weak line, Devan, especially when I'm trying to give you information that may save your life, but, okay, I get it. You'd rather flirt than live. Whatever."

I went back to looking at the map and hoped he couldn't hear my heart beating rapidly.

"Sorry," he said softly.

I glanced up at him and caught his eye. The map fell out of my hands, and he picked it up and gave it back to me without breaking eye contact.

"For some reason, you make me nervous and then I say incoherent things," he said in a serious tone. "It's like you see past everyone's bull or something."

I raised an eyebrow at him. "I think you're perfectly capable of saying incoherent things without me, but it's all right. Just more planning, fewer bad puns, okay? We should head out as soon as we can."

"Righto." Devan jumped off the bed like his cute British arse was on fire. "I'll go pack. You can hold Ganesha," he said, handing me the palm-sized statue from the shelf.

I turned the little elephant-headed figure over in my hands. "He's cute, but what am I supposed to do with him?"

"My grandmother gave him to me when I was young. I'm not very religious, but I like to have him nearby. He's my favorite Hindu god." Devan hesitated. "He's the remover of obstacles. I guess I feel like him sometimes, like I have multiple arms and I'm balancing too many roles and responsibilities," Devan said, while throwing stuff in a backpack.

I studied him, surprised. "I feel that way, too, pretty much every day." My expression softened, imagining Devan much younger.

We exchanged wary smiles that I hoped meant we could get through this challenge without butting heads as much as we had in the past week. But I wouldn't count on it. Last time we had a nice moment, he went and ruined it by insulting my sister before I stormed out of the cabin.

I went into the kitchen and rummaged through the cabinets until I came up with some chips and wasabi peas for Devan, and a box of Pop-Tarts. Sadly, all the cinnamon ones were gone. The blueberry ones would have to do. We were in survival mode, after all.

Hal and Dave stopped by to set us up with body mics and film us packing our gear. Hal said he'd catch up with us in our quadrant of the property later on in the day, but first they had to get footage of some of the other team's preparations. Devan and I hiked to my family's campsite and raided it for wilderness survival essentials. There was no sign of my parents. They must have already relocated. Lucky them.

"I think we're good to go." Devan slung the heavier pack over his shoulder and trudged further into the forest.

Chapter 21

"Most people refer to Bigfoot as a male creature
probably because we don't often spot females of the species.
I like to think it's because the females are
smart enough not to get caught."

—*Brenda Berger, from remarks made at the*
Lady Bigfoot Hunters annual luncheon

I insisted on navigating. Devan finally agreed to let me take control, when he couldn't figure out which direction was north, even with a compass. We trotted along in companionable silence, enjoying the first sunny weather we'd had in days. The location we had been given wasn't far, but we had to climb over a big ridge and maneuver down a steep slope to reach the valley where we wanted to camp.

When we got to the lake, we were pretty sweaty. We found a grassy patch by the water's edge and dropped our packs. My shirt was plastered to my back where the pack had been and a few damp curls had adhered to my forehead. Very attractive.

"Fancy a swim?" Devan asked.

"I didn't pack a suit. Unless your plan was to skinny-dip?" I asked, trying to keep my voice from shaking.

He gave me a mock offended look. "I had no such plan. I was just going to wear these shorts. They'll dry pretty quickly."

I debated swimming for a moment. The vivid blue water was clear and glistening in the sunlight. I was hot and sticky, and it did look refreshing. But I generally didn't like to swim in water that wasn't chlorinated. I may have been able to face down a wolf, but marine life was a different story. I never recovered from watching *Jaws* as a kid.

"I don't know," I tilted my head, weighing the options. "It looks pretty cold. And I'm not sure we have time."

"We've got three days. I think we can afford a short break. I'm going in. Swimming relaxes me. I'll be of better use once my head is clear."

"That's how I feel about reading. Why don't you go ahead and I'll sit here and read?"

"Suit yourself," he said, unclipping his microphone and taking off his T-shirt to reveal a slim but toned figure perfectly built for swimming.

I tried not to think about other things that it might be good for, as I purposefully studied my book and read the same sentence at least six times. Devan did a pretty intense butterfly stroke for about five minutes. I turned a page, not comprehending a single sentence. I snuck a peek at his graceful yet strong form. Was there anything he couldn't do? Other than Bigfoot hunting, camping, or maintaining a polite conversation with me for more than a few minutes?

Never mind. Maybe he should stick to swimming. I laughed out loud at the thought, and it must have been louder than I realized, because he lifted his head out of the water, to see what was so amusing.

"What?" he asked.

I pointed at my book. "Funny stuff."

He twisted his mouth. "There are swords and blood on the cover. Are you sure it's not something I did?"

I rolled my eyes at him. "Paranoid much?"

Huh. I guess I got under his skin, too.

"I'll show you paranoid!" Devan said, a wicked grin spreading across his face as he splashed me with freezing cold water.

"Hey, stop!" I ran out of the splash zone and dragged the backpacks with me. "All the equipment is here. What's wrong with you?"

Apparently, he knew that the gear was waterproof and I was bluffing because he continued splashing, trying to make the water go even further. At one point he got me good, and as I pushed my drenched, soon to be frizzy, curls out of my face, I decided that I had no choice but to retaliate.

"Oh, my god!" I stood still, pretending to stare at something behind him. He stopped splashing and turned to see what I was looking at.

"What?" he asked.

"Nothing, probably," I said, trying very hard not to smile or laugh. "I thought I spotted a Pacific Northwest Poisonous Water Snake, but it was probably just a shadow or something."

Devan stood up in the water and looked behind him. "Wait, seriously? Poisonous water snakes?"

"Yeah, they're rare, but very deadly. Don't panic, but, there it is!" I pointed to his left.

I don't think I ever saw him move so quickly as he scrambled up the bank of the lake. I was in mid-laugh at his horrified expression when my mirth was cut short by an awful noise as he tripped and crashed to the ground. He collapsed in an undignified heap, clutching his arm and swearing like a sailor.

"Damn it, Devan! I was teasing! Are you okay?"

"I think I broke my arm," he spat out in between mumbled curses.

"Let me see." If he had actually broken his arm, he'd probably be in a lot more pain, but I needed to feel the bone, to know for sure. I reached out for his arm.

"Ow!" He held onto his wrist like I was about to saw it off.

"Hold still, you big baby," I said in my most no-nonsense voice.

I lowered him so he was sitting with his back against a tree. Lake water dripped off him making him shiver. I yanked a towel from the gear and draped it over his shoulders. I ran my fingers up his arm, trying to focus on his wellbeing and not his beautiful, muscular body. His eyes found mine as I traced his forearm muscle with my fingers. He sighed and I let go right away and blushed, wiping my hands on my pants.

I picked up his elbow in a less gentle manner, careful not to look directly at his face this time. "Does it hurt when I do this?" I twisted his elbow a little from side to side and around in a circle.

Wincing, he gasped, "It hurts, yes."

"The good news is that I don't think it's broken. You'd be screaming more if it was, and we'd maybe see a bone poking out."

I pulled the little first aid kit out of my backpack and cracked open an instant ice pack and placed it on his arm, which was already starting to swell and get a little purple.

"Do you have anything in there for the pain?" he asked.

I passed Devan a few pain killers. I found his canteen and helped him take the pills. "You should rest here for a little while and then I'll wrap it with an elastic bandage. You'll have to be careful not to move it too much, but you should be okay until we can get you back to camp. The doctor can x-ray it to be sure there're no fractures. Do you want to call Beth now and head back?"

I chewed my lip, realizing this probably meant the end of the challenge for us.

"No. No. I can go on, I think." He was breathing heavily, trying to fight the pain.

"You sure?"

"Yes." He nodded and tried to summon a smile. "As you said, it's not broken. And I certainly don't want to be the reason we lose."

I nodded, relieved.

"Devan, I'm sorry," I said.

His eyebrows knitted together, confused. "For what?"

"There aren't any poisonous water snakes out here. I just made that up to get back at you for splashing me. I didn't think this would happen." I waved a hand at the ice pack.

"It's all right. I'm the one who tripped," he said. The perspiration formed beads on his forehead. He was really suffering and it was my goddamned fault.

He patted me on the knee with his good hand. "Sam, really, it was an accident. Don't worry. And you're very convincing. But, next time you try to take the piss out of me, make sure there aren't any snakes involved. I'm only afraid of a few things, and one of them is snakes."

"Okay. No more snake jokes. Although, it was pretty funny." I giggled.

He gave me a weak smile.

I peeked under the ice pack. "I think it needs to chill for a few more minutes before we wrap it up," I said.

"Okay, you're the doctor." Devan studied my face. "I'm not going to lie, I'm impressed," he said quietly. "How do you know how to do this?"

"I volunteer in a hospital. I hope to be pre-med in college, if I can scrape up the cash." I couldn't decide if I was flattered or annoyed, maybe both. Granted, I was used to being underestimated and it was an advantage in the contest. But, I wished Devan could have seen my hidden talents without having to practically break his neck first.

He nodded, speechless for once, then closed his eyes and lay down on the towel, grimacing.

"So that's why *you're* doing this?"

"Doing what?"

"This show—for the prize money so you can go to college?"

"Yup. Well, that and I just love making a spectacle of myself on reality TV. I mean, who doesn't?" I tried to fend off his serious question. "And how did you get stuck doing this contest?" I asked.

"Oh, I didn't have much of a choice. Dr. DeGraw said that the top three anthropology students had to do this. I couldn't turn her down because I need her recommendation. She knows people at all the top college programs. One word from her and I'm golden."

We sat in silence for a bit. Just like in our earlier hike, there was no awkwardness in not talking. It was easy to get lost in my own thoughts, and not worry about trying to fill the quiet with inane conversation.

The only problem was that my thoughts tended to be focused on the fact that he still wasn't wearing a shirt, and with each breath his chest muscles gently flexed under his smooth skin. His eyes were still closed, and he had put his good hand behind his head, like he was relaxing on some beach, and not nursing an injury, in the middle of the wilderness, with a girl he couldn't stand. I averted my eyes, only to find them drifting back to his serene face.

His hair was still wet, and one lock stuck to his forehead. I had an almost irresistible urge to smooth it, but before I could give in to the temptation, he spoke.

"I think you'll make a great doctor."

He opened his eyes and put his hand on my knee.

Once again, my limb burned where he touched me. "Thanks." The fire spread to my cheeks in an obvious blush. I stared at him until it was just too humiliating, then I jumped up. I threw his shirt at him, hoping my skin was returning to its normal color. I hunted in my pack for the bandage and then found a sturdy stick.

I gestured for Devan to sit up so I could ease his shirt back on one arm at a time, before I placed the stick under his injured forearm. He sucked in his breath, so I quickly got to work wrapping the bandage around it to create a splint that would limit his range of motion.

"Well, I hope you win," Devan whispered in my ear.

"Really?" I asked, so surprised I wrapped his arm a little too tightly.

"Ouch!" he said then looked a little embarrassed.

I made a makeshift sling out of a spare T-shirt and a bandana and slipped it over Devan's neck, hyper aware of the fact that I was practically embracing him.

"I mean, you know, if I can't win," he added.

"Of course," I whispered back. We were still so close, I could feel the heat radiating off his cheek.

"Why are we whispering?" I asked.

"Sorry," he responded even more quietly. "It's just, I have an illustrious school and family reputation to uphold, and I can't say that I don't want to win with that bloody camera watching."

"Wait. What camera?" I stood and slowly turned around and wouldn't you know it, there was Hal, grinning, while I still had my arms wrapped around Devan's neck.

Oh, hell no.

Chapter 22

"The mating season of the Bigfoot is short and intense. Males of the species must prove themselves worthy of the female and she, in turn, chooses the strongest and most persistent suitor."

—"Love and Loss in a Bigfoot Pack"

Hal must have been practicing walking quietly, because I sure as hell didn't hear him approach.

"This is going to be great!" he said.

"No it's not!" I snapped.

I ran my hands over my frizzy curls.

Devan laughed, which turned into howling. "What did you give me? I can't stop laughing."

I closed my eyes and breathed deeply, and pretended this wasn't happening. "It's Advil, Devan. Pull yourself together," I said.

"You should have seen your face, though!" he said between guffaws.

I turned my back on him. First things first.

"Hal," I lowered my voice and spoke deliberately, restraining myself from yelling. "How long have you been standing there?"

The cameraman gave me a huge smile. "Let's see, Devan was talking about skinny-dipping, and you were gazing at him longingly, then you two had a flirty splash war, he tripped, and you played nurse. So romantic." Hal sighed like he was watching a soap opera. "Then you had a heart-to-heart talk about your hopes and dreams."

My mouth dropped open as I struggled to catch a breath, so astonished I couldn't even talk at first. "Oh, my god! It wasn't like that."

Hal smirked at me. "It will be once it's edited. This love/hate romance is TV gold." His eyes went all dreamy again.

I looked to Devan for support, but he was still caught in a fit of laughter.

What the hell was wrong with everyone?

I stomped over to Hal and snapped my fingers in his face. Hal blinked and frowned at me.

"There is no romance going on here," I said. "If you want romance, go read a novel." My voice rose in desperation, which seemed to make Devan laugh even harder. I turned around and narrowed my eyes. "Do you want me to twist your other arm?"

That shut him up, mostly. Although his face contorted as he swallowed his laughter.

Hal shrugged, looking sheepish. "I'm sorry, I just love romance. Call me a softy, but this is the part I really like, when I can capture something real."

I threw my hands up. "Enough! We need to get to work." I offered Devan an outstretched arm and helped him up. "Are you okay to go on?"

He picked up his backpack and put it on his good arm, sucking in breath through his teeth. "I don't know how much I can carry, but otherwise, I'll manage."

I surveyed the area, and thought maybe I could save his pride, despite the fact that we were probably a good quarter of a mile from where we had planned to camp.

"What if we set up camp here?" I asked. "You can sit for a while and I'll go see if I can find any clues before it gets dark. Then hopefully tomorrow morning, you'll be a little less sore and able to help. What do you think?"

"Okay. That sounds good." Devan agreed and lowered himself onto a tree stump.

I trudged through the thick underbrush that was just inside the tree line, in search of some branches for a fire. Hal followed with his camera. *God, I thought I had no privacy growing up with two sisters.* This was definitely worse. I liked Hal, but being filmed all the time was pretty invasive.

Hal's insistence that there was some sort of blossoming romance between Devan and me was extra annoying. But I realized he wasn't the first to suggest such a thing. Lyssa had hinted that there was something going on, too. *Strange.* Yes, Devan was really cute. Hadn't I been ogling his bare chest and staring at his handsome face for the last half hour? But on the other hand, we hated each other, and this was just a momentary truce. And yet, I couldn't help the stomach drops or the dizziness every time he gazed at me. It was like being on a perpetual roller coaster when he was around.

It was way too confusing and I had to focus on winning the challenge and getting my family out of debt. But first I needed to get the campsite set up.

It took a few minutes, but eventually I found enough dry branches to make a fire. I dropped the wood and gathered some stones to make a fire ring.

Devan offered me a wide smile. "You're useful to have around. If there's ever a zombie apocalypse I know who to call."

"How do you know I won't be the one to start the zombie apocalypse? I could very well be carrying a deadly zombie virus right now," I joked.

"I haven't seen infectious undead monsters that look as good as you," he said, giving me another one of those gazes that made me forget how to breathe.

Behind us, Hal sighed like a teen girl watching the prom episode of her favorite show.

"Cut it out!" I said without turning my head. "Now I know why celebrities beat up the paparazzi," I grumbled in Hal's direction.

Devan added, quickly, "I just meant that zombies are usually more decayed, you know, rotting flesh, entrails, not cute. Opposite of cute, really . . ." He was rambling, trying to backpedal out of the compliment he accidentally just gave me.

I raised an eyebrow at Devan. "Remember what Dr. DeGraw said. You need to stay focused, too."

The amusement disappeared from Devan's face in a hurry. "I can help you unpack at least," he said, standing. We hadn't brought much with us in the way of gear so it didn't take long, even with Devan's right arm out of commission. Hal filmed us pitching the little pup tents and then he set up his own tent.

It was late afternoon, so I left Devan with another ice pack for his arm, the walkie and a whistle to use if he needed help, and a paperback if he got bored.

Hal followed me through the woods as I began to systematically survey our quadrant for fake clues. I managed to find a chunk of unusual hair stuck conspicuously in some tree bark. It looked like synthetic doll hair to me—no follicles, texture, or split ends. It was too perfect.

By then it was getting dark enough that I was eager to get back to the warmth and safety of a campfire. To my pleasant surprise, Devan had already lit the fire and was cooking some soup for us all.

"Nice work, Mountain Man." I plopped down next to him. "I found a fake clue. Only one, but hey, it's something." I held up the hair, waving my hand around it like a product model on an infomercial.

Handing me the soup, he grinned. "Brilliant!"

I warmed my icy hands by the fire. "Remember a few hours ago when we were sweating our asses off? Now I'm freezing!"

Without standing, he reached his good arm over to the packs, pulled out a fleece sweatshirt, and handed it to me. I shrugged it on, inhaling the woodsy British cologne I now associated with him. Mmm. Warm all over, I crossed my arms over my stomach and let out a happy sigh. "Thanks," I said to Devan who shivered next to me. I frowned at the goose flesh forming on his arms. "Won't you be cold?"

"Nah, I'm good for now," he said, always the stoic. A few minutes later, he reached into his bag again and pulled out a long-sleeved thermal shirt.

"Do you mind helping me?" he asked.

I took the sling off of him and gently helped him get the sleeves over his arms while he gritted his teeth. I put the sling back over his neck and helped position his arm in it, hoping he couldn't feel me shaking.

When I was done, I forced myself to scoot a few inches away from him and mentally slapped myself for thinking about how the tight shirt showed off his physique.

I glanced away, but he gazed at me until I met his eyes. "Thank you," he said.

Hal emerged from his tent in a parka and wool cap. A bit of overkill, but whatever. He set up the camera on a tripod facing our fire, so he could be sure to capture all the excitement of us eating soup and making small talk.

Dinner was fairly uneventful. We were all starving, and more focused on food than conversation. After dinner, Hal crawled into his tent, but I stayed by the fire. Devan handed my book to me.

"You can hang onto it if you want," I said. "I've already read it. Like twelve times."

"Really? You like it that much?" he asked, sounding surprised.

"Yeah, I know I'm a nerd."

"I'm going to be an anthropology major," he replied. "Doesn't get any nerdier than that."

I smiled at him and he returned my smile. "Good point. So what makes you want to study anthropology? Is it the family business?"

Devan shook his head. "Not exactly. There're some similarities, but my parents are both really focused on ancient art and artifacts. I want to study societies and cultures right now. I think it's the best way to try to help solve contemporary problems, like poverty and inequality."

We just gazed at each other for a moment. It was surprisingly nice getting to know who he was outside of the contest. I think I looked away first, but he started babbling nervously.

"Anyway, the troll book is an excellent read, but I haven't read the first book in the series, so the elf and troll politics were a bit difficult to follow," he said seriously.

"Sorry. I forgot it was the sequel," I said.

"So give me the rundown of the first book." He leaned forward, looking genuinely interested.

I rambled on and on about the different tribes of trolls. Devan listened and asked questions. He laughed at my enthusiastic retelling once or twice, and told me about a few books he had liked in the same fantasy genre. Eventually he rubbed his eyes and I glanced at my watch. It was past midnight. We were having such a nice time, I hadn't even noticed.

"I'm sorry I kept you up so late," I said.

He tilted his head so his eyes found mine. "Don't be."

Hal's mighty snoring reverberated from within his tent. Devan lifted himself up with his good arm and walked around the campfire to the camera, still on its tripod. He flicked the power off and the red light went out. Staring at the dormant machine, a huge wave of relief swept over me. I hadn't realized how tense I had been with the camera constantly watching.

"Oh, my god, thank you!" I said, twisting my neck from side to side, letting all of the tension go.

"I can't bear having that thing staring at me anymore tonight," he said.

We both took off our body mics and turned them off as well. Enough was enough.

He sat next to me and leaned a little closer. Our shoulders were almost touching, and the heat practically radiated from him.

"I can't believe you just threw this splint together. You're really incredible," he said.

I pushed my hair behind my ears, flustered that he was so close. "I'm really not. I just paid attention in Girl Scouts." When he didn't laugh I added, "Never mind, just a joke."

"I get it. But . . ." He trailed off, looking at me quizzically.

I bent my head down, feeling like I had lettuce in my teeth or had done something equally embarrassing. "What?"

"You do that a lot," he said.

Okay, now I felt like fake Barbie hair under the microscope.

"Do what?" I asked.

Devan softened his voice. "You make a joke whenever people compliment you. When you were at the cabin, Sophie would tell you how wonderful you are, and every time, you'd laugh it off."

Devan's eyes were on me when I lifted my head. I held his gaze, trying not to blush or shrug. I ended up doing both. "I know. But come on, it's not a huge deal. Of course, I take care of Sophie. She's my sister."

He continued to study me. It was becoming more and more unnerving. "I think you enjoy taking care of everyone. You took care of me and my arm."

I barked out a quick laugh. "I was pretty much to blame for your arm, if you'll remember."

His mouth twisted in a sardonic grin. "Vividly. But that's not all. I saw your face. You were ready to go two rounds with Dr. DeGraw for me."

"Well, that's because she called my family rural rednecks. She's a bully. I hate the way she treats you. I mean, I hate the way she treats people." With each word, my voice got louder and my indignation increased. Hal's snores stopped for a moment, but then resumed with a snort.

More quietly, I said, "I'm sorry, I know you admire her and she's your mentor, and she's super accomplished and all, but that doesn't mean I have to like her."

Devan's mouth suddenly returned to its usual grim line. I worried I'd ruined our pleasant truce, but Dr. DeGraw was a heinous, snobby witch. I didn't care if he agreed. But then, for the millionth time that day, Devan surprised me with a conspiratorial grin.

"I don't like her either, if you want to know the truth. You're right about her being a bully," he said, poking at the glowing embers in the fire pit, which bounced up and made him jump back.

"Do you really think your dad would be upset if you didn't win this stupid TV contest?" I asked.

"I don't know, to be honest." He stared at the ground, rubbing one eye and then the other. "I guess I'd rather not find out. I just think about how if they're distracted, one wrong move could jeopardize their lives. They go into the most dangerous places. I get why they do it. They're not just rescuing art, they're rescuing cultures, and ancient history and someone's heritage from looting and war. It's important work."

He shook his head. "I don't want to put them in the position of not being one hundred percent focused while they're there. So the easiest thing is to do what's expected of me. I'll just get through this last year at Netherfield, somehow, and then I can escape and go to college."

"Sounds like you really hate it there. I can't imagine your parents want you to be miserable, just to make them happy."

"Perhaps," he said. "But if I'm safe and getting good grades that means they don't have to worry about me." He didn't utter any other words, but tension took up residence in his shoulders and his jaw.

"I always thought boarding school kids were so lucky. You have so much more freedom, and you're practically guaranteed a spot at an Ivy League school," I said.

"I guess that's true, but what's so great about living out of suitcases and not having your own room?" Devan asked. "And never celebrating your birthday with your family?"

"I guess it does sound a little lonely, when you put it that way."

He nodded thoughtfully as he reached out his good hand to warm it by the fire. "It was really hard at first, especially being at such a white school. When I got there, I remember looking all over for the other brown faces that I saw in the brochure for the school. I even asked someone my first week, 'Hey, where are the people in the photo?' The guy told me, 'Oh, Omar and Angela? They graduated two years ago.'" Devan let out a small rueful laugh.

I bit my lip, a little sad for him. "Are people mean to you?"

He shook his head. "I've had some run-ins with people in the town who've yelled racist crap at me, and one even pushed me, which was scary."

"Oh my god!" I said. "That's awful."

Devan shrugged. "It's not like that at school. It's more that they're unintentionally rude, or they treat me differently. I really felt like I didn't fit in at first, which made being away from home harder. But then I eventually made some friends, like Kyle and Caroline, and now it's not so bad."

"I know what you mean about not fitting in," I said, choosing my words carefully, still shaken by what he'd told me. "We're pretty much the only Jewish family in my small town. When I was younger, I hated that we were different. My dad would write letters to the editor about how the paper wasn't reporting on anti-Semitic graffiti in the cemetery where my family is buried or the bomb threats to our temple. He'd get hate mail because of it."

Devan shook his head. "I'm sorry," he said quietly.

"Thanks," I said. "I understand why my dad spoke out, and I can appreciate it now, but when you're little, it's embarrassing to be different."

"And at least he doesn't embarrass you anymore," Devan smirked, apparently changing the subject to a lighter topic.

"Ha!" I barked, then caught myself before I started to really laugh, conscious of not waking up Hal. "Yeah, now we're not just the weird Jewish family, we're the super weird Bigfoot hunters. I'm dreading going back to school once this show has aired."

Devan sighed and I could see the pity in his eyes. "Me too," he added in a whisper. "If DeGraw even lets me back in."

My stomach churned with indecision. I would hate it if he got kicked out of Netherfield his senior year because of me. I wanted to go to college more than anything, but not at his expense. However, I had my own problems. Regardless of the fact that Devan wasn't as bad as I originally thought, I still had to put my family first. I reached out my hand, and then pulled it back. I fought the urge to give Devan a hug. We might be getting along, but I wasn't confident we were on hugging terms. I settled for putting my hand lightly on his back, over his shoulder blade.

When I touched him, electricity shot up my arm, and everything around me became blurry, except for Devan. He peered at me sideways, like he was surprised, too. I thought maybe I should back away, but my arm wouldn't obey—it wanted to stay attached to his shoulder. He didn't pull away either, but instead leaned against my side. It was a tiny, gentle movement that caused my heart to pound so loudly, I was afraid he would hear it.

I had no idea how long we sat together like that, staring into the glowing embers of the fire. The logs had burnt down to coals, and low flames flickered. A cool breeze swooped through the valley, but Devan's strong back under my hand, rising and falling with each breath, warmed me all the way up to my intoxicated head.

The wind stirred up the embers and one of the sparks floated up to the sky. A boundless sea of stars shone down on us. I gasped at the unexpected beauty. How had I not noticed it before? Devan's mouth turned upward in a hopeful smile. Without a word, we both laid down on our backs, hands at our sides, to marvel at the clear, twinkling night sky. He reached out and took my hand in his uninjured one and the stars seemed to grow even brighter. It was magical how the soft warmth of his hand drove away every anxious thought I'd had that week. I let go of all the worries, anger, and memories of hurtful words.

"So beautiful," I breathed.

Devan sat up and turned toward me, his handsome face staring at me, lips slightly open. I rose to meet him.

With his good hand, he brushed a wispy stray curl off my forehead then put his warm palm against my cheek.

"Very beautiful," he whispered, gazing at me while his finger traced my chin, making me shiver.

Devan closed the distance between us and kissed me gently right next to my ear. I couldn't help myself, I sighed. He looked at me with a shy smile, which I returned. He then angled his face toward my lips and I trembled with anticipation, like some inexperienced geek, which, honestly, I kind of was. But, then I noticed he was shaking too, and before I had time to worry anymore about whether I knew what I was doing, he kissed me.

He was tentative at first, his soft lips moving slowly against mine, kissing my bottom lip, then my top. He tasted slightly like toasted marshmallows, which was now my absolute favorite taste. Who knew s'mores could be so sexy? I tilted my head up, wanting more. I nipped his lip in encouragement, teasing him with my teeth.

A deep chuckle escaped the back of his throat. Devan pressed himself closer to me, kissing me more deeply, intensely, his tongue seeking mine out, warming me all over.

I moaned, pulling him even closer to me until my major organs melted into molten lava and I just didn't care. All that mattered were his lips on mine, his hand winding its way through my hair, all tangled up.

Holy crap! I'm kissing Devan. And it's freaking wonderful. And confusing.

We kissed and kissed. I threw my hands around his back and he traced circles along my spine. Eventually, Devan ran out of breath and pulled away, staring into my eyes, gauging my reaction.

I gulped and my eyes widened, trying to slow my heart down, to no avail. The boy had serious kissing skills. I was in completely over my head. All that energy I had put into controlling everything, and a few amazing kisses later, I could barely control breathing in and out.

"Mmm. More," I said, pulling him back to me for another kiss. The crackle of the fire echoed the heat between us.

Eventually we stopped to catch our breath again. He returned to his position at my side, but this time he wound his arm around my waist.

I snuck a glance at him, trying not to stare. His hair was rumpled and his eyes were shining. He returned my gaze and we sat in a happy post-kissing haze for a long moment, until I broke the spell with a frown.

What had just happened? What the hell was I doing? How could I kiss Devan, the enemy? Devan, who had insulted me and my family at every turn, and who was clearly so appalled by the idea of my sister dating his friend?

Because he wasn't just "Devan, the Competition" anymore. He was now also "Devan, the Sweet, Caring Guy Who Thought I Was Beautiful and Made Me Feel All Sorts of Things I Hadn't Felt Before." My head swirled, and I suddenly needed to get away. I had to think about Devan and the contest.

I couldn't be this close to him and not end up cuddling or making out with him again. If this night taught me anything it was that we were both drawn to each other. That wasn't what I needed right now.

I pulled out of his embrace and opened my mouth to say something, but nothing came out. I studied the fire in front of me, avoiding his eyes. Devan grabbed my hand, but I wrestled it away.

I scooted away from him, hating myself more with every inch I retreated. "We should get some sleep," I muttered. His eyebrows knit together, and he squinted in confusion. Then I stood and stammered, "Sorry, I . . . I don't know."

I practically ran to my tent without looking back.

Chapter 23

"The females of the species are quite picky
about their partners, often choosing to be alone rather
than with the wrong mate. Luckily, the females are strong.
They can defend themselves."

—"Love and Loss in a Bigfoot Pack"

Shortly after I stormed off, I heard Devan throw water on the embers of the dying fire, causing an angry hiss of steam to cut through the night. It was followed by the zip of his tent flap, and then silence. Not the sweet kind, the tense kind.

I threw my head back, and gazed at the stars through the mesh of my tent, and let out the huge breath constricting my chest. Maybe I overreacted. It was just a kiss. Okay, a few kisses. Really awesomely good ones, but I didn't have to lose my mind like that, right?

"Arrgh." I struggled to get comfortable, lying on one side, then my back. The small inflatable pillow leaked out air, just like my brain let out a steady stream of arguments for and against those kisses. The jury in my head knew I couldn't allow myself to become attached to Devan. But my still-tingly lips wanted to keep deliberating.

I groaned and stretched when the sun rose over the mountains. My knees and hips made loud cracking noises like those of a little old lady. I exited the tent, breathing in the tangy, tension-scented air. The overcast sky closely resembled the murky shades of gray rumbling around in my undecided mind.

"Morning." Devan approached me, quietly, like I was an unpredictable wild animal.

I turned and faced him. "Hey."

He stood a good five feet from me, a stark contrast to the previous night. The distance almost hurt. My lips were still swollen from our make-out session, and my heart hadn't recovered either, judging by the bass drum roll in my chest.

His eyes searched mine, looking for an answer. I knew the question on his mind: why the hell did I run off the night before? But he didn't ask and I didn't offer an answer.

"Um, where should we start today?" he asked instead.

Devan deferring to me was further proof things were weird between us.

I played with my hair, unsure what to do with my traitorous fingers that wanted to touch him. Instead of his warm skin, my hands found crunchy leaves in my hair, left from last night's kisses, no doubt. I picked them out and dropped them to the ground. Anything to dodge his accusing eyes. Chewing my lip, I willed myself to focus. If he was going to let me take charge, I'd do it. I was still undecided about how much I should help him, but since we were working together as a team, I could put off that worry for now.

I surveyed the area to our west. "We're way behind because of your arm," I said. "We need to get serious about the challenge. I haven't seen any more fake clues, which means they're either really well hidden or we're in the wrong place."

He frowned at what I said, or how I said it. Who could tell?

"Right. Let's have a quick bite and set out," he said.

We ate a few granola bars quietly, with only Hal's oblivious chatter breaking up the awkward silence. Then we started our search.

"Why don't I look up at the trees, and you stick to the ground? This way we can cover twice as much territory," Devan suggested.

I nodded. "Makes sense. We'll work in a circular pattern and overlap each other. Did they say how many clues they planted?"

"Five."

I was glad to have the distraction of an actual task. I lowered my eyes and walked a few paces away from Devan and all that awkwardness.

Ha! My eye caught a partial footprint under a bush. It must have been too dark to see it the night before. It was a total fake for sure. Besides the fact that the toes were all wrong, it was clear that someone had simply tried to draw a footprint in the dirt with a stick. "Got one!"

Devan nodded briskly when he saw the footprint. "Good catch."

"We don't have time to make a plaster cast, not if we want to keep looking," I said. "Let's just photograph it and move on."

We worked efficiently, searching for additional clues for the next forty-five minutes, followed by Hal and his camera.

Devan's shoulders drooped under the weight of his backpack, but he kept going until he couldn't anymore. "Sorry." He struggled to drop the bag.

I slowed down and handed him my canteen. "We can stop here," I said, while keeping my eyes on the path ahead of me and off of his scruffy, yet adorable, face. We hadn't gotten far on our fake-evidence search, but he had a hard time with his arm, and was too proud to admit he was in pain.

"I know how to read a map, so I know we haven't traveled nearly far enough," Devan said, his voice thick with frustration.

I pointed at a fallen tree trunk closer to the direction of where I was headed. "Why don't you sit there and rest and I'll see if I find anything else? Unless you want me to call Beth."

He inhaled deeply through his nose. "I'll be fine."

He lowered himself carefully onto the tree and wiped the sweat off his brow. *Damn it!* He even looked gorgeous in a rumpled button-down shirt and cargo pants. I clenched my hands and stared straight ahead, furious at myself for thinking about him romantically when all I should be concentrating on was the contest.

He raised an eyebrow. "Everything okay? You were zoning out."

I blushed up to my messy hairdo. I gestured to the woods behind me. "I'm gonna go over there now and see if there are any clues." That's when I noticed Hal's camera positioned on my face. It was amazing how I kept forgetting we were being filmed. "Hal, why don't you come along, too? Who knows, maybe I'll find a fake Bigfoot corpse and we can name him Roswell."

"You know, I worked on a documentary about aliens, too. It was pretty rad." Hal followed me and we chatted about life on other planets. I noticed that someone or something had been through this part of the woods recently. The foliage was broken and matted in a clear trail that led off to the east. I guessed that these obvious tracks probably led to another fake clue, so I changed course and followed it, Hal in tow, still rambling on about ETs and UFOs.

"I mean, the possibilities are staggering. How could there *not* be intelligent life elsewhere?" he was asking when I shushed him.

"I hear something. What is that?" I asked.

A rustling sound came from some underbrush. I gestured for Hal to shadow me, reminding him with a finger to my lips to keep silent. We walked slowly, careful not to step on any branches.

As we got closer, we heard a grumbling sound.

I turned back to Hal. "It could be a hurt animal. Don't make any sudden moves," I whispered. I would have loved to help a bear in need, but I knew better than to do so without a tranquilizer dart or three.

I stopped right away when I spotted a shirt on the ground. Last time I checked, bears didn't wear rhinestone-studded T-shirts. Neither did Bigfoot. I turned to Hal, who walked toward the discarded shirt.

"Hal," I whispered as loudly as I could. "We should go. It's probably Jake and some chick," I said, feeling strangely a little sad for Caroline. Hadn't she learned her lesson?

Sure enough, after a few slurping face-sucking noises, a male voice said, "Did she notice anything?"

My suspicions were confirmed. It was definitely Jake. Again.

I tapped the cameraman's back. "Hal!" I said in my regular voice. "I feel like a pervert. We shouldn't be here. Can we go now?"

"Dude, I can't. I'm under orders to capture the romantic stuff and anytime anyone fights. Colin wants drama," Hal said, shrugging.

"But it's prime time! You can't show any nudity or anything."

"I wouldn't film anything like that. You worry too much," he said with an indulgent smile.

"I'm going back." I turned and walked about five feet until a girly giggle rang through the trees. I bit down on my lip, hard. That voice was too familiar to ignore.

"Jake!" Lyssa cooed. She erupted into laughter again.

That did it. Fire threatened to escape the top of my head and my vision turned red. I was going to kill Jake.

"Oh for the love of god!" I screeched, storming the couple, trailed by the camera. "Get your goddamn hands off my sister, Jake."

"We were just hanging, no big deal." Jake protested when he saw me. They sat on the ground together, but jumped up immediately.

Jake was shirtless, in his jeans, and my younger sister was in her infamous short-shorts and a strappy tank top. I let out the breath I was holding. At least Lyssa was dressed.

I wrenched Lyssa away from Jake, and planted myself between them.

I pinched the bridge of my nose, willing my headache to go away. Instead, a wild rushing sound filled my ears. Without thinking about it, I launched myself at Jake and punched him squarely in the jaw. There was a fantastic cracking sound as my fist made contact with his face.

"My face!" he squealed like a little baby.

I wished I had hit his nose. God, how I would have loved to break that jerk's nose. I started to go back in to finish the job, but someone was holding me back.

"Sam!" Lyssa spat out my name.

I ignored my sister and continued to bark obscenities at Jake about his lack of respect for his girlfriend and for women in general, while I tried to evade the arms that were around my waist.

"Just two weeks ago you were making out with Caroline, and now you have to go after my little sister? And what about your actual girlfriend? Does she know what an ass you are?"

"He's not really with Melody. That's just for show," Lyssa said. "Right, Jake?"

Jake distanced himself from Lyssa and my fist but didn't answer.

"I'm sure that's what he said, but I doubt it's true," I practically shouted. "I've heard them on the phone. It sounds real to me."

After a few moments of struggle, I gave up. Reason was starting to filter back into my brain and my need to destroy Jake's face was fading.

With a sinking heart, I heard the unmistakable sound of Devan's voice behind me say, "Jesus, Jake, what the hell were you thinking?"

"Shit." It was Devan who had held me back. His arms, both the good one and the sprained one, were still securely around my waist.

"I'm okay," I snapped. "Let me go, damn it."

Once I was free, I swung around and confirmed his presence. "Of course you'd have to be here to witness this."

Devan looked down at me, his mouth open in surprise.

I narrowed my eyes at Devan and gritted my teeth. "You don't have to get involved. I can take care of this," I said, my face burning from the mortification of Lyssa and me living up to his image of my family. I had to take charge of the situation.

Devan blinked, and a hurt expression spread onto his face, like he was upset I didn't want his help. He shook his head, and turned from me to Hal.

Shit. Shit, Shit, Shit!!!!!

I forgot that Hal was filming.

Hal's eyes were as wide as an alien's and his hand shook as he held the camera.

"Did you get everything? Enough underage drama?" I advanced on Hal, hands on my hips.

Hal took the camera off his shoulder and looked down in embarrassment. "I'm sorry, Sam, really I am . . ."

Devan held out one hand to interrupt Hal. "But, you'll be erasing that footage, correct?" Devan pulled out his British charm and boyish smile. "You're a good guy, right, Hal?"

I knew there was no chance this tactic would work, based on what Hal had told me earlier about his mandate to film anything remotely scandalous.

"Listen, I like you guys," Hal said. "And I feel bad about it, but Colin and the executives will have my ass if I don't provide the footage. It's not my call."

He did seem sorry, but sorry wouldn't save my sister and me from nationally televised humiliation, not to mention the gossip blogs and magazines, which would love to know about Jake cheating on Melody.

"Listen, my agent is not going to be happy," Jake tried to reason with Hal. "And neither is my publicist. Or Melody's publicist. I have a squeaky-clean reputation to uphold. And if my agent's not happy, Colin isn't going to be happy either, so why don't you just give me the footage and we can pretend this didn't happen." He held out his hand but Hal didn't move.

Jake pointed a finger at Hal and whined, "Not cool, man. You'll be sorry!" Then, grabbing his shirt and nodding at Lyssa, he added, "I'm outta here," and stomped off into the woods. Lyssa stared after him as if he were on a freaking white horse, and not the repulsive source of this mess.

"I don't see what the big deal is. We were just kissing." Lyssa tried to smooth her own messy hair. "Who knows? Maybe the video will kick off a modeling career for me or something. A lot of reality TV stars started off by dating celebrities."

I clenched my fists and shook them out so I wouldn't be tempted to use them again. My eyes shot nuclear missiles at my sister. "You need to stop talking! Now! I don't know how you could do that to another girl. How would you like it if someone made out with your boyfriend and everybody knew it?"

Lyssa's mouth snapped closed, her eyes wide at my uncharacteristic explosion of anger.

My head pounded. I shut my eyes and pressed the heels of my hands against them. "Just . . . please, don't say another word." I kept my eyes closed, hoping it would make my headache go away, but it didn't.

"Lyssa," I whispered in her ear, dragging her away from Hal and his camera. "I'm going to walk you back to Mom and Dad, and you're going to stay there until we figure out what to do with you."

"You can't tell Mom and Dad!" Lyssa said in a tiny voice.

"Oh my god! How are you so naive!?" I wanted to shake her. "Didn't you hear what Hal just said? All of America is going to see your little act—including Mom and Dad! Do you know what happens to people who get caught cheating with famous people? I'll give you a hint. It's not good. We're going to have sleazy photographers camping out on our lawn and following you to school."

My sister started crying, and not the pretty tears she perfected during her pageant days. These were ugly, snotty sobs that emanated from somewhere deep inside her gut. "Now Mom and Dad will hate me," she said. "And Caroline's going to hate me. And you hate me . . ."

"I don't hate you." I inhaled, and took a step toward her, but then I realized exactly what she had said. "Wait. Why is Caroline going to hate you?"

"Because I told her I'd be back after lunch to help her finish the challenge, and now we're going to lose." Lyssa began bawling again.

Oh, freaking hell, the challenge. Another disaster. Defeated, I threw my hands in the air and said, "Fine. Do whatever you want. I'm done." Without another word, I plunged into the woods, stumbling as quickly as I could through the brush, until I knew I was completely alone.

I leaned my head against a big tree. Tears rolled down my cheeks as I stood motionless, my forehead pressed against the rough bark. This was a catastrophe, and I couldn't fix it. I had tried. There were no other tricks up my sleeves or tools on my Swiss Army knife.

How could I lose my cool like that? Once that footage aired, Lyssa would forever be branded as the trashy girl who Jake cheated on America's tween sweetheart with, and I'd be her trainwreck of a sister. And I'd never get into a good school—who would accept a student with such overt anger management issues? Hell, Jake would have every right to press charges, and then I'd have an assault on my record, too.

But it didn't matter because I'd never be able to afford college now. I had completely ruined our chances of ever winning this contest. I'd let my self-control falter for one moment, and managed to destroy both my dignity and my future medical career.

The swish of overgrown foliage behind me announced Devan's arrival. How could I face him now that he had witnessed the worst in me?

"Your sister and Hal took off to find Caroline. They want to finish the challenge," he said softly.

"Good." I didn't think I was capable of more coherent thoughts. I just wanted him to go away.

"Sam . . . I . . . I'm really sorry about what happened." He touched my shoulder. I remained facing the tree, and he pulled his hand away. "I want you to know I don't think any less of you."

Boy, was that the wrong damn thing to say. My eyes narrowed and I turned on him. "You mean, you don't think any less of me because my sister was taken advantage of by a D-list reality show host? That's so kind of you to not lump me in with my sister." It felt good to get some more of my anger off my chest.

"No! Sam, listen . . ."

"I don't need your approval. Or anyone's."

I pushed past him, and Devan stumbled a little. Then he reached out and grabbed my arm and turned me around to face him.

"Samantha, I can't stop thinking about you and last night by the campfire. Maybe I'm imagining things, but you've completely gotten under my skin like . . . like a . . . festering rash, but in a good way," he babbled.

I squinted my eyes and tried to keep up with him.

"Well, that's kind of disgusting. But here's the thing, even though you're infuriating, and your family's beyond embarrassing, I can't stop thinking there's something between us." He gave me a hopeful smile. "If it weren't for this ridiculous contest, I wonder if you and I could be . . ."

"Whoa. Stop right there." I pushed his hand off my arm. "Yes, we had a moment. But it doesn't make up for the fact that you just said I'm like a festering rash, and my family is embarrassing. Then you say you like me, even though it sounds like you really wish you didn't. And what was with the hedgehog comment? How the hell am I like a hedgehog?"

"You know, they're spiky and irritable, but adorable."

The veins in my neck were throbbing, and my pulse sped up from the adrenaline. My body was prepared for a fight, even if my heart wasn't.

"God, I hate this contest! I hate Bigfoot, and I hate you!"

Devan winced, like I had poured fire ants down his boxers, which I totally would have, if I had any handy.

I stopped and took a deep breath. "I'm sorry. I don't hate you." I swiveled around to face him. "But, look, Devan, you've made it obvious what you think about my family and me. You've called us trashy and ridiculous since day one, and now you've been proven right. So, yay for you. You win."

Devan's face fell. "I never called *you* trashy or ridiculous!"

"You might as well have. You said my family was and that's the same thing. And I could have handled that on its own, if you hadn't been so horrified by the idea of my sister dating your friend. Kyle likes Sophie. How dare you stick your nose in and try to mess that up?"

Devan clenched his jaw. "First of all, I was never trying to mess that up. Dr. DeGraw made it very clear she expected us to focus exclusively on the challenge. I simply reminded Kyle he didn't need any more distractions."

"Honestly, Devan, I don't care what you or your professor think. As soon as this challenge is over, so are we. Let's just get it over with and find a few more fake-ass fake clues."

"Fine," he said with ice in his voice. "You'd know all about fake clues, wouldn't you?"

My stomach dropped. "What?"

"I know it was you who made those claw marks in the tree near our cabin." Devan was eerily calm as he said this.

I opened my mouth to protest, but he cut me off.

"Don't deny it, Sam. We have proof. Caroline found a scrap of fabric at the scene and she matched it to the threads in your sweatshirt when you were staying at the cabin."

I felt sick. The tears I had held back when I was yelling at him, burst forth. "That was just a prank," I blubbered. "I'm so sorry . . ."

Devan stood watching me cry, without expression.

"Why didn't you say anything?" I gulped and wiped at my eyes.

He sighed, "In the end it worked out fine, so . . . besides, we're even now."

"What do you mean?" I sniffed.

"You were right. Caroline was using Jake to get information, but not the way you thought. She only got close to him so she could hack his phone to give us a heads up on the upcoming challenges, just in case. I didn't know at the time. But she admitted it the other day. She was trying to cheat and if she had gotten caught, she could have gotten us disqualified, too."

I knew it! But the superior feeling of being right was short-lived. It didn't matter. Everything was still a chaotic mess and All My Freaking Fault.

"What do we do now?" I whispered.

Devan shook his head and stared at the ground. "How about we split up the remaining territory and spend the rest of the day sweeping for clues on our own. Then we can pack up and head back with whatever we find by the end of the day."

I just nodded. That sounded like the best I could expect at this point.

Chapter 24

"I've heard of Bigfoot hunters who use a recording
of a crying baby for bait. They hope a female Bigfoot will be
compelled to take care of the infant. I think causing
emotional distress on purpose is cruel and unethical."

—*Sophie Berger, volunteer, North Ohio Animal Shelter and Sanctuary*

The walk back to camp was unnervingly quiet, other than the occasional branch breaking under my feet, or the buzzing of mosquitoes
in my ear. I never noticed before how much I relied on my big
mouth in uncomfortable situations. But this was one situation I
couldn't talk my way out of. Nothing I said would have made it any
better, so I willed my lips to stay shut.

Devan rolled his shoulder and issued a sigh, but otherwise
seemed more than willing to pretend to be in a silent movie.

Halfway there Beth and Dr. Sawyer pulled up in the Jeep. I
guessed Hal must have called them ahead of time.

Dr. Sawyer gave us a little salute. "Hey there," he said, reaching
out his hand to help Devan into the Jeep. The doctor took my
makeshift sling off of Devan and handed it to me with a grin before
pulling out a real one for him.

"Can I take a look?" the doctor asked Devan as he unwrapped
his injured arm. "Nice job, Samantha!" He whistled to show how
impressed he was. "Devan, you're very lucky to have been with this
young lady."

"Quite." Devan's dry tone suggested he felt exactly the opposite
of lucky.

"Samantha, you'd make a great medic out in the field if you ever wanted to join the army."

It was something I'd considered in the past, as a way to pay for medical training, but I ruled it out. I couldn't imagine being in a war zone, especially after everything Devan told me about his parents.

"No thanks. I'm a lover, not a fighter."

"Ha!" Devan scoffed, earning a death glare from me.

I might have even grinned a bit when the doctor wrapped a fresh bandage so tightly that Devan yelped.

The doctor patted Devan on the shoulder. "Well, kid," he said. "You're going to be fine. As Samantha probably told you, it's sprained, not broken, but try to take some time to rest. Maybe with a pretty nurse?" Dr. Sawyer's eyes twinkled. Clearly, he had completely missed the palpable animosity between Devan and me.

Carefully avoiding Devan's eyes, I smiled at the doctor. "No offense, but I hope we don't see you again."

"None taken." He shook my hand warmly and smiled. "Stay healthy."

I declined the ride in the Jeep that Beth offered. I couldn't wait to get away from Devan and have a few moments alone to digest all that had happened in the previous two days. As the Jeep drove away, Devan turned to look at me over his shoulder. I crossed my arms and watched him go.

I trudged the last quarter of a mile toward my campsite, suddenly feeling the full exhaustion of a sleepless night, followed by a very emotionally charged day.

Sophie stood behind one of the tents, out of sight of the remote cameras, and as far as possible from my mom and Lyssa, who were yelling and crying.

I sidled up next to her. "Hey, you okay?"

She jumped. "Oh! I didn't hear you come up the hill."

"I can't imagine why. It's so quiet and peaceful here," I said, pursing my lips.

She threw her arms around me, and started bawling. Stunned, I returned her hug and didn't say anything for a few moments.

"Is this about Lyssa?" I asked.

"No. It's about Kyle," Sophie said in between sobs.

"What happened?" My stomach dropped with dread.

"I don't know!" Sophie said, tears running down her cheeks "We had such a nice time together, then the cameras were off, and he told me that he has to concentrate on the competition." She wiped her red-rimmed eyes on her arm. "He said I'm a distraction, and he needed space. How can he need space when we never really dated?"

I chewed the inside of my cheek, pausing to answer her. Even though I knew it wasn't entirely Devan's fault, I blamed him. He must have convinced Kyle to break up with Sophie because of the challenge and Dr. DeGrouch. "So he waited until the middle of the challenge to end it with you?"

Sophie nodded and loudly sniffled. She was a goopy mess. "This is pathetic," she choked out. "You can't break up with someone you barely know, right?"

"It's not pathetic. It's longer than any relationship I've ever had."

"Our family is so embarrassing. It's no wonder he got scared off." She started crying again.

"This isn't fair," I said with more force than I intended.

Sophie, who was usually so composed in a yoga teacher kind of way, struggled to catch her breath in between sobs. "I'm sorry. I don't want to cry over a guy. I'm not that pitiful." She hiccuped and choked at the same time. "It's more about wanting what I can't have, like going to a great college and dating someone like Kyle, and for a little while, I forgot about all that . . ."

My head throbbed from everything I was holding back from my sister. I took a deep breath and said, "Kyle does like you. I think he's just confused about his priorities. That DeGraw lady was all over them to focus on winning and forget about being nice human beings."

Sophie nodded and dabbed at her eyes one more time.

"So, what else did I miss?" I asked, changing the subject.

"Mom's going apoplectic over Lyssa's adult film debut. Lyssa said it's no big deal. That it will help us win. Mom and Dad talked to Colin who wouldn't do anything." Sophie wrung her hands. A stray hair fell in front of her eyes.

"I can't say I'm surprised, but it still sucks." I moved the offending hair back behind my sister's ear. "How are we related to them, again?"

My father sat quietly watching from the sidelines, while my mother was confiscating clothes from Lyssa's tent, which was a little like closing the barn door after the horse escaped. "No!" Lyssa shouted. "Those are my favorite shorts," she said. "I promise I won't wear them on television."

"Ugh. I hate when people automatically blame the girl because of what she wears," I said.

Sophie nodded. "And what about Jake? It was just as much his fault as Lyssa's. If not more. He's the one with the girlfriend and the paparazzi following."

"Yeah, I doubt he's crying now," I said, frowning. "I guess I better go into the breach and see if I can help."

My sister gave me the hint of a smile. "Better you than me. I'm awful in a crisis. I never know what to say."

"I don't either. I just make shit up and try to calm everyone down. Sometimes it works, sometimes it doesn't," I said.

Sophie crawled into our tent out of the line of fire.

I stomped into the fray and my mom immediately grabbed my arm and dragged me over to Lyssa's tent. My dad had joined them, too. "Myron, tell your daughter what a foolish thing she did. Tell

Lyssa that she'll end up a joke on the Internet and no nice boy will want to date her now."

I pulled my arm away from her and gave Lyssa a sympathetic glance. Her face was so pale, I worried she would faint. Lyssa retreated to her tent and zipped the door closed.

"Mom! This isn't helping," I said. "It's done and we can't undo it."

"Well, it wouldn't be as bad if you hadn't decided to punch that boy and swear a blue streak!"

I was miserable. "I know. I agree. I don't know how it happened. I just lost it."

My mom huffed, "Well, I don't know what to say. You girls have truly embarrassed the whole family."

"*We're* embarrassing?" I snapped at my mom. "Don't you realize how your ridiculous 'Wood Ape' obsession has ruined all of our lives? We've been the laughingstock of our school since sixth grade when you were interviewed for the *Shopper's News*!"

Her mouth fell open. "Samantha, I . . . I had no idea you hated all this so much . . . I'm sorry . . . I never meant to . . ." Her face crumpled and she burst into tears. She turned and zipped herself into her tent.

I called after her, "Mom, I'm sorry. I was angry. I didn't mean it." But she didn't respond.

Now it was just me and my dad, who waved for me to join him on one side of the tree line.

"Dad, I only said that about Bigfoot because I was upset with Mom. I feel terrible."

"It's okay, Sammy," he said. "I understand. And I'm sorry you always seem to be in the middle of everything." He drew little circles in the dirt with his foot. "I feel awful that I exposed you girls to this pressure. It's hard enough being a teen without cameras watching. I just thought it would be fun and that we could maybe win some money for college."

"We still can. It's not over yet. Not until the fat Sasquatch sings, right?"

"Right." He grasped my hand and gave me a weak smile. "Take care of yourself, Sammy. Believe it or not, we'll be fine. I'll figure out how to send you to school. It may have to be a state school, but more than anyone else, it would be good for you to get away from the rest of us. Find out who you are when you don't have to worry so much about everyone else."

It was the most serious I'd seen my dad in a while. I could tell he was much more upset than he let on earlier.

"Thanks, Dad. I appreciate it. I really do, but I know about the bank calling."

I didn't think it was possible, but his face fell even further. "Dad, I won't bankrupt the family. I'll find another way. Maybe I'll sell Lyssa's tape."

My dad just grimaced at my attempt at humor.

"Too soon?" I asked.

"Let me do the worrying, and the joking, too," he said.

"At least mine are funny." I attempted a small grin, which went unanswered.

"I'm serious, Sammy. You take on too much. Your mother and I will handle Lyssa, and Sophie can manage herself. You can't control everything."

I nodded. Maybe he was right. All the worrying I did, and I still couldn't fix anything for either of my sisters. And I certainly messed things up for myself, too.

"I better go check on your mom," he said, and climbed into their tent.

I was alone, surrounded by tents filled with my weeping family. I plopped down, defeated, onto a log and tried to let them cry it out like cranky babies. But, it was impossible.

"Oh, screw it." This whole situation was absurd, and I couldn't stand it anymore. I jumped back up, scraping my hand on the rough bark in the process. "Enough! There isn't a show, or a contract, or money, or even a college important enough to put our family through this," I hollered.

My bleary-eyed sisters and red-eyed parents emerged from their tents when they heard me yelling.

"Seriously. Let's just walk away and quit," I said.

When no one answered me, I continued. "I'll start!" Stepping back and making a megaphone around my mouth with my hands, I called out, "I quit! You hear that? Colin? Hal? Squatch? I don't care if you exist. I'm done with all of you! I QUIT!" I shouted so loudly my throat hurt. I probably blew out the microphones attached to the cameras in the trees.

I looked around at my family, waiting for one of them to quit along with me, but they were surprisingly quiet.

My dad's eyebrows joined together in solidarity. "We're not quitters, Samantha."

My mom nodded and stood behind Lyssa, wrapping her arms around her daughter. She kissed my sister's cheek. "We'll get through this. It's not all on you."

Lyssa started to cry again, but she nodded through her tears.

"Sophie, how about you?" I asked.

She studied her feet. "I don't crave the spotlight, but I'm not ready to quit. Especially not when we have a good shot of winning."

"You sure?" I asked.

Sophie met my eyes and nodded quickly.

"Fine. Okay, it's settled. We won't quit," I said with a scratchy throat. The woods around us were silent. "Do you think I need to take back my resignation?"

"No. We got it." Colin's voice echoed from behind a nearby tree. He and Hal stepped out into view and gave me a thumbs-up.

"Can you redo the quitting scene again? So I can get a second angle?" Hal asked, positioning his camera on his shoulder.

"Don't push me," I said, wiping my bloody hand on my pants, and wondering if I was doing the right thing or not.

Chapter 25

"Some people believe that Bigfoot is the living
ancestor of a giant ape called *Gigantopithecus* who roamed Asia
millions of years ago. I'm not convinced. It would be hard to
miss bones that size, never mind actual animals."

—*Dr. Roberta DeGraw, advisory expert for* "Myth Gnomers"

Luckily, we weren't called on set until late the next morning. Sleep, even in a duct-taped tent with my older sister snoring in my ear, was exactly what I needed. I woke with awful breath and tangled hair, but also a fire in my belly. Instead of blaming it on the canned beans I ate, I chalked the feeling in my stomach up to a new resolution to kick both British and Bigfoot butt and go home. And in order to do that, I needed a pilfered Pop-Tart. Stat.

While still in the tent, I poked Sophie with the box, which I had kept hidden in my backpack. Fortunately, no bears had come sniffing around in the night.

"Ouch! What is that?"

"Pop-Tarts. Stolen ones from the cabin. They taste better that way," I said.

Without opening her eyes, my sister held out her hand and made a grabbing motion. "Gimme."

I unwrapped the foil and handed her one.

"Thanks," she said while chewing the dry part. "Yuck! This isn't cinnamon." Her eyes opened wide and she grimaced as if offended by the fake blueberry filling.

"Someone ate all of the good flavors. I could only get my hands on the blueberry ones. Do you not want any?"

"I didn't say that." She sat up and wiped the crumbs from her mouth and the sleep from her eyes, then went back to chewing, loudly.

"How are you feeling?" I asked. Her color was better, but she was still looking thin and tired. And even still, she was lovely in the morning. It was more than a little unfair.

"Better; although, I guess I would have to be, compared to a couple of days ago." Sophie let out a wistful sigh and flopped back onto her pillow sporting a bittersweet smile.

"What's with the Mona Lisa look?" I asked.

"I was just remembering how sweet Kyle was when I was sick. He took care of me and kissed my cheek and forehead."

I wiped the last crumb off her chin. "Yeah, but Grandma used to do that, too," I said. "Did he make you red Jell-O with little pieces of fruit in it?"

Sophie sat up again and whacked me with her pillow. "I didn't say he acted like Grandma. He didn't smell like sugar-free oatmeal cookies, or call me anything in Yiddish."

"I would hope not. It's not a very sexy language," I said.

"Grandpa would probably disagree."

"Ew!" I threw the pillow back. Sophie's eyes got misty, and she stopped laughing and sighed. "What I was going to tell you, before you interrupted to discuss Grandma's sex life, is that Kyle had said he couldn't wait to kiss me for real, when I was feeling better."

I was in no position to offer her advice. My own recent kissing session had been such a disaster. Not that I was ready to talk about it.

"That's really sweet," I said. "I'd assumed he already made a move."

My sister's lips turned down a little more. She waved the rest of her breakfast pastry in frustration. "How could he? Devan and Caroline were always there. Plus, I was really sick and phlegm and kissing don't exactly go well together. I wish I could have had some more time with him, you know, just the two of us . . . Then maybe he wouldn't have ended things."

"Hey, do you want me to cause some sort of distraction so Devan and Caroline and the cameras leave you alone and you can talk?" I offered. "I could dress up in a Bigfoot costume, or punch Devan or something. My preference is the latter."

Sophie opened her mouth widely and popped the rest of her breakfast in. When she finished chewing she said, "No. Don't punch anyone. You've done enough punching lately. It's over now."

And just like that she was serene Sophie again, but my urge to sock it to Devan didn't go away as quickly.

"Not even a little slap? Or a pinch?" I asked. "You gotta give me something. A paper cut at least?"

I was still trying to cheer Sophie up when my dad poked his head into the tent.

"Girls, it would be a great idea to wear our team uniform today, to show solidarity," he said.

"We don't have a team uniform, Dad. Do I even want to know what you have in mind?" I raised an eyebrow, maybe two, at him, and wished I had a third when he pointed to the shirt he was wearing.

"Oh, hell no!" I said.

Sophie gasped.

My dad was wearing a bright orange T-shirt with Hebrew-style lettering on it that said "Shalom Sasquatch," complete with a drawing of Bigfoot holding a menorah.

"What the eff is that?" I choked out. Words couldn't describe its ugliness. Gagging could possibly do the trick. Or maybe there was a Klingon word with a whole lot of vowels and glottal sounds that could vocalize just how hideous this shirt was.

My dad beamed. "I got us all matching shirts for Hanukkah, but I thought we could wear them now."

Even Sophie, who was admittedly less of a fashionista than I was, looked like she was going to hurl fake blueberry filling all over the tent.

"Dad, why are they bright orange?" she asked.

"For safety reasons. So you can be seen by hunters and not get shot. Aren't they hilarious? Wait until you see how cute your mom and Lyssa look in them," he said with a boyish grin.

Lyssa was wearing that monstrosity? She must have been desperate to get on my parents' good side again. I struggled to put my boots on, not bothering to change out of my pajamas. I had to see my mom and Lyssa in the traffic-cone colored shirts. I stared at the shirt, speechless for a good fifteen seconds before I could form sarcastic words again. "We don't have to worry about guys coming on to Lyssa anymore, so mazel tov on that."

Lyssa crossed her arms in front of her chest and opened her mouth to say something, but probably thinking the better of it, shut it.

My mom smiled at my dad and patted his arm. "Well, I like them," she said to us. "It's good to have a sense of humor about yourself. It's one of the things I love most about your dad."

"It's clearly not his fashion sense. Lyssa, what do you think?" I goaded her.

"Whatever makes everybody else happy." Lyssa stared at her sneakers.

Realizing that the appalling T-shirt wasn't even close to the most embarrassing thing about my family, I gave in and took the shirt my dad held out to me.

He frowned at my hesitation. "Aren't you proud of who you are?" he asked. "Jews don't have to hide in this country. My grandfather fought in World War II so you could wear this shirt."

"Oh, don't get me wrong," I said. "It's not the Jewish part that's embarrassing. It's the Bigfoot part. And orange isn't really my color." I gestured to the possibly flammable fluorescent shirt.

"Well, Sammy," my dad stroked the stubble on his chin. "Perhaps they are a bit bright."

"Just like you girls, bright and cheery," my mom said, flashing her eyes at me. The subtext was clear: make your father happy and wear the damn shirts.

Sophie threw her shirt over the tank top she was wearing and I did the same. Shortly thereafter my family marched back to the base camp for the judges' table, one behind the other, like prisoners on a chain gang. Nothing good ever happened in this shade of orange.

"If Dad was so into ugly uniforms and team sports, why didn't we all take up bowling like Mom?" I grumbled the entire way.

We were the first team to arrive, which was fine with me. My parents and sisters sought out Mindy for makeup to complement the orange shirts. *Good luck with that.*

I leaned up against a nearby tree, letting it support me. Constantly carrying around so much family stress was exhausting, and I suddenly felt like I was going to collapse under the weight.

The slam of a metal door made me jump. Jake burst out of the production trailer with Colin hot on his heels.

"Jake, wait," Colin said. "This is a good thing! This is really going to catapult your career. Think apologies on late night talk shows, and spreads in celebrity magazines. Plus, romantic tension is great for ratings. You'll see." Colin had a wolfish grin, which disappeared when he saw Jake's stormy expression.

"You mean it will catapult *your* career. I'm the one who has to deal with the angry fan base and the paparazzi," Jake snarled, marching off.

"Oh, sorry, Sam," Colin said a bit sheepishly when he noticed me standing there. "Listen, I told your parents the same thing. I wish I could help you guys, but that footage is fantastic. It's going to be picked up by every major news outlet. Sorry." He shrugged and shuffled to his director's chair, where Beth was standing by to hand him a huge stack of folders.

He accepted the bundle, barely glancing at her. "Colin!" she said in a harsh tone. "Here are the production sheets for today and in this folder is everything you need for the rest of the shoot. And this is my letter of resignation." Beth handed him a thin business-sized envelope.

Colin stood up from his chair and the folders fell from his lap onto the grass. He made no move to retrieve them. "What? You're quitting? Why? We're almost done here." He started pacing. "Beth, I need you! I can't replace you so quickly." He kept talking, not waiting for an answer from her. "Did you get another job? Because, unless it's CNN, you need to stay here and finish this out."

Throughout his tirade, Beth stood with her arms by her side and calmly watched him like he was an agitated tiger in a cage at the zoo. Everyone on set had stopped what they were doing to watch their exchange.

"I'm leaving because of the footage you insist on using," she said. "I don't want to be part of a show that degrades young girls." Her voice started to falter. "That's not the kind of work I want to do. I'll find something else. I'm sorry, but I have to quit."

Colin hung his head. "I could try to talk you out of this, but I know it probably wouldn't work. I respect your decision." He gazed at her with wide, almost admiring eyes. "I don't know what the hell I'm going to do without you, though."

Beth turned and strode away to the production trailer, leaving Colin standing defeated, amidst the mess of papers and folders, watching her go.

I searched around for Sophie, and found her sitting at one of the picnic tables alone and dejected, tearstains evident on her face. I guessed she hadn't had a chance to talk to Kyle yet.

Sophie rubbed her eyes and blew her nose. Traces of mascara were on her hands and on the tissue. "I hope Mindy can fix me up again. I must be a mess."

"Nah, you're fine. You just look like someone who's had their heart broken, slept on the ground, and was forced to wear the ugliest polyester T-shirt to ever grace the earth. No biggie."

Sophie started laughing a little at first, then hysterically. My joke hadn't been that funny, but before I knew it, I joined her and laughed until my stomach hurt in an I-ate-too-many-tacos way. We must have been loud because Devan and Kyle homed in on us as they walked toward the base camp.

"Stop, stop," Sophie whispered to me between bursts of laughter, when she noticed the boys staring and Steve's camera fixated on us.

"No, don't. The boys probably think we're laughing at them. It will make them completely paranoid."

"Awesome."

My sister and I stood and linked arms, snickering, and trotted right by the bewildered boys and into the makeup trailer.

Chapter 26

"I was helping my wife pick tomatoes in our backyard when our Yorkies started barking their little heads off. Wouldn't you know it, there was this big hairy thing flashing by me. I'm just glad he didn't take any of her prize-winning tomatoes."

—*Jim Duckworthy, interview in* "Witness to Bigfoot the Majestic"

Colin straightened the edge of his button-down shirt and cleared his throat. "Okay, let's get everyone in places for the judging."

"Devan and Sam," Colin said, "I'm going to need you to stand closer. You need to be in the same frame. At this point, I'd settle for the same state."

I inched closer to him, but refused to meet his eyes and did my best impression of a statue.

Devan's eyebrows squished together when he took in my shirt. "Why do you look like a giant Cheeto?"

"Why do you care is a better question."

"I don't care, but I *am* morbidly curious."

I turned to glare at him and that's when I realized he was out of his sling.

"How's your arm?" A bandage peeked out from the bottom of his sleeve. His eyes got soft and melty on me. "It's better. Thank you."

"Good. You're welcome." I gave him a professional nod.

"Sam . . ." Devan whispered. "I want to apologize."

I cut him off with a brisk shake of my head. I didn't want to second-guess my decision, not right before we were going to be filmed.

"I didn't mean those awful things about your family. If you had let me continue . . ."

"Not now," I said through gritted teeth.

He had voiced his opinion more than enough earlier. I couldn't bear to hear him utter one more word. I closed my eyes, to further shut him out, and waited for the judges to get into place.

I opened my eyes just in time to see Jake slither into the clearing with a snarl on his face. He knew we were all watching him and loathing him. I couldn't decide which was more obnoxious, his pouty babyface or his shiny skin-tight embroidered dragon shirt. Jake may as well have worn a shirt that said Bad Guy on it.

"Asshole," Devan spat out, directed at Jake.

"You know the microphone is on, right?"

"I don't care."

"What do you care about?" I asked with a huff.

He opened his mouth to answer, but he clamped his mouth shut when the guest judge ambled onto the set. It was Dr. DeGraw, decked out in a beige linen dress, big floppy hat, and a mic pinned to her collar. My eyes narrowed. "I thought she was only here in an off-camera advisory capacity."

"The other judge got malaria and had to bow out."

"Oh. That's awful," I gasped. Malaria could be deadly. And here I was worrying about a Bigfoot hunting contest.

Devan noticed my concern and his expression softened. "The guy'll be fine. They caught it early."

"Good." I let out my breath, which I hadn't realized I was holding.

"You really do worry about everyone, even people you don't know."

I shrugged, trying not to show him any more pesky emotions. They always popped up when I tried to be mean or detached. "She's not a fair judge," I said. "She kind of hates me."

"But you're on my team, so it will be fine." Devan said.

He had a point. If Dr. DeGraw had to step in to judge, this was the best challenge for it. No matter which pair she chose as the winners, it would include one of my teammates.

"I'm not concerned," I said, but that could be filed under "L" for lying. The shoot began and I half listened to Dr. DeGraw rattle off an extensive list of the digs she had been on, the papers she had published, and a bunch of other crap I really didn't care about.

I glanced at Devan's strong profile. Yeah. He was right, not that I'd tell him. There had been something between us. And even if I hated his attitude toward my family, I had to admit that I couldn't stop thinking about him and our campfire kisses. But it didn't matter. I had the contest to think about. And I had blown any chances of any happiness between us when I told him I hated him. He probably hated me back now.

I snapped out of my angsty contemplation when Dr. DeGraw asked for the three teams to present their findings.

Jake preened into the camera, hiding his crankiness behind Hollywood bravado. "We'll start with our lovebirds, Kyle and Sophie."

The two looked miserable. You could have put an iceberg between them and their coolness toward each other would have kept it frozen through the summer.

Kyle was a wreck. His usually wrinkled clothes looked like they had been in a hamper for months. His sneakers were untied, and I could spot the toothpaste on his shirt from a few feet away. It was possible he was really unhappy with his decision to cut things off with Sophie. *Good.* I was glad it wasn't easy for him.

"I guess they aren't exactly birds of paradise," Jake joked. "Show us what you've got anyway."

Kyle gestured for Sophie to speak. With a hoarse voice she said, "Kyle and I heard some howling, which we traced back to an audio recorder in a tree. We could tell it was a fake because of the way it was repeated on a loop over and over. We also found some hair, which resembled the hair from a standard poodle."

Dr. DeGraw peered over her glasses at them. "A good effort, but we planted three other clues in your area. I'm very surprised that you didn't spot the fake blood." She waved to dismiss them.

"Next up, we have Caroline and Lyssa. If they find Bigfoot, he'll be a lucky dude." Jake winked.

"God, I hate him," I growled, until Devan shushed me. I waited for Colin to yell cut, but he just rolled his eyes.

Neither girl seemed offended, although it was hard to tell considering they both plastered big fake smiles on their faces for the camera and ignored Jake entirely. Caroline did the speaking. "We found three clues. There were animal bones, probably from a chicken. We know that Bigfoot doesn't have access to chickens in the forest, and tends to eat berries and other scavenged foods. Then we found some very suspicious um, feces," she curled her lip, annoyed at having to talk about poop.

Lyssa quickly added, "We also found the recorder with looping animal noises."

Dr. DeGraw pursed her wrinkled lips and the girls' beauty queen smiles faltered just a little.

"Good. But, you should have picked up on the footprints and the costumed intern we had running around out there."

Jake jumped into frame. "Devan and Sam are next. Let's see if they could stop fighting long enough to find anything." I rolled my eyes but Jake continued in a more conversational tone. "Yes, it seems Devan and Sam were arguing by a lake and he fell in and hurt his arm. At least they *say* that's what happened. Anyone else think there may've been some skinny-dipping involved . . . or other activities?" he waggled his eyebrows.

Dr. DeGraw cleared her throat.

"So what do you have for us?" Jake added.

I wanted to offer him a kick in the ass, but let my teammate answer.

"We found four clues." Devan's tone was clipped and businesslike but his face was a storm cloud about to burst. "A fake footprint, fake claw marks, and some other rubbish that was a gigantic waste of time. I can't do this!" Not waiting for a response, Devan marched off the set.

Dr. DeGraw called after him, "Devan, what do you think you're doing? There is no room for these kinds of antics. Get back here immediately!"

Caroline stepped forward, "Oh let him go, you old bag."

Everyone gasped at Caroline's slam, which seemed to have flown directly out of left field.

"Miss Bing, what on earth has come over you?" Dr. DeGraw demanded.

"I'm tired of you bullying us and telling us what to do every moment of the day." Caroline was calm but fierce. She took a step toward Dr. DeGraw's chair, but Kyle reached out and pulled her back. "You think you own us just because we were lucky enough to be accepted into your stuffy school. Honestly, it should be the other way around. Do you have any idea how much money our parents donate to Netherfield on top of our ridiculously expensive tuition? We pay your salary. You can't do anything to us."

Dr. DeGraw's lips were pressed into a thin white line, while her face was turning purple with rage. "This is absurd! I won't tolerate this behavior."

Kyle stepped in front of his sister. "I totally agree with Caroline. You can't tell me who I can be friends with anymore." He crossed back to Sophie and took her hand in his. "Sophie, I've been an ass and I'm sorry. I don't know why I let Dr. DeGraw's opinion, or anyone else's, matter to me. If I like someone I should tell them, right?" He glanced at her for approval.

"Right," she whispered, wide-eyed with a surprised smile blooming on her face.

"Will you give me another chance?" Kyle asked.

Sophie wiped a couple of tears from her eyes and nodded yes.

Kyle gave her a friendly one-handed bro-hug then glanced at the cameras and shrugged before he grabbed Sophie and kissed her. Half the crowd gasped, the other said "Awwwwww."

I was glad Kyle had finally figured out he was being a tool. I was also relieved to not have to kick his ass, which I had fully intended to do. I may have been smaller than him, but I was scrappy and I didn't fight fair. Not when my sister's heart was on the line.

"I won't sit here and listen to this nonsense!" Dr. DeGraw stood up and tottered off the set on her sturdy troll legs. "And you two are sorely mistaken if you think there's any way I'm allowing you to come back to Netherfield in the fall."

Colin threw his binder on the ground in frustration and shouted, "I guess we're taking a break! Let's come back in fifteen minutes and try to contain our outbursts, this time, please." He walked away muttering, "This is turning into a goddamned soap opera . . . Not what I had in mind."

Sophie and Kyle hugged. Caroline grinned like a Cheshire Cat. And everyone else started whispering about what had just gone down.

I went in search of Devan.

Chapter 27

"What if the search for Bigfoot is more about
looking for life beyond us? Or a desire to discover something
new in the world? But I don't take Philosophy 101
until next year, so check back with me then."

—*Devan Das, senior at Netherfield Academy*

It took a few minutes, but I finally found him tripping down the stairs of one of the production trailers.

"Devan, wait," I called, running to catch up with him. "What was that all about?"

He stopped when he heard me call. His breathing was shallow as if he'd just run a race. "I can't . . . Jake just makes me so angry . . ."

I put my hand on his bad arm by accident and he flinched. "I know you're upset. I hate Jake, too." I raised my voice and pleaded, "But we need this win. *I* need this win. I know you don't owe me anything, but please, we're so close to the finish. Please, come back."

He nodded his head once, and turned to walk back to the set with me.

Devan sighed and ran his hand through his hair, which had grown longer in the two-and-a-half weeks we had been here. It was a little floppy, but it suited him.

"Oh, by the way, you missed quite a show," I added. "Caroline and Kyle both flipped out on DeGraw. It was unbelievable."

"Really?" He seemed less surprised than I thought he would be by this news. Maybe the preps had all been complaining to each other about their hideous mentor.

As if I had summoned her with my thoughts, Dr. DeGraw was huffing and puffing her way directly toward us.

"What kind of thing do you think you were pulling back there, Devan?" She blinked her toadlike eyes at him, waiting for a response.

Devan just looked at the ground. His frustration rolled off of him in palpable waves.

"I thought I made myself clear," Dr. DeGraw continued. "Our school needs to win this money for research. I don't know what is going on with Caroline, or with you and Kyle and these *girls*, but you've all been unfocused and undisciplined since you arrived."

She said the word *girls* like we were common streetwalkers or an unknown sticky substance on her shoe.

"I'm very disappointed. In fact, if I were asked to write a college recommendation for you right now, I am not sure what I would say about your future." She pointed a stubby finger at his chest. "This is the last warning you will get from me, and that goes for your teammates, too."

Dr. DeGraw walked back over to her mark and arranged a sweet expression on her face. "I'm ready to begin again, Colin, whenever you are, dear."

Once everyone was wrangled back into position, and behaving, we started the shoot again. Colin let Devan present our faux evidence over. This time he went straight through it without throwing a fit, so yay for that.

Pushing her glasses up on her nose, Dr. DeGraw nodded once. "I believe we have our winners. Devan and Samantha, you two did a respectable job of searching every quadrant in a scientific and skeptical manner that was well suited to the task. And you found four clues, which is more than the other teams." Sweeping off her glasses, she said, "I wish you luck in the final challenge."

When the cameras cut away Devan put his hands on his knees and bent down, letting his breath out in a relieved stream, all traces of the cocky future Ivy Leaguer disappeared thanks to Dr. DeGraw. Now that it was gone, I actually missed his confidence. It was like he was a deflated balloon version of himself.

"I'm glad that's over." I attempted a chipper tone, but ended up sounding sarcastic. I had that kind of voice. Chipper was a stretch for me.

He nodded without looking at me. "Excuse me for a moment."

I swept my hand to the side in a formal gesture. "By all means."

I ripped my body mic off and threw the orange shirt over my head, not caring that the tank top underneath was more revealing than I would normally have worn. At least it wasn't the color of a pumpkin that spent too much time in a tanning booth.

My family clustered near the *Myth Gnomers* banner and seemed a whole lot happier than they did yesterday.

My dad gave my hand a quick squeeze when I joined them. "You did good, Sam. So did Devan."

Lyssa snorted. "After they all told Dr. DeGraw to go screw herself."

I imitated Dr. DeGraw's snobby tone, "I'm going to need you to find five fake clues that demonstrate you are indeed in hell."

Even Sophie cracked a real smile. "I think this shirt may be one."

"Put yours back on, Sam," my dad said. "It's family photo time!"

"Oooh. Great idea, Myron," my mom said. "Let me get Mindy. I think she has a good camera."

Not happy, I put the polyester blend nightmare back on. Mindy arrived with her camera and started directing the photo shoot. "I bet the publicity team will like these," she said. "Myron, why don't you stand in the middle? Brenda, you can be on one side, and Sam, you go on the other. Sophie and Lyssa can crouch down." I put my hands on my hips and tried to look as serious as I could while wearing the aforementioned shirt.

"Where is it?" Colin bounded out of the editing trailer and charged at us like a very angry badger.

Hal stepped in front of him and held him at arm's length. "Colin, calm down. Where's what?"

Colin directed his laser beam glare at me. "The footage of Lyssa and Jake—the memory card is gone and the file on the hard drive is erased."

I instinctively stepped back and held up my hands. "I don't have it, although I wish I did."

Colin's raised eyebrows told me he wasn't sure he believed me. He addressed the crew. "Everyone needs to stop what they're doing and figure out what the hell happened."

"Fine. But I'm sure an intern just erased it by mistake or something as simple as that," Hal said, pulling his saggy pants up and heading back to the editing trailer. He grabbed Steve and an unlucky intern on the way. Based on his cowering, the intern had overheard the conversation and was terrified he'd be the one to take the fall for the missing film. *Poor guy.*

After forcing myself to stop worrying about the intern's wellbeing, I allowed myself a little hope.

Colin grumbled, but then dashed over to his associate producer who was throwing her suitcase into the back of the Jeep. "Beth!" he said. "Please, don't leave yet. We may not be airing that footage after all."

She looked at her luggage for a moment, but the corners of her mouth turned up slightly. "Okay," she replied. "I'll finish out the day. Then we'll see . . ."

After Colin left, I turned around and caught Lyssa glaring at Jake who was sitting on one of the picnic tables playing with his phone.

I groaned. "To quote Devan, Jake really is a first-class wanker. I'm only sorry I didn't get to break his nose, too."

That made Lyssa smile. "Yeah, I don't know what I saw in him."

"And I'm sorry I was so harsh on you."

"It's okay. I shouldn't have been so naïve. Or done that to another girl. I just got carried away. I think I just wanted to be special."

"You are special, and you deserve a great guy who is going to treat you that way. And who wants to be with only you." I reached out and touched Lyssa's shoulder. "I just worry, and I forget that you're not me and you don't want to hang out in libraries or play nerdy board games all day. So, I'm gonna back off and let you be yourself, and make your own mistakes. But I'll be here if you need me."

"Thanks, Sam." Lyssa gave me a genuine smile.

Taking a deep breath, I grabbed my sister for a tight hug.

Lyssa squealed in surprise. "Ouch, Sam! It's okay. I love you, too."

"Sorry." I smiled at her wistfully.

"Hey, things are starting to go our way, for once," Lyssa said. "Kyle and Sophie are patching it up. And someone stole that footage."

"Didn't *you* steal it?" I asked. It seemed like the most logical explanation.

"No. It wasn't me."

Lyssa must have been telling the truth. If she had stolen the footage she would be the first to take credit for something so devious. "Who do you think it was? Jake?" I asked.

"No idea, but I doubt it was Jake. He's not smart enough. Plus that footage didn't go missing until after we started shooting and Jake was on set the whole time. Who knows, maybe it really did get erased by an intern."

Lyssa gave me one more squeeze before running off to talk to Mindy. I plopped myself down at the base of a big tree on the edge of the woods. I was relieved that the footage was gone, but something tugged at my brain. It was one of those feelings like when you know you've forgotten something important, but can't figure out what it is.

I was ecstatic that things were going to be okay for Sophie and Lyssa, of course, but it hurt that no one seemed to realize that things weren't okay for me. Sure, my dad tried to assure me that our finances were okay, but I didn't believe him. Plus, I was a mess, pining over a guy who maybe liked me for two seconds, before going back to despising me.

My throat tightened and my eyes prickled with itchy hot tears. I buried my nose in my book so no one would see me struggling to get my emotions under control.

"For all I know, you stole that footage." Dr. DeGraw's pinched voice echoed from around the other side of the big tree.

I peeked behind me and saw Devan with his hands on his hips. "That's farfetched."

"I can't believe you would throw away the contest for that girl." Her voice was measured, like she was finally trying to reason with him.

"Why not? It's just television." Devan was just inches from Dr. DeGraw's angry face. "It's not worth messing about with real people's lives."

She took a step closer to him and reached up to put a hand on his shoulder. "It's time to learn, Mr. Das, that some people are inconsequential."

"Sam is *anything* but inconsequential," Devan said through gritted teeth.

"This is your future, and it's important to keep your eye on the prize."

"Is that your lesson for the day?" Devan's voice took on a surprisingly cheerful tone.

"Maybe it is. I didn't realize you had to learn it," the older woman said.

He started laughing. "I think the only lesson I've learned today is that I wish you'd bugger off."

Dr. DeGraw straightened her spine so she could almost meet Devan's eyes. "I think it's time I have a chat with your father."

"Go ahead. I just talked to him myself. He'll probably have some choice words for you."

Dr. DeGraw sputtered and opened her mouth. "I'll talk to you when you've had some time to consider your actions. Now, I have a meeting with Colin in the production trailer. And you have a final challenge to win." She started to walk away and stopped like she was confused about the direction.

Devan gave a wry smile and pointed. "It's that way, Dr. DeGraw. Just go through those trees and cut through those bushes. You'll run right into it."

The professor stalked off without another word, into the shrubbery.

I couldn't believe what had just transpired. Without remembering to wipe my tears or brush the dirt off my pants, I stood and strode toward Devan, leaving everything behind. "Did you just send her through the poison oak?"

He smirked. "I may have."

My respect level for him rose exponentially. If anyone deserved to be an itchy mess, it was Dr. DeGraw.

"But what about your dad?"

Devan grinned. "I told him what was going on and you were right. He's proud of me no matter where I go to school. He was especially proud of me standing up to DeGraw."

"I'm so glad." I searched Devan's impish expression. Then it hit me. The only person who wasn't on set when the footage was erased was Devan.

"You took it, didn't you? You got rid of that footage." I studied him closely.

"I had help," he said, obviously pleased with himself. "Caroline coded a software bug that would cause any footage from that day to disappear permanently. All I had to do was get into the production trailer and install it on one of the computers."

"Oh. So that's why Caroline and Kyle chose to duke it out with DeGraw during the shoot. It was a distraction. Clever. But why would they do that for me?"

He shrugged. "Because I asked them to. The only really good thing about boarding school is that your friends become your family. We take care of each other. You've proven yourself to them, and to me, so they were happy to help. They created a diversion to give me time while everyone on the crew was occupied outside of the trailer. Although, I imagine it was obvious that they actually can't stand DeGraw."

"Very obvious." I smiled at the thought of Dr. DeGraw's purple face. "I can't believe you pulled that off."

"I think you'll find that I'm capable of a lot of things, especially when you're involved." His tone was flirty, but his eyes were serious. He took a step closer to me, and I couldn't help but lean closer to him, like we were connected by a magnetic force.

He bumped my nose by mistake.

"Ouch!"

He rubbed it for me, and lowered his voice. "Sam, if you still hate me, I'll leave you alone," he whispered. "But, I'm not sorry I got rid of that footage. Lyssa made a mistake with Jake, and you defended her. People make mistakes and get angry. That's not something you should have to pay for forever." He held my chin, and gazed into my eyes.

"I can't believe you'd do that for her. For my team. I . . ."

"I did it for you, Samantha," he said. "I wanted to make you happy. I wanted to fix things between us. I wanted to take care of you, the way you take care of everyone else. I'm sorry I don't always get it right the first time."

He reached out to touch my cheek. "But let me tell you now. I'm wild about you—all of you. The strong part, the gentle part, the hysterically funny part, and the scary serious one. I adore them all, because they're all parts of you. And that's why you make me nervous as hell. Because I like you. A lot."

I stood motionless, mesmerized by his beautiful dark eyes. The true impact of what he was saying washed over me. Big, fat tears made their way down my cheeks, dripping on my shirt. I was so grateful someone would do that for me. That Devan, of all people in the world, cared enough that he risked his career, the disappointment of his father, and the wrath of his mentor, for me.

"I think we can try to take care of each other," I said, punching him lightly on the arm. Yeah, he was trying to get mushy and my big move was to punch him.

Devan laughed and I joined him, before I went back to crying. The absurdity of the situation was too much.

I threw my arms around his neck and buried my face in his shoulder. He hugged me tightly, holding me together, making sure that my huge, ugly sobs of relief wouldn't shake me apart. He stroked my hair and kissed the top of my head, letting me cry without asking any questions.

When I finally stopped, I leaned back in his arms, and with a soft smile said, "I have to warn you, I like to be in charge."

"I noticed." He grinned down at me. "Are you done crying? Can I kiss you now?"

I chuckled. "You Brits are so pushy. First you want our colonies, then you tax our tea."

I could have gone on, but Devan had other ideas. He stopped my mouth with a gentle kiss that turned hot and heavy within seconds. And it was revolutionary, for sure. We're talking Fourth of July fireworks and the *1812 Overture* with cannons, all in one.

Best of all, there wasn't a camera in sight. Or so we thought.

Chapter 28

"Everyone needs a quest.
Knights had dragons to slay. We have Bigfoot to find."

—*Myron Berger, president-elect, Northern Ohio Wood Ape Conservation Society*
(previously known as the Northern Ohio Bigfoot Society)

"Nice!" Hal was behind us with the camera. "Can you guys put your mics back on and do that again?"

Devan rolled his eyes. "If we ignore him will he go away?"

"Better not chance it. Run!" I shouted playfully and I grabbed Devan's uninjured arm, pulling him up the trail away from Hal.

Devan squeezed my hand and we giggled maniacally, scurrying into the heart of the forest. In a matter of minutes Hal was pretty far behind us, his boots and gear slowing him down.

"I can't run with this big camera. No fair!" he shouted.

When we got to a sunny spot, far enough from base camp to feel completely alone, we collapsed onto the grass still laughing. Devan brushed a stubborn curl away from my face.

"Running away was a good idea," he said.

"It's not my usual way of dealing with things, but I didn't overthink it. I just wanted to be alone with you," I said, blushing. That had come out cheesier than I had intended. Devan didn't seem to mind. He took my chin in his hand and kissed me in a way that was far from suitable for prime-time television, but A-OK with me.

"Mmm. You taste like a Cadbury bar," Devan said, once he came up for air.

"That may have been one of the nicest things anyone has ever said to me." I rested my head on his chest. "Plus it means I have a very good reason to keep up my chocolate intake."

Devan lifted my chin and kissed me again. "Mmm, delicious," he said.

I couldn't agree with him more. The only thing more fun than bickering with him was kissing him.

I giggled. "If I had known it would be this easy to shut you up, I never would have insulted you so much. I would have just grabbed you and kissed you whenever you annoyed me."

Devan's face twitched into a wicked smile. "Your lips would be sore from all the snogging. I can be pretty infuriating. So I've heard."

We sat together in our little woodsy hideaway for a long time, my head resting on his chest, his arm around my waist. We talked and kissed and occasionally fell into a comfortable silence.

It was starting to get late, and I knew I should get back to my family for the instructions for the final challenge, but I couldn't move. I didn't want to. Devan shifted and seemed to know what I was thinking. He picked up my wrist and looked at my watch, and then tracing circles on my arm, sighed. "I guess we should head back soon."

I forced myself to sit up, not wanting to face reality, which was kind of ironic considering it was a reality television show.

"Yeah. I guess you're right," I said. "What happens now? I mean with the contest?"

"We go back to our teams and finish the game," Devan answered.

"Yeah, but . . ." Suddenly I felt very shy. I was unsure what his reaction would be if I told him the truth about how I was feeling. He gazed down at me warmly, while I struggled to find the right words. Looking up into his eyes, I realized I didn't have to always worry that I was going to say the wrong thing. We'd already established that we could fight and debate and make up afterward.

The words escaped my lips, before I could change my mind. "I'm scared that if I win, you'll be upset," I said. "And I need to win, for my parents, and for college. I'm not going to back down at all."

"I won't be upset. I don't really care about the contest anymore," he said, pulling me close to him. "And honestly, I hope your team wins. You deserve it, Sam," he said, squeezing me harder. "You deserve to go to a fantastic pre-med program—and so much more."

I blushed and snuggled close to him, putting my hand on his chest.

"Okay, good. May the best team win." I smiled up at him and began to untangle myself from his arms to stand up. He gently pulled me back down with his functioning arm and initiated a whole new round of kissing and nuzzling, and again the world disappeared.

Until we caught a whiff of something truly foul-smelling. Devan's face scrunched up in an adorable grimace.

"Ugh, what is that?" he asked.

"It smells like a wet dog that rolled in fresh manure and then got sprayed by a skunk," I said, turning to face upwind in the direction of the stink. My breath caught in my throat.

I froze, partially with fear, and partially with amazement. On the top of the hill, only thirty feet from where we sat, something big covered in brown fur darted behind a tree. I blinked, wondering if I imagined it. "Um. Did you see that?" I asked, more casually than I felt.

Devan followed my gaze and gasped. "Was that a bear?"

"I'm not sure. It looked awfully tall to be a bear."

The creature was still hidden behind some trees, but the top of its head had to be eight feet off the ground. Devan and I both slowly stood up, trying not to make any noise. I took a step forward to get a better view, but Devan held me back.

"I know you've faced wolves, but I wouldn't recommend getting too close to something that could eat you," he whispered.

I nodded. He was probably right. I took a step back, and a twig snapped loudly beneath my foot.

The creature turned toward the sound, and I could just make out its small, dark eyes shining through the branches, gazing directly at us. Its intense stare never wavered as it licked its paw—or was it a hand? The beast seemed injured. Then, suddenly it let out a mournful howl, unlike any bear I had ever heard. My heart pounded in my chest, and somewhere in the fog of confusion and fear, my mind calculated a means of escape should this thing come after us.

But, instead of charging, it disappeared back into the forest.

Devan and I exhaled the breath we'd been holding, and turned to each other, the same confused look on our faces.

"Was that . . . ?" Devan's voice trailed off.

"I don't know what that was." I turned back to stare at the empty space where the animal had stood. That had to have been a bear—a weird bear with long fingers, walking on two legs.

Suddenly, the strange howl sounded again, but from a bit further up the hill.

"Oh my god," I said.

Devan jumped up, and began rummaging through the pockets of his cargo pants until he came up with a small recording device. "Now I'm not saying it's anything more than a bear, but we might as well get a recording, right?"

A throaty whooping sound floated down to us through the trees. Devan hit record. The whooping howl continued for a moment, and then silence.

"Maybe we can still get a photo!" Devan moved to follow the beast, but I grabbed his arm and turned him back to face me.

"Wait," I said. "Let's think about this for a second. What if that was just a bear? And it's wounded? The best thing we can do is leave it alone."

Devan's eyebrows knitted together. "But what if it wasn't? What if it's what we've been searching for all this time?"

"I just . . . I always thought there was a logical explanation. I never believed in even the possibility of Bigfoot being real until I saw . . . whatever that was. And, now . . ." I said, "I'm not sure I want people to know about it."

Devan stared at me with his mouth open. I was shocked to hear myself saying this, too. Proof of Sasquatch would mean instantly winning the competition, being assured of the money and my college dream.

I grasped his hand and pleaded with my eyes. "Now that we've seen something, it feels wrong, almost evil, to exploit an obviously gentle creature. He deserves some privacy, right? I'm sorry, but maybe we should just let the Sasquatch remain imaginary. Which he probably is anyway," I said, crossing my arms, prepared for a fight.

I was sure Devan would argue with me, or even go off on his own to hunt the creature down. But instead, he nodded and wrapped his arm around my shoulder. "Okay. If you love the Bigfoot, let it go, right?" Devan said and pressed play on the recorder.

The whooping howl rumbled out from the recorder. *"A-whooo, a-wooo, a-wooo."*

"Is it me, or did Bigfoot tell you to kiss me?" I asked.

"A *bear* told me to kiss you, but either way I think it's good advice." Devan grinned, and replayed the recording, full volume, to enhance the sound.

"Woooo . . ."

Devan wrapped both arms around my waist, pulled me to him, and, with his lips hovering above mine, whispered, "Even if he is imaginary."

Joyfully, I closed the distance between our lips. We kissed, giggling at the now far-away howl of our new maybe-not-so-imaginary friend echoing down the mountains.

Heavy breathing, not our own, interrupted our fun. An out-of-breath Hal traipsed up the hill. "Guys, we gotta go. It's time for the last challenge. Ugh, what is that stench?"

We just wrinkled our noses, shrugged, and followed him back to the set hand in hand.

When we arrived at the base camp, Devan pulled me toward him and put something in my pocket. It was the audio recorder.

His eyes bore into mine. "I want you to have this."

I opened my mouth to refuse, but he held my wrist.

"Let me do this for you. If you can use the recording, you should." His eyes crinkled when he let my wrist go. "You never know when I'll need a personal physician again, so you better go to school and study."

I sighed but nodded. I did promise I would let him take care of me, too. "Okay. I'll take it. I was thinking about NYU for pre-med. I hear their anthropology department isn't too shabby either."

Devan's eyes sparkled at that idea. I gave him one more kiss then went to where my parents and sisters were huddled over their equipment.

• • •

"Bigfoot hunters, we've come to the close of the competition." Jake paused for dramatic effect. "As we move into the last challenge, the teams are tied: the Bergers scored big in the tracking challenge with their extra big footprint, but the Netherfield team took the trophy in the audio-visual challenge with their snapshot of a possible

Sasquatch. Then Devan and Sam split the points for identifying the fake clues. So this is it. Winner takes all.

"As you may know, most Bigfoot hunters go their entire lives without ever seeing a Sasquatch, but we have faith in our contestants. For the final challenge, our competitors will have one last chance to bring in conclusive proof of the existence of Bigfoot. Each team will have twelve hours to use every resource at their disposal to find the best evidence they can. This can be audio, visual, DNA, or any other type of physical evidence. Maybe one of you will capture the beast alive!" Jake's weak laugh was almost as obnoxious as he was.

"Remember, contestants, you only have the next twelve hours to collect the best piece of evidence you can before you must return here for judging," Jake continued. "And don't forget, this is for the win! Good luck to both teams."

Jake clomped off the set.

I caught Devan's eyes and wondered if he regretted giving me that recording now. A gentle grin formed on his lips as he returned my gaze, and I knew he was okay with his decision.

I mouthed "thank you" and he gave me another reassuring smile.

I grabbed my pack and followed my family, Hal, and Dave.

"We're going to head further up this time," my dad said. "I think we'll have the best shot up there. I suggest we focus on luring a Wood Ape toward us with calls, and then try to capture a photo or vocal response. It's low-tech, but it could work."

I touched the recorder in my pocket. This was perfect.

We hiked for the next hour and a half, set up the tents in record time, and prepared the fire for later. Luckily, we went in the opposite direction of the Bear-squatch. I didn't want to lead anyone to the animal.

"Okay gang, are you ready to get started?" my dad asked.

My mom gestured for us to join them. "Yes, honey," she said. "We're good to go."

"We're going to spread out in opposite directions and each take a video camera and an audio recorder. I'll go with your mom and Sophie. Lyssa and Sam, you can go in that direction. We'll practice howling and see if we get a response. We'll meet back here in time for sundown. I don't want you wandering in the woods at night, even with a tranq gun."

Before we headed off, Hal cleared his throat. "Can I get a quick shot of all of you howling together?"

My shoulders slumped. This was almost as bad as the Shalom Sasquatch T-shirts.

"Of course," my dad said. "Ladies, let's first do a moaning howl." Then to the camera he added, "This is the sound fully grown male Sasquatches are known to make."

He cupped his hands around his mouth, forming a megaphone and let out a long, rising howl, which we followed. "A-woooooo."

"Good. Now we'll do a whooping noise, that's also often commonly heard."

This time we all placed our hands by our mouths, ready to repeat his whooping sounds.

"A-whoop, a-whoop, a-whoop," we all said. By the time we were finished, a giggling fit had overtaken us, and I had forgotten about feeling embarrassed in front of the camera. Sophie and I danced a little jig in time to the howling and only stopped when our ribs hurt from too much laughing.

"Got it. That was great," Hal said, chuckling at our silliness. "I'm going to follow along with Myron, Sophie, and Brenda this time, since I got a lot of footage of Sam already."

My mom kissed Lyssa and then me. "Be careful girls. We'll see you in a little bit."

Lyssa and I walked to our designated spot. She took out the camera from her pocket and I pulled out the audio recorder. "You're louder. Why don't you howl first?" Lyssa said.

"Okey dokey." I went through the motions until my throat hurt. I thought I heard a coyote or something in the background and Lyssa got excited. Good. When I produced the tape that Devan and I recorded she wouldn't be surprised.

We continued until we were both out of breath and were losing our voices. A few more animal sounds made it into the background, so we left, satisfied with our work.

By the time we got back, my mom was making everyone hot dogs, Sophie had a pot of soup going, and my dad was cooking corn on the cob in tin foil over the fire. They looked more or less content.

My mom twisted her neck back and forth. "I don't know about you guys, but I'll be glad to get back to our own beds."

"And our own showers," Lyssa said.

I took in my family sitting around the campfire and smiling, even after everything that transpired since we packed up the minivan. "I don't know, I think there are some things I'll miss about being here," I said, stuffing a hot dog in my face and then nibbling some corn to the amusement of Hal, who caught me on camera with a face full of food.

"Seriously?" I asked. "Don't you have better things to film?"

He shrugged and put down the camera to eat his own dinner.

I took advantage of the camera being off to tell my parents about my new relationship with Devan. They weren't all that surprised. My mom said she had seen it coming a mile away, and had already told my dad. Lyssa, of course, had known all along. Sophie was the only one who didn't realize what had been going on.

"But I thought you hated him," she said, with wonder.

"I thought I did too, for a while. But I guess I judged him too quickly. He's really great. Beyond what I could have imagined. He's so caring with his friends. He's ridiculously smart and funny, and honestly, almost as nerdy as me." I was suddenly shy trying to describe my feelings for him.

Lyssa saved me. "I knew it! I'm totally getting you a gift card for Dairy Queen for your birthday." I elbowed her in the ribs, and she shoved me away, with a smile.

Once everyone was full, the food was put away and the fire out, we shared the evidence that we all had collected with each other. My parents had some audio that was fine, but not great, plus a few very blurry snapshots that didn't show much of anything. When I played the recording Devan and I captured, which was much clearer and deeper than the others, my dad stood up and gave me and Lyssa huge hugs.

"Wow! Wonderful job, girls."

Mom got in on the hugging action, too, but quickly pulled away. "We should all get some sleep. We have a big day tomorrow."

I squirmed in my sleeping bag for hours, nervous about our final judging. Every few minutes, I reached into my bag to make sure the recorder was still there. I hoped the recording would be enough to give us the win, but I wasn't confident. What if the judges liked whatever the Netherfield team presented better or if DeGraw swayed everyone against us?

I groaned, but eventually managed to fall asleep for a few hours, still clutching the digital recorder in my sweaty palm.

The next morning, we packed up the camp for the last time and headed to the *Myth Gnomers* base camp.

Colin and Beth were standing with Jake, Dr. DeGraw, Dr. Bruckmeier, and Jeff Duckworthy. Devan, Caroline, and Kyle were already there, waiting with their equipment and camping gear.

I swallowed. I didn't think I would be sad for it all to be over, but the reality of not getting to see Devan every day just hit me. He gave me a little wave, seemingly thinking the same thing.

Colin and Beth set up the shot, told Jake where to stand, and called "Places!" before I could talk to Devan. I had no idea what they were about to present. Their stony expressions gave nothing away. Although I assumed they would be more excited if they had actually seen something.

So maybe we still had a shot at winning. My stomach churned with anxiety.

"Bigfoot hunters and Sasquatch fans, this is the moment you've been waiting for," Jake began. "It's time to reveal the evidence for the final challenge. And for this last round, we'd like to welcome back all of the previous judges."

When he said that, the three judges stepped forward into the shot.

"We'll start with the Bergers," Jake added.

My mom smiled at me. "I think Sam should present this time."

I patted down my hair and stepped forward. "Well, we took turns howling and whooping, which is low-tech, but seemed to work because this is what we captured." I played the two samples, first my parents', which was faint and could've been a coyote. Then I switched recorders and played the whoops that Devan and I had captured.

Jeff Duckworthy clapped. "That's what I'm talking' about. I'm not sure what kind of animal that is, but he sounds pretty big." Dr. Bruckmeier nodded her tiny, bird head furiously. Dr. DeGraw seemed unimpressed, however.

Jake strode across the set to the other team. "Okay, well, thanks, Bergers. Let's see what you're up against."

I took a deep breath and held it, glad my presentation was over, but tapped my fingers against my thighs, nervous to see what would come next.

"I understand Caroline will be presenting today," Jake continued.

Caroline cleared her throat. "We set up an iPod and portable speaker system and blasted a section of the woods with sound. The recording we used was that of a supposed Sasquatch, in distress. We hoped this would encourage others of its kind to investigate. We then retreated about a quarter mile downwind, and sent up a drone with a high-definition camera to observe the area from the sky."

"A what?" Duckworthy interrupted.

Devan jumped in. "A drone. It's a small, lightweight, remote-controlled helicopter type thing. It's virtually silent and equipped with the best HD and infrared cameras."

"Hmm . . ." Duckworthy stroked his beard, then added, "Well, what'd ya get?"

The Netherfield team glanced at each other and hesitated. Caroline wore a stoic expression. "We were able to capture this image."

A very blurry shot of the tops of the trees appeared on the monitor, and below the thick branches was a black shadow.

"We believe that this black mass here," Devan pointed to the shadow, "is perhaps a Sasquatch."

"More like a blobsquatch," Lyssa said under her breath. I held back a laugh.

Dr. DeGraw snorted. "Anything else?"

"Unfortunately, at this point, there were, um, mechanical issues," Devan replied.

"I crashed the drone," Kyle added, looking at his feet. "Totally my fault."

Caroline rolled her eyes. "I'm so done with you putting yourself down, Kyle. It's not like we knew how to operate the drone either."

"Yeah, but you would've been smart enough to figure it out."

Caroline groaned. "You're smart, too. Your IQ score is two points higher than mine."

"Seriously? How do you know that?"

"Hacker, remember?" She mimicked typing on a keyboard.

Kyle grinned and high-fived his sister.

There was a tense moment of dead air, as the judges waited for the Netherfield team to add any final remarks.

Finally, Duckworthy jumped out of his chair and said, "I think we have a clear winner here. You ask me, that photo wasn't much to look at. But those howls, now they were something."

"And what do the other judges say?" Jake asked.

Dr. Bruckmeier pushed up her glasses onto her head. "I tend to agree with Jeff. While I remain a skeptic, the Bergers' recording is certainly intriguing."

"Dr. DeGraw?" Jake turned to the final judge.

She waved her hand to dismiss the conversation. "Yes, yes. It's a better piece of evidence."

"It's unanimous. Congratulations to the Bergers, who have won this *Myth Gnomers* competition and will walk away with bragging rights and two hundred thousand dollars!" Jake smiled into the camera before shaking my family's hands for the benefit of the television audience.

I exhaled the breath I had been holding for what seemed like hours as the facts sunk in. Everything was going to be okay, now. The house was saved and college was possible. We had won. We came, we saw, and we kicked very cute prep school butts. I even managed to make a couple of unlikely friends, despite myself.

As soon as the cameras were off I flew into Devan's arms and kissed him. Sophie and Kyle were pretty cuddly next to us, too.

We stopped kissing just in time to witness Dr. DeGraw unclip her microphone and toddle our way.

"I hope you're proud of yourselves," she said to Devan and Kyle, and Caroline who had walked over to where we were. "This should have been easy money and good exposure for the school."

"You know what?" Devan asked, putting his arms tightly around my waist. "We are proud of ourselves."

She let out a dramatic sigh. "Then you aren't who I thought you were."

Devan winked at me and kissed the top of my head. "Good."

Dr. DeGraw didn't say anything further, but just let herself into the Jeep.

Caroline threw an arm around her stepbrother's shoulder. "You know the best part of this being over?"

"What?" Kyle asked.

"The after-party. How about we invite the whole crew over to the cabin and order some soy cheese pizza and play video games."

"Take out the soy cheese and add pepperoni and you've got a deal," Kyle said.

"What do you think, Sam?" Devan asked.

"I'd say it's time Bigfoot finds himself." I smiled up at Devan, happy that while I still couldn't be certain of the existence of any mythical creature, our feelings for each other turned out to be the very opposite of imaginary.

Acknowledgments

We'd like to offer a big, hairy, Bigfoot thank you to all those who joined us on this adventure and helped make this book a reality. We are forever grateful to:

Our own idiosyncratic families, who never embarrass us as much as the Bergers embarrass Sam (but sure try their darndest). Endless appreciation to Bill and Paula Mingo, who helped shape Betsy into her current bookworm form, and shuttled her to Hebrew school for a million years, but never made her go camping. Heaps of gratitude to the DuBois family—Charlie, the eccentric inventor dad, who plans all the DuBois family adventures; Helen, the ever-clairvoyant mom, who knew Carrie would be a writer well before she did; and Dana, the little brother who encourages all of Carrie's outrageous ideas without (too much) judgment.

Our nerdy love interests. Big thanks to Marcus Aldredge, Betsy's geeky significant other, who first got her hooked on cryptozoology. All those hours watching *Monster Quest* finally paid off! And three cheers for Dan Shaw, Carrie's partner in sarcastic commentary. He may be a skeptic when it comes to the existence of Bigfoot, but he's a true believer in this book and his wife's big dreams.

Our amazing agent, Christa Heschke, who was *Sasquatch*'s first champion and who, along with Shannon Powers and the rest of the McIntosh & Otis team, read and reread our many drafts, offering excellent editorial advice along the way.

Our extraordinary editor, Jacquelyn Mitchard, whose wisdom and acumen transformed our little monster of a manuscript into a ferocious beast of a book, as well as Bethany Carland-Adams, Karen Cooper, Stephanie Hannus, Meredith O'Hayre, and the whole Merit Press/Simon & Schuster team whose enthusiasm for *Sasquatch* has taken our breath away.

Our excellent critique partners and early readers Amanda Lanceter, Emily Lake, Christy Mafucci Wendell, Julia Putnam, Judy Shatzky, Sherry Soule, and Constance Tarbox Windish, with special thanks to Mathangi Subramanian for her thoughtful comments which helped bring additional layers to the characters.

Our wonderful world of writers, especially our friends from Query Kombat, including hosts Michelle Hauck and Michael Anthony, our QK Cabal group, author Micol Ostow and the lovely writers we met through her Media Bistro class, and the super talented and encouraging 2017 debut author group.

Our relentlessly supportive friends who've offered infinite love, encouragement, and expertise over the years, including Alexis Buatti-Ramos, Sonya Carpenter, Jim and Lori Crispi, Michael Hicks, Ella Leitner, the Meola family, Elizabeth Miles, Poornima Ravishankar, the Shaw family, Kimberly Small, and Cara Winter, as well as all those in our "extended" families at the Museum of Jewish Heritage, New Victory Theater, San Francisco Ballet, Purchase College, SUNY, The Faux-Real Theatre Company, and New York University's Tisch School of the Arts/CAP 21.

Our inspirations: Ms. Jane Austen and our fellow Janeites, the Bigfoot believers and cryptozoology community who search for Sasquatch on TV, blog about beasts online, and stand behind their sighting stories, and, most especially, the adventurers who explore the mysteries of our world and seek to find that which has yet to be discovered—we salute you!